In This Way
I Was Saved

Brian DeLeeuw

Simon & Schuster
New York   London   Toronto   Sydney

Simon & Schuster
1230 Avenue of the Americas
New York, NY 10020

This book is a work of fiction. Names, characters, places, and incidents either are products of the author's imagination or are used fictitiously. Any resemblance to actual events or locales or persons, living or dead, is entirely coincidental.

First Simon & Schuster hardcover edition August 2009

SIMON & SCHUSTER and colophon are registered trademarks of Simon & Schuster, Inc.

For information about special discounts for bulk purchases, please contact Simon & Schuster Special Sales at 1-800-456-6798 or business@simonandschuster.com

Designed by Davina Mock-Maniscalco

Manufactured in the United States of America

1 3 5 7 9 10 8 6 4 2

Library of Congress Cataloging-in-Publication Data

ISBN-13: 978-1-4391-0313-5
ISBN-10:   1-4391-0313-5

Dedication

Kafka imagines a man who has a hole in the back of his head. The sun shines into this hole. The man himself is denied a glimpse of it. Kafka might as well be talking about the man's face. Others "look into it." The most public, promiscuous part of his body is invisible to himself. How obvious. Still, it takes a genius to say that the face, the thing that kisses, sneezes, whistles, and moans is a hole more private than our privates. You retreat from this dreadful hole into quotidian blindness, the blindness of your face to itself. You want to light a cigarette or fix yourself a drink. You want to make a phone call. To whom? You don't know. Of course you don't. You want to phone your face. The one you've never met. Who you are.

—Leonard Michaels, "Journal"

"When I'm alone, I stop believing I exist."

—A. Alvarez, *The Savage God*

PART ONE

Meeting Midnight

1

I ENTER THE LOBBY of Claire Nightingale's apartment building, here to tell her I have murdered her only son. As always, the marble foyer is hushed and dim, almost sepulchral, and, as always, two doormen stand watch over the evening shift. The one who opens the door for me is named Victor. He recognizes my face—of course he does, he's worked here for years—and he says, "They starving you at that college? I can see your ribs, buddy."

"Hunger strike," I say, trying on a smile, but my voice comes out too loudly and echoes clumsily around the hollow space. My mouth still feels new, these lips, this meaty tongue. I cough to cover my mistake and walk toward the elevator at the back of the lobby. The second doorman looks up from his copy of the *Post*. Our eyes meet briefly, and he looks down again, uninterested.

"Ms. Nightingale just got in," Victor calls after me. "She'll be happy to see you. She's always talking about you."

I want to tell him that I already know she's upstairs, that I saw her step out of her taxi fifteen minutes ago from my hiding spot across Central Park West. Instead I just give him a wave and press the elevator button. I sat on a park bench for hours, waiting for Claire to return from wherever she was—holed up in her Chelsea office, suffering through some hopeless date, alone at the movies— all the while holding myself tightly against the November cold. When a cab finally pulled up to the building and I saw Claire get out, her slight, familiar outline backlit by the lobby's glow, I suppressed the urge to run across the street and grab her right there on the sidewalk. I had to remind myself about the doormen and the neighbors and the dog walkers, about strangers heading for the subway entrance on the corner or tourists who'd walked the wrong way after leaving the Museum of Natural History. This was a private matter; there was no need for anyone else to get involved.

From my bench I watched her hand Victor a leather bag, laugh along with something he said, touch his shoulder. Even at her lowest, she can always pull herself together for these brief encounters, these rote, mannerly interactions. There is always decorum. There is always propriety. I lived alongside Claire and her son, Luke, for thirteen years, and I know that trusting any particular Claire to hang around for too long is always a mistake. Luke never liked to admit this, to himself or anyone else, so I used to say it to his face: You're not dumb, just incurably naïve. As I sat on the bench, Victor opened the door for Claire and pulled it shut after her. Behind my back, Central Park shivered along with me, bare branches and spindly bushes rasping in the wind. I stood up and stamped feeling back into my legs, still amazed at the brittleness of my new body.

But don't mistake this for a complaint. I can now pick a coffee cup off the counter and carry it over to the table on the other side of the room. I can shake a man's hand. I can drive a car. I can press my palm onto a square of wet cement and leave a mark. I have a voice that can be heard by anyone who cares to listen. I am here, in the world, in the flesh, a body moving in space. And, of course, Claire can no longer ignore me. She never liked how much time Luke spent alone with me; even when we were children she suspected that our friendship was the face of something dark and hidden. But tonight she will be forced to listen to what I have to say. It's something for which I've waited a long time—fourteen years—and part of me wants to jab at the elevator button like a maniac, to sprint up the three flights to her apartment in one breath, to yell and scream and bang my head against the marble lobby walls.

But I don't. I stand with my hands clasped behind my back, my body rigid and still, my frenzy contained. Above my head, floor numbers light up in reverse. In the brass doors, my reflection is murky and distorted, as though submerged in a pool of dirty water. Outside on the street, someone shouts, a car door slams. The second doorman shakes his newspaper. I wait and watch the numbers tumble downward.

<hr />

The day I met Luke, I was alone in the playground when I heard someone call my name. I turned around and his face was there in front of mine. He was six years old then. His skin was pale, his features delicate and precise, just like his mother's. His left eye was yellow-flecked green, the right brown, as if, instead of melding, his parents' genes had been split evenly, an eye for each. Later, I liked to remind him that he came looking for me first. I didn't ask for any of it.

"Hi," he said. "I'm Luke. Want to play a game?"

He explained the rules: "The dinosaurs try to eat us, but we hide and use these"—he waved a neon-orange water gun—"to shoot them instead. Get it, Daniel?"

I nodded slowly. Daniel? It was true, that was my name. This was how things were at first: Luke said it and that made it so. He looked at me, not quite satisfied. "You need a laser pistol too. Here." I felt something cold and heavy weigh down my hand. I looked at my gun. It was dull silver metal, double-barreled and snub-nosed, a scope mounted atop the barrels. "You aim through that," Luke said, pointing at the scope.

We were in the playground across from the Metropolitan Museum. It was November then, too, and cold. We stood in a sandpit in the shadow of a toy brick pyramid, fifteen feet tall at its peak and dotted with footholds to help children scale its sloped sides. I watched as two older boys fought their way to the top, clawing at the gritty bricks and each other until one slipped, ripping a hole in the knee of his khakis and sliding down to the base. Luke winced, and the boy cried, clutching his knee while his rival peered down at him from the top of the pyramid. I couldn't help laughing at the boy's scrunched-up face, such an obvious exaggeration. The theatrics of a loser.

"Stop laughing," Luke told me. "It's not funny." He waved me toward two tire swings, where a little girl spun in lazy circles, humming to herself. She pinned us with a pair of watery eyes and said, "I was leaving anyway," before she hopped off and disappeared behind a family of concrete turtles. We got down in the cold dirt and squeezed under the tires. We lay there on our stomachs, a pair of snipers propping up our guns in the desert sand. I looked around while we waited. Plump babysitters pushed strollers and held the hands of toddlers in bulky parkas. Girls in pale blue skirts shared cigarettes and eyed the boys jostling one another out by the bus stop in their maroon blazers. I didn't see any dinosaurs.

"There!" Luke whispered, pointing toward the museum. "A *Tyrannosaurus rex*. Be very quiet and don't shoot until I say."

I followed his finger. At first I saw nothing except the glare of the sun on the glass wall of the museum, but gradually a two-story outline took shape and filled in on the lawn in front of the wall. Two giant legs rippled with sinewy muscle and ended in tri-clawed feet. Tiny, almost dainty arms hung tight against a massive torso. A triangular head opened its mouth to display rows of fist-sized teeth. Old white scars marred brown, pebbled skin, and one fresh-looking red wound splashed across a thigh like war paint.

"See him?"

I nodded. The tyrannosaurus lurched toward the playground and the earth shuddered under our stomachs. Its shadow dwarfed the trees, and I could see the reflection of its spiny back receding on the glass wall as it stalked across the road between the museum and the playground, hunched forward, its black eyes sweeping the space at its feet. A wailing police car sped between its legs as it stepped over the playground's fence. I checked my vision through the scope, finding the creature in the crosshairs.

"Go!" Luke shouted, and we rolled out from under the swings, scrambled to our feet, and ran toward a chain-metal bridge. The tyrannosaurus spotted us from the edge of the play-ground and began moving faster, dipping its head low, showing us its teeth. Wrist-thick ropes of saliva webbed the space between its two rows of incisors, and a chunk of flesh dislodged itself and tumbled wetly to the sand. We were almost at the bridge when I heard her voice, strident, insistent, scaling upward like a warped record: "Luuuke!"

Her name fit. Claire Nightingale was small-boned and bird-like, full of sharp, quick movements. She stood at the far end of the playground, the setting sun flush in her face, her body bi-

sected by shadow. She fluttered her hands at us. "Time to go."
Luke didn't move, and I glanced over my shoulder: the tyrannosaurus was nowhere to be found. Claire's hands were now on her
hips. "Luke!" She wore a navy pantsuit and black flats, and was
coatless despite the bite of the early-winter afternoon. She
stamped her foot, pointed at the ground in front of her. "Come
here this instant."

Luke sighed, looked at me, shrugged. My gun disappeared as
he walked toward his mother. Halfway there he stopped and
turned back to me. "Come on. You don't want to stay here by
yourself, do you?"

As soon as Luke was within reach, Claire kissed his cheek
and grabbed his wrist, hard. "I lost track of time. We're late."

"Daniel's going to come with us," Luke said. "He's my new
friend."

I nodded at Claire, but she didn't give me more than a glance.
"Is that so?"

"I won't make any trouble," I said.

Claire smiled, a private thing. "I suppose that's fine."

Luke stuffed the water gun in his pocket and took my hand,
making himself a bridge between his mother and me as we
walked onto Fifth Avenue. A second police car and then an ambulance screamed past us, parting the downtown traffic with their
urgent authority. I followed their course over my shoulder and
saw them pull to a halt a few blocks south, where a small crowd
had gathered on the sidewalk across from the museum, but then
Luke dragged me on and I didn't look back again.

"I told you not to roll around in that filthy sand." Claire glanced down at the grit streaking her son's sweatshirt. "You could get a disease."

"How?"

"Anything that lives in the sand, if it gets inside you it will live there too. I'm trying to keep you safe, Luke." He nodded, but I could tell he didn't understand. "I mean living things you can't see. They're everywhere. They're all over you and you can't even feel them. And us, people, we're vulnerable to even the smallest. Our skin is permeable. Do you know what that means?" "Porous," I said, but she continued as though she hadn't heard me. "It means we're dotted with holes. Cheesecloth. Sieves. And then these things get inside us and mingle with what's ours until we can't tell the difference between the two." She kept on like this the whole way. I tried to sort through her speech, but I didn't know what was important and what could be thrown away.

The Nightingale apartment was on 106th Street, across Fifth Avenue from the Conservatory Garden, which was almost never crowded, not even in the spring when flamboyant tulips and roses splattered its lawns. In winter, the garden was reduced to an arrangement of sharp-cornered hedges, an homage to discipline and order. Benches nestled hidden in dense folds of brambles; sheltered corners offered up a wealth of shadows. Even that first time, I felt a strong, simple appreciation for the garden as the three of us passed by its gates and crossed the street to their apartment building.

The elevator deposited us on the penthouse floor, where the

doors opened directly into the apartment's plush but cramped space. Over Luke's shoulder, in the living room, a massive wooden armoire abutted a mirrored liquor cabinet, which in turn crowded a low glass table cluttered with bamboo baskets. In the foyer, a watercolor landscape looked down upon a wicker rocking chair. In this rocking chair Luke's father sat, ankles crossed and hands behind his head, stretched out to his full length. The air in the apartment was close and heavy. I trailed behind Luke and Claire, unsure of my place in any of this.

James Tomasi sat up straight. "I believe you said four-thirty."

Claire flicked her head toward Luke and me. "Your son was busy making friends at the playground. It was all I could do to drag him away."

"I'm sure you had nothing to do with it." He winked at Luke with half of his face, like a mime. "Isn't that right, chief?" Luke put his finger in his mouth and looked at his mother. "All I'm saying is somehow I managed to escape the office and get here on time. It would have been nice if you had attempted to do the same."

"The sacrifices you make. I'm lucky to be married to a hero like you."

James turned his head to the side and snorted like a horse. I studied him from my spot behind Luke. He was tall and rangy, long-fingered and loose-limbed. Tufts of wiry black hair sprouted from his knuckles. He wore a blue- and white-striped Oxford shirt, the top button open above the knot of his loosened tie. Over a once-broken nose two dark brown eyes retreated deep into their sockets. He had given Luke one of these eyes, but there were few other similarities between father and son; Luke's features were concise, while everything about James was elongated and roughly cut. Though tense, Luke's father looked more than a little resigned, as though the outcome of whatever battle he was fighting had already been decided. He gestured at the briefcase resting beside the wicker chair. "I brought everything." His eyes flickered over to Luke and me, and then back to Claire. "I don't feel like there's much either of us should say right now."

"Your altruism is breathtaking." Claire took off her suit jacket and hung it on a hook near the front door, and I saw for the first time how thin her arms were, how her skin was almost translucent, blue veins vivid as tattoos against the white skin. She squatted in front of her son. "Luke, your father and I have some things we need to talk about in private. Why don't you and your new friend go to your room for just a little bit. Can you do that for me?"

Inside the bedroom, the last thin bands of sunlight slid through slits in the drawn bamboo shades. Luke spun a giant freestanding globe, and let his fingers graze across oceans and continents smeared into one unbroken stream of color. An antique four-poster bed stood against one wall and a meticulously detailed dollhouse was wedged into a corner. Luke saw me looking at the dollhouse and said apologetically, "It's for girls, but my mother says there's nowhere else to put it."

Inside the miniature rooms, porcelain dolls with painted faces and tiny clothes took tea and played chess. Each time I looked into the house, the dolls seemed to hold slightly different positions than before, yet I could never catch them in motion. Luke hopped onto a stuffed leather chair and kicked off his boat shoes. His feet didn't touch the floor, but he'd fashioned a footrest out of several old hardcover mystery novels. His bare toes worried the cover of the top one as he announced: "My father doesn't sleep here anymore but he still comes home for dinner sometimes. On Mondays and Thursdays, I think. My mother keeps changing the days."

I didn't know what to say. "And tonight?"

Luke frowned. "I asked my mother and she said they're on strike in Delphi, so it's anyone's guess. Do you know what that means?"

I wanted to say, *It means your father probably isn't going to stay for dinner,* but I couldn't explain how I knew that, so I just shrugged. Movement caught the corner of my eye, and I spun to face the dollhouse. "What is it?" Luke said. The figurines had moved, I was sure of it. A woman hung by her feet from a chandelier, her little pink evening dress billowing out toward her head; two men lay facedown on the floor in the parlor, their hands crossed behind their backs as though bound. "Oh, they always do that," Luke said. He slid off the chair and took a step toward the house. I stepped behind him, and the house loomed large in its corner, and then I took another step and Luke's bedroom and all its objects fell away. I stepped onto the porch—white-painted wood, it gave with a creak—and into the foyer, where Luke was already waiting for me. The smells of sea salt and pine drifted in through the open windows; a grandfather clock kept the time.

"Where are we?" I said.

"Newport," Luke said. "Rhode Island. My grandmother's house. Want to meet her?"

In the dining room, the woman still hung from the chandelier. Her porcelain head swiveled to fix us, and her upside-down mouth moved, but nothing came out. "I guess she's not talking today." The woman's feet unhooked from the chandelier's iron arms, and she crashed to the floor. "Well," Luke said. "Another time, maybe." In an adjacent nursery sat a crib, navy blue with white trim. A baby lay swaddled in blankets, its blank face unblinkingly regarding us. "That's my mother," Luke said. "They didn't make any more after her." Dangling over baby Claire was a mobile of stars and quarter-moons. Bright light wiped away any scenery on the other side of the windows.

"Luke?"

Suddenly the walls and floors and ceilings flew apart, and James stood in the doorway of the Fifth Avenue bedroom. "Are you playing with that creepy old thing again?"

"I was just showing it to Daniel," Luke said, his face flushed and damp.

I wasn't sure what I should say, so I kept my mouth shut. James looked in my direction, and then back at Luke. "It's just that we might not be seeing as much of each other as we're used to. What you need to understand is that it's not because I want it to be that way."

Luke paused for a moment, then said, "Who does?"

"What?"

"Who wants it to be that way?"

James tugged at the knot of his tie. "Nobody does, Luke. That's just what's going to happen."

Dustlike quiet settled over the room, and Luke hung back, letting the dead space sag between them. I knew that each had disappointed the other, but I didn't know how or why. I wanted to speak up now, to reach out and pinch James's cheek or ruffle his hair, to slap Luke on the backside of his head and tell him to snap out of it, but I found myself unable to say or do anything.

James put on a fake smile. "Hey, cheer up, chief. It's not the end of the world. Things won't be that different."

You don't have to lie, I wanted to say.

Luke shook his head. "They're different now," he said.

Claire's voice suddenly echoed through the apartment: "You guys okay in there?"

"No, the roof caved in, we're all crushed to death," James yelled back. "Christ," he muttered under his breath, and then he kissed Luke's forehead and left the room wiping his son's sweat from his lips. Luke and I waited a moment before sneaking down the hall after him. From the doorway to the foyer, I saw him say something low and seemingly tender to Claire. He put his hand on her elbow but she jerked it away and walked into the kitchen. He stood alone in the foyer for a moment, and then he picked up his briefcase, and without another word he made his escape.

In the foyer mirror, I saw Claire pick a coffee cup off the marble countertop and raise it to her mouth. She brought the cup down from her lips, paused for a brief moment, and then, with the slightest flick of her wrist, sent it flying in a slow-curving arc across the kitchen. The white china cup rotated elegantly on its axis, its handle tracing lazy curlicues in the air. The moment before it exploded in the sink, before its delicate shrapnel spun out across the counter and onto the floor, was utterly and completely silent. In the mirror, after the impact, I saw Claire bend down to pick up a stray shard. She handled it with uncertainty, as though trying to figure out how such a thing had happened.

2

THE FIRST NIGHT I spent in the apartment I fell asleep just like everyone else. When Luke asked if I could stay over, his mother smiled. "Don't you think we should call his parents?" Luke frowned, then shook his head and told her it would be fine. She shrugged: "Whatever you think is best." Those nights at the beginning of our friendship I could sleep leaning against a wall, curled up in the leather armchair, prostrate on the floor: it didn't matter. After Claire read us our story for the night—Sherlock Holmes, the Brothers Grimm, *A Thousand and One Nights*—and turned out the lights, Luke's breathing would quickly grow long and raggedy, and I would just as quickly fade with him, unconscious until the next morning, when he'd wake me with an elbow to the ribs. Sleep then seemed to be such a simple thing, the dimming of consciousness at the dimming of our lamp, automatic and unremarkable.

Children believe the situations to which they are first exposed are simply the way things are. And so, after Luke shook me awake before dawn on my first morning in the Nightingale household, I thought perhaps all children got up at a quarter to six to read the newspaper aloud with their mothers. It seemed entirely possible to me that in countless other apartments across the Upper East Side of Manhattan countless other little six year-olds were busy learning words like *multilateral* and *interventionist* rather than lying in bed asleep, dreaming their dumb, harmless dreams.

We sat around the kitchen table, which was covered by the spread-out first section of the day's *New York Times*. Claire's finger jabbed at a headline. " 'NATO, Expanding Bosnian Role, Strikes a Serbian Base in Croatia,'" she quoted as Luke stirred his bowl of Lucky Charms. I watched sodden clovers and stars float on top of the rainbow-streaked milk in my own bowl. Luke had pointed to the empty space at the table in front of me, and Claire had said, "I don't know what he's used to at home, but Daniel can help himself to anything we have here." I had no appetite, though, and the cereal sat untouched.

"This man says, 'If we did not act, we would be viewed as incompetent and spineless. But if we acted too vigorously, we could provoke an escalation leading to tragic consequences. We try to tread this narrow path.' Well," Claire said brightly. "Hmmm. That's a good way of looking at things, I think." Outside the kitchen window, the sky had just begun to lift over Central Park. Claire spun the paper around so it was facing us. "Now you try a sentence."

Luke pushed aside his cereal bowl and squinted at the blocks of text. I stood behind him and looked over his shoulder. The page was covered with groupings of black marks that resolved themselves into a field of mostly unknown combinations.

" 'In the past,'" Luke started, then paused. I saw where he was looking, and the three words he had just read aloud suddenly lay naked, open and unguarded on the page. " 'In the past,'" he started again, then stopped. The word following *past* curled in on itself like a worm poked by a stick.

Claire read it upside down. " 'Treading.'"

"Treading?"

"Treading, like walking. Going forward."

On the page, the worm uncurled.

Luke read, " 'In the past, treading this path has led to . . .'"

"Sound it out."

"Con . . ."

I examined the unfriendly word. Its two halves resisted each other, failing to become one.

"Con . . ."

"Does Daniel have any ideas?" Claire looked around. "Maybe he can help you."

With an almost audible click, the two syllables slotted together. "Conflict," I whispered in Luke's ear. He jerked his head up as though he'd forgotten I was there.

Claire smiled at us expectantly, nearly ecstatically. "Yes? Yes?"

" 'In the past, treading this path has led to conflict.' "

"Beautiful." She smiled. "Seems like it might be a good idea to keep Daniel around for a while."

I understood it was the newspaper's words that were important, not what they meant. That they described something beyond a lesson in language, something that was actually happening somewhere else, was ancillary. But the lesson seemed valuable, and I wanted to learn more. The other sections of the newspaper were strewn about underneath this top one, and my eyes were drawn to a photograph that jutted out over the edge of the table. It was a headshot of a sullen-looking young man that had the blurred quality of something scanned from a passport or driver's license. A sour, hollow feeling opened up inside my chest when I saw it, although I could not place the man's face. I pointed: "What about this story?"

Luke glanced at me, and then pushed the first section aside to uncover the rest of the article. Below the headshot was a block of text, and below that a larger photograph in which a cluster of people stood on a sidewalk, looking down at something outside the frame. The spectators appeared well-dressed and stunned. A police officer spoke into a walkie-talkie; a gray-haired woman held a hand over her eyes. I could make out the steps of the Metropolitan Museum in the unfocused background as Luke put his finger to the headline. "Can we do this one?"

Claire scanned the article and frowned. "I'd rather try something different."

"Why?"

She sighed. "It's just . . . Something very sad happened to that young man."

I looked closely at the headshot: brown hair, brown eyes, a bland, unremarkable face that betrayed nothing except slight irritation, or maybe just boredom. I couldn't understand the unease roiling around in my stomach, a hot, greasy sensation, but I couldn't ignore it either. "What does it say?" I asked, although I was not sure I really wanted to know.

" 'Fall,'" Luke said. He pointed to the middle of the headline's five words.

"Yes," Claire said reluctantly.

I concentrated on the first word. " 'Fifth,'" I said, and Luke repeated it after me.

Claire hesitated, which meant I was correct. But the other three words were too complex for me, and for Luke as well. Abruptly, Claire flipped the paper over. "Enough." She put the first section back on top, and guided us to an article about the birth of a panda in a Chinese zoo.

After the rest of the paper had been parsed, Claire moved on to her day's work, pulling out a manuscript from the pile that engulfed her desk, getting on the telephone to her staff at the Chelsea offices of the Nightingale Press. Claire's mother, Venetia, had founded the publishing house with the remainder of the Nightingale banking fortune when Claire was a child; after her mother's abrupt death, Claire took over just as the will instructed. It was an independent mystery press and it made no money, but Claire considered the house to be more like a family member than a company, and you don't kill a relative just because she's crippled. Yet on that first morning I did not know any of this. All I knew was that Claire shut the door to her study at 9:00 A.M. sharp and—after emerging briefly at lunchtime to fix Luke a peanut butter and banana sandwich—did not open it again until five that afternoon.

"Luke!" she called from the doorway then, tethered to the room by the phone cord wrapped around her wrist. "Where are you, sweetie?" We had been exploring the Newport house all afternoon, and we were just taking a rest, lying on our backs in the tawny light of Luke's bedroom. He told me that Claire had pulled him out of kindergarten weeks before, soon after James had left, and now his afternoons were slow and dull. Lying there on the floor next to me, he turned his face to mine and said he was glad I was there to divide the time with him. I was about to reply when Claire turned the doorknob to her study. I heard the sound all the way across the apartment—the soft, dry click loud and distinct as a gunshot—and I jumped to my feet and was at the far end of the hallway, Luke close behind, by the time she called for him.

"There you are." She clucked at Luke as he slid around me to reveal himself. "What are you wearing? They'll be here in less than an hour."

I looked at his sweatpants and T-shirt. "They who?"

The phone squawked on Claire's shoulder. "Yes," she said into the receiver, "but excuses don't interest me, Gregory." A buzzer rang. "You might be spared." She hung up the phone and walked to the service door, where she received a riotous vase of flowers, then she trundled us into Luke's bedroom and laid out a gold-buttoned blazer, gray flannel slacks, a white dress shirt, and a pair of black loafers. She dangled a plaid bow tie like a dead mouse.

"What about Daniel?" Luke asked.

"I'm sure everybody will think Daniel looks fine." The buzzer rang again, and Claire disappeared. Luke undressed down to his briefs. His body was so pale and small, like a mollusk stripped of its shell. Larval. I was repelled but fascinated enough that I couldn't resist reaching out to probe his soft belly. He slapped my hand away. "Stop it." Soon the pasty skin was again hidden from sight, and I was glad I didn't have to look at it anymore.

The first group of guests arrived just after six. They wore suits and cufflinks, evening dresses and sparkling jewelry. We darted between their legs and almost knocked over a tuxedoed waitress bearing a silver tray of champagne flutes. A man with a gray face and yellow teeth bent down to shake Luke's hand, but Luke turned to the wall and refused to move. "Well, what do you expect," I heard a woman trill. "Plucked out of school, hunkered down in this apartment."

Claire consulted with a slim man in a black suit, some sort of pin with writing I couldn't read affixed to his lapel. The foyer slowly filled up with adults, their chatter clogging the air above our heads. At six-thirty, the slim man tapped his flute with a gold pen and led the crowd into the living room.

Like every other room in the apartment, its walls were crammed full of paintings and photographs, their frames sometimes touching to make space for as many pieces as possible. A photographic portrait rubbed shoulders with a pastoral landscape; a calligraphic scroll split two stark geometric prints. I didn't understand the arrangement, its chaos, its illogic, and I hated the way individual pieces were lost among the clutter.

The slim man stood at the head of the crowd and started talking. I couldn't catch what he was saying—something about a museum, something else about gratitude and a grand tradition. "Does this happen often?" I asked Luke. "Every month now," he said. "I hate it." We stood at the back of the crowd, and I edged forward until I was absorbed into the genteel organism. No one paid any attention to me. I looked up and saw each face pointed at the slim man, who was still talking. "God, what a mess," a man whispered into a hoary-haired ear. "Stored like cheap family snapshots." I slipped deeper into the crowd. "She's not as rich as she looks," I heard somebody say.

The slim man directed a laser pointer at a portrait of a white-frocked little girl. Claire, where was Claire? Through the forest of legs, I saw her on the far side of the room, alone, leaning on the grand piano for support. She looked to be on display, a painting herself: *Woman with Piano*. Expressions cycled across her face as though she were trying each on for size. Some were too tight, others too loose. Finally, she found one that fit: terror, sheer terror. Of what? I didn't know, but the emotion plastered itself onto her face like a wet rag. Then the speaker gestured toward her, and in a flash her gracious smile appeared, fast enough that I almost believed no one else saw what it replaced. She nodded back at the slim man, acknowledging something. Courteous, indulgent. I smelled Luke's milk-sweet breath on the back of my neck; he was smiling at his mother, his eyes wide and soft. The slim man turned again to the painting of the girl. "The shading," he said, "you'll find to be deceptive."

The length of a child's day is elastic. A moment can be stretched out into an entire afternoon, an afternoon compressed into the delving of a single moment. During the weeks that followed, while Claire sat at her desk in the study all day long, Luke and I had the run of the rest of the apartment, and time simply did not exist.

"Look at this one." Luke stood in front of one of the larger artworks in the living room, a painting of a peasant woman working at a fence, filling her basket with flowers that grew among the weeds at her feet. Its colors were light and soft, its brushstrokes staccato. The sky was pale blue, dotted with the cotton-candy clouds of a dry summer day, and the fields stretched out behind the woman in shades of green and sun-bleached yellow. In the near distance, a single willow tree cast a small pool of shade. A creature seemed to be hidden there within the texture of the brushstrokes, something that looked like a rabbit or maybe a dog, splayed out, possibly sleeping. It was more a suggestion of an animal than an animal itself, but there was something indecent about even this suggestion. It was as though the painter had changed his mind and, ashamed of what he had created, tried to conceal his original thought.

"Sweetie?" Claire appeared in the living room doorway. We blinked at her, startled out of our inspection of the painting. She moved to her son and put her hand on his forehead. "God, you're sweating." She looked where he looked. "Your grandmother bought that painting for the old Newport house, which is where it belongs." With her hand resting on her son's head, Claire seemed to forget where she was or who she was talking to. She looked into the painting and drummed her fingers on the top of Luke's skull, tapping out a secret code. Luke's eye caught mine, and he winked at me, his co-conspirator. We all stood together for a few more silent moments until Claire clapped her hands. "No more work for me today. Let's go to the park." She smiled at us. "Wouldn't you like that?"

Outside, it was colder than it had looked through the window, and as we crossed Fifth Avenue, a sharp wind funneled between the buildings at our backs. It was the first of December. We entered the Conservatory Garden under the iron curls of the Vanderbilt Gate and descended the steps into a garden empty of both flowers and people. Even the hedges were bare, presenting themselves as spindly outlines, placeholders for a greener spring. Claire was coatless in all black. She wore only slacks, a turtleneck sweater, and a scarf wrapped around the lower half of her face, a revolutionary dressed for a cocktail party. Who else frequented the northern reaches of Central Park at noon on a winter Thursday? A crumpled woman pushed a shopping cart loaded with bottles and broken radios; slow-eyed teenagers sauntered in no particular direction; a lean man, fit in fleece and spandex, strode along behind ten leashed dogs. I let my eyes linger on each face, on the way each person walked or spoke or arranged the angles of his body. I felt starved for information. No one noticed me. Not one person looked me in the eye.

We walked south, and Claire and Luke talked about why there had been no Thanksgiving dinner that year. "Your father's parents decided not to come to New York," Claire said. "He went to Philadelphia to see them instead."

"I remember Grandma and Grandpa's house. The one with all the lights outside."

"Hmmm?"

"The lights." Luke wiggled his fingers in front of his face. "Thousands of lights all over the house."

"Oh. That's only at Christmas, but yes, that's where your father was last weekend."

"When are we going there again?"

"We're not," she said.

He considered this for a moment. "That's okay," he said. "I didn't like it there anyway."

"That's not nice," Claire said, but her voice sounded half-hearted to me, false. I wondered whether Luke was smart enough to know he had said exactly what Claire wanted to hear.

We walked until we emerged into a clearing. A long field spread out in front of us, bare and freezing, six baseball diamonds ringing the patchy turf. Claire pointed across the field at a small castle perched on top of a pile of schist. "Camelot," she said. On the path leading up the hill, the bronze statue of a warrior frowned down from the saddle of his gigantic warhorse, twin broadswords crossed above his crown, turning his head to follow us as we made our way up the inclined path. Below, swans glided across the black surface of a pond; I looked down into the water and saw the sky as it appears at midnight.

We walked through the castle's entrance and onto an observation deck looking out over the field. We were alone except for a middle-aged couple dressed in shades of charcoal and brown, well-tailored layers of wool and cashmere. They held a guidebook and a camera with a telephoto lens they trained on each other like a gun. The man—as tall as James, but thicker and more handsome—spoke to his wife with a brittle and unfamiliar accent. "They're British," Claire whispered to us. "We like that." She walked right up to the couple and held out her hand. "Hello! I'm Claire. If you're lost I can help."

The woman turned. She was attractive but soft, her cheeks full and her chin weak, as though the sculpting of her face had been abandoned halfway through. "Oh! You startled me." A red kerchief, one lone burst of color, was tied under the neck to hold back her short hair. She took a step backward and her husband filled the space. "We're fine, thank you." Claire did not drop her hand, so he finally grasped it between his own. "My name is Simon, and you have very cold hands."

"A pleasure," Claire said. She looked as though she might execute a curtsy.

"The pleasure is all ours," said Simon.

He looked at Claire with something as covetous and nearly physical as hunger. It was the first time I realized how strangers saw her, how she displayed her beauty to them like an exotic mask, something both exaggerated and reductive.

Simon broke his gaze to gesture toward the towers floating above the trees on both sides of the park. "Each time I have business here, I come to stand at this spot, and I am always afraid they will be gone, poof, or different, 'improved.' But no, they stay as they should be."

Yet the buildings would not always stay as they should be, I thought. Each of them—somehow, sometime—was going to come down. That was the truth. Every single building in the world would be leveled at some point, humbled either in the rush of a destructive moment or by the slow creep of time and neglect. Each had its own secret endpoint. Was it more natural that I saw the buildings and thought only about their endings, or that everybody else saw them and didn't?

"There is some beauty left in this city," Claire said.

"More than some." Simon took his eyes off Claire for a moment. "That's true, isn't it, Jackie?"

"It is quite a lovely city, yes." Jackie's tone was flat, and she kept her distance from Claire.

Simon squatted down on his heels in front of us. "And who might you be?"

"Oh, excuse me." Claire eased Luke forward. "Say hello to Simon and . . ."

"Jackie."

Luke hid behind his mother and clutched at the fabric of her sweater. I inspected Simon's ruddy face, boyish and simple behind the wrinkles, and I noted Jackie's twitchy brown eyes and worried mouth. She did not see Claire the same way Simon did; she saw a different person entirely.

Claire grabbed Luke's shoulder and tried to pull him out from his hiding spot. He wouldn't budge. His mother smiled grimly at the couple; she wanted to show Luke off. "Sometimes he just doesn't want to talk," she said.

Simon straightened up and shrugged. "We all have those moments."

Without warning, in the still beat that followed, Claire reached out her hand and tucked a strand of Jackie's hair back under the kerchief. The touch was intimate, careful, almost erotic. But there was also something controlling or condescending in it. A painter correcting a canvas. The woman recoiled sharply, but Claire pressed forward to smooth the red silk across her forehead. "It was getting in your eyes," she said.

Jackie swatted Claire's hand down. "Excuse me. Excuse me."

Claire sighed. "I wish I had the face for that kerchief. A

woman needs some fullness in the cheeks for it to work, like you have. I'd look like a skeleton."

"Is that supposed to be a compliment?"

Claire touched her own cheekbones sadly. "Skin and bones."

Jackie looked over our heads for the deck's exit, a tight fury gathering in her face. Her husband was embarrassed, but I wasn't sure for whom. Luke let go of his mother's sweater to peer through a slit in the low wall onto the rocks and pond below.

"This is boring," he said. "Why does she always have to talk to everybody?"

"I don't think that woman likes her very much," I said.

"Who cares? Who is she anyway?"

"Nobody. Let's get out of here."

A large group poured out onto the balcony behind a man carrying a neon-orange flag on a stick. The observation deck was suddenly crowded with elderly couples wearing pastels and the dazed look of the herded. As Claire rubbed her arms and softened her words, Luke and I melted into the gaggle of wrinkled faces and disappeared.

A network of paths fanned out from the castle into the wilder areas of the park. Trees leaned over the walkways and closed off the view above their branches, and sometimes we lost sight of any buildings at all. We could have been anywhere then, miles from anything. The few people we saw did nothing, and let us pass by without question. They let us go because that was the easiest thing for them to do.

"My mother is gonna to be angry," Luke said, but he didn't seem anxious. He was just stating a fact.

"Yes," I said. "But you don't want to go back, do you?"

He didn't even slow his pace. More clouds moved in, and it grew colder. If we had ever known where we were going, we were certainly lost now. The path became steeper, and we entered a hilly area where walkways intersected at drunken angles and bushes crowded the cracked blacktop. The paths turned in on themselves, drawing tighter knots. Luke laughed to hide his fear. I felt him grow nervous as he realized what we'd done. There was no way we could ever find our way back. We would have to ask for help and break that cardinal rule of all children: never talk to strangers.

"We could play a game," I said. Anything to delay our reunion with Claire. When Luke was with her, it sometimes seemed as though I was not even there.

"What game?"

"Hide-and-seek." It was the first thing I could think of.

He considered the idea for a moment. "It's a good game," he finally said.

He told me to close my eyes while he hid. I did as he said, sneaking a last glimpse at his little body tunneling wormlike into the underbrush before I lowered my eyelids. I felt unmoored in the sudden blackness, floating in deepest space. After counting to sixty, I opened my eyes. I stepped off the path to follow Luke and moved into dense clutches of shrubs and leafless trees extending out on every side, crowding in on each other and leaving little room between their branches. I tested how it felt to be alone again; I couldn't remember the last time. A strange anxiety came over me. I suddenly thought this game was a terrible idea, our separation a bad mistake. I wanted to find Luke as soon as I could, and I began to move faster through trees that loomed prehistorically huge all around me. I focused all my attention on trying to discover his hiding spot. Since sight told me nothing, I closed my eyes again and tried to locate Luke some other way. I concentrated until there seemed to be a slight pull in the darkness to my left. The pull grew stronger and then it became truly forceful, a magnet I could not have ignored even if I had wanted to. I opened my eyes and the feeling remained. I walked through a small slot between two black cherry trees and then—"Boo!"—Luke burst out from behind a bush, and I jumped despite myself. "Got you." He grinned, at ease. Obviously, he had not shared in my panic, and I put on a fake smile because I didn't want to seem the weaker one.

Luke stuck his tongue out at me, and suddenly I heard voices echo through the trees. Luke heard them too. We looked at each other, trying to figure out where they came from. Luke pointed at a small rise beyond which we couldn't see. We heard a man's laughter and something harsher following it, an exhortation or a command. We got down on our stomachs and crawled up to the crest of the rise, the last fall leaves rustling like burnt paper beneath our bodies.

Down in a hollow hidden from any path, a man and a woman were under a tree. She faced away from him, her hands splayed on the tree trunk, her fingers scratching at the bark. She was bent over at the waist, and her jeans had been pulled down (or maybe she had pulled them down herself) around her ankles like denim manacles. Her thighs were an inconceivable white in the middle of all the muted grays and browns; her head was hidden so cleanly between her outstretched arms that for a moment it seemed to be missing. The man was positioned behind her, one hand gripping her waist, the other locked around her wrists, pressing them against the tree. His own jeans were unbuttoned and loosened but not pulled down. The man's head was big and heavy-looking, sinking into his shoulders like a boulder into mud. He wasn't young, and when I saw the woman's face, I could tell she wasn't young either. She gave out a low noise, and the man took his hand off her waist and roughly covered her mouth with it, pinching her nostrils shut and mashing his palm into her lips. The man was showing his power over the woman, but the woman, by submitting, was showing her own power too. She looked up and saw us hiding there on the rise. Behind the masking hand her face wore an expression I had never seen before, and it took me years to understand what it meant. Pride was part of it; so was pure physical pleasure. But the largest portion was a kind of defiant cunning. The man was animalistic and base; he'd take whatever he could get. It was the woman who was permitting the moment to happen. Everything we saw was of her design. She snared us for a moment with her eyes, and then we got up and ran.

3

WE WAITED IN the lobby for an hour. After a teenage girl, our rescuer, deposited us under the awning, the doormen had been discreet and asked few questions, setting us on a low leather bench and letting us be. We had almost knocked the girl over in the park, tearing out of the trees and plowing straight into her book bag; she had soothed us then with her owl-eyes, her slow, soft speech and chapped fingers. She coaxed an address out of us and then paid for the crosstown cab, presenting us to the doorman like an unrequested gift before crossing Fifth Avenue and disappearing back into the park.

Finally, Claire and James emerged out of the backseat of a black car. Claire saw us first, and she froze just outside the open lobby door, her hands clasped across her stomach. It had been at least two hours since we had left her side. James brushed past her, walking into the building with clipped steps. He bent down to hug Luke, kissing him once on the forehead, and then he straightened up, grabbed his son's arm, and headed toward the elevator without saying a word. When its doors opened and Claire still hadn't moved, he turned around: "It would be a good idea to get in this elevator before I start to get angry."

Upstairs, Claire wouldn't let Luke leave her sight. She paced around the kitchen as we sat at the table and James leaned his long body across the doorway. I hunched down in my chair and hoped everybody would forget about me.

"Claire," James said. "I don't want to upset our arrangement. You've made concessions, and so have I. We have an agreement. But you can't expect me to ignore this lapse."

"I want to go to my room," Luke said.

"There's been enough of what you want today," Claire snapped.

"Let him go." James's eyes were sunken into deep wells of purple skin, but underneath this exhaustion buzzed an alertness, a sense of opportunity. He smiled at Luke, but Luke was looking at his mother instead.

"You will not blackmail me in my own home," Claire said. "You don't live here anymore."

"Just tell me why I should stand here and listen to you instead of calling my lawyer."

"I don't need to defend myself." Claire jabbed her finger at him. "You gave up on both of us a long time ago."

"The way you flip things around is un—"

"Keep your mouth shut."

James held up his hands. "Give me a reason to."

And she did. Within a month, Claire sold the Fifth Avenue apartment to James and put most of the art up for auction. During those four weeks, she did not sleep. She talked on the phone all night, urgently whispering behind her bedroom door. She ate nothing at dinner three evenings in a row, and then roasted a whole turkey the next morning. It sat there on the kitchen counter for five days, a carving knife planted in its breast, a crime scene.

The Fire Island house was simple enough to arrange. Claire took a leave of absence from the press, although she still packed an enormous trunk full of manuscripts and galleys. She used the money from the art auction to rent the beach house, which wasn't difficult since nobody wants to be on Fire Island in the winter anyway. The villages dotted along its length are almost deserted from November through April, and at night it felt like we were settlers of a remote and frozen northern coast, somewhere hostile to human inhabitance.

We left Manhattan on New Year's Day. "Fitting," Claire said. The car—her mother's, a rust-spotted maroon Saab that had been rotting for a decade in a garage somewhere in

Queens—sat double-parked on Fifth Avenue. Luke and I stood on the sidewalk outside the lobby, watching two doormen in their green coats and peaked caps carry Claire's luggage out from the building. The suitcases and trunks were finely made, with leather trim and brass rivets, gold clasps and velvet lining, but they were old and overused, the leather cracked and the metal dull. The Saab was not a big car, and the doormen were having trouble fitting everything inside. After the trunk was full, they moved on to the backseat, stacking and restacking under Claire's direction until finally everything fit. "Well," Claire said, "that was more difficult than I had imagined." She smiled at us, something small and desperate beating itself against the cage of her smile.

Luke looked at the packed car. "But where's Daniel going to sit?"

I had of course assumed I was coming with them. What would I do here in New York by myself?

"Hmmm." Claire blinked rapidly. Luke would sit up front with his mother—there was no question about that—and the backseat did not have an extra inch of room. "How about in the trunk?" Claire suggested. "The trunk?" I said. We walked around to the back of the car. The arrangement of the bags left an odd-shaped gap, too irregular for any suitcase but perhaps large enough for me if I scrunched myself into a tight ball.

"Do you think he'll be okay in there?" Luke asked.

"Why don't you ask me?" I said.

Claire nodded. "I'm sure he will be fine."

"Is anybody listening to me?" I said. "I will *not* be fine. What's wrong with you?"

Luke glanced at me. "Calm down, Daniel."

"I refuse."

"Don't be difficult," he said.

"Lower your voice," Claire said. "Daniel will go in the trunk and that's the end of it." She walked around to the driver's-side door and buckled herself in.

"Luke," I begged, "please."

"You'll fit in there," Luke said, "and you'll be fine because I say you'll be fine." Claire jammed on the horn, and Luke put his hands on my shoulders and pushed me forward. I shook myself free. "I can do it myself." I climbed into the tiny space, hanging half in and half out of the car. Luke grabbed my floppy stray leg and tucked it into the trunk with the rest of me, completing my humiliation. "There," he said. My bones softened, pressed into new shapes by the hard-sided suitcases, my body folding in on itself like a flower closing before a rainstorm. Luke slammed the trunk shut and darkness collapsed on top of me.

The Saab rumbled to life. We jerked forward and the luggage shifted, flattening me against one side of the trunk. My body offered no resistance to the more permanent things crowding upon it. Soon I was just an idea to be folded and stored like an item of clothing. We hurtled out of Manhattan and over the East River in our metal box. By the time we came to a stop an hour later and Claire opened the trunk—the sky gray and wide above her head, the white ferry bobbing on green water—I knew what part of me had always known: I was not a normal child.

———

That night, I stood at the top of the stairs of our rented house as Claire hollowed out a squash, its stringy yellow guts splattered across the kitchen counter. She pinched her brow in effort and blew a strand of hair away from her face. January swept in through the open kitchen windows, and outside, the lights of the few occupied houses glowed sparsely across the island. She attacked the squash, raking at its insides, but her spoon was too dull and kept getting snagged in the pulp. Soon she gave up and tossed the halved thing into the garbage. Dinner that night came out of a can, and after Claire washed the dishes, she swallowed a small yellow pill with a glass of water and went to sleep.

The next morning, she didn't get out of bed. Luke and I climbed the stairs and stood at the deck windows, watching the ocean beat itself against the shore. It was an upside-down house, with the kitchen, living room, and master bedroom on the second floor, two smaller bedrooms and a den on the first. I listened at the door to Claire's room and heard nothing. After waiting half an hour, Luke made himself a bowl of cereal, spilling Cheerios all over the floor. At nine o'clock, he knocked on Claire's door. There was no answer. He tried the handle, but it was locked. I didn't understand; I had never seen Claire get up any later than seven. In fact, when I went to sleep at night, she was awake, and when I got up in the morning, she was awake then too. I'd never had any evidence that she slept at all.

Unease slunk into the house. It draped itself over the plaid couch, fingered the bookshelves lined with the creased spines of paperback thrillers, handled each miniature lighthouse and ship-in-a-bottle. I wondered if Claire were dead, or if she had abandoned us, locking her door and lowering herself out the window like an escaping convict. I tried to distract Luke by guessing about the house's owners. They were international spies, and this was their hideaway. Beneath the floor, there were underground chambers, hidden bunkers, a passageway to China. Or they were witches and sorcerers, and this their gingerbread house. In the dirt under the porch, we would find the bones of little children, picked clean and buried after a cannibal's dinner.

"The last time she locked her door, it was summer," Luke said. "She didn't come out for three days. I went to my father's office and learned how to use the abacus, and then he took me to the museum to see the dinosaurs."

"What did she say when she came out?"

"Nothing. She was tired. But my father made us dinner and then she said she felt better." He saw me looking at the closed door. "It'll be okay. Let's go outside."

We spent the rest of the morning behind the house, out in the dune grass and pines. We found an old tennis ball among the pellets of deer droppings that littered the ground, and when Claire finally came out onto the deck, Luke was flinging the ball against the back wall of the house over and over again. I envied him the simple mechanical motion, the satisfaction of making such a casual impact on the world around him. Each time the ball hit the house, it made a hollow thump, like dirt shoveled onto a coffin. Inside, Claire fixed Luke an onion and mayonnaise sandwich and offered no explanations. All afternoon she stared at a single manuscript page, her own mood closely matched by the particular loneliness of a house and town so out of season.

My sleeping problems began soon after we arrived. Claire's habits had changed. She now closed the door to her bedroom around nine at night, and didn't reemerge until after nine the next morning. She tucked Luke in downstairs—ignoring me now, pretending I wasn't there—before turning out the lights, but she hardly ever read him a good-night mystery like she had in Manhattan. Luke wasn't interested in mimicking his mother's new schedule. He still rose at dawn, and we had the house to ourselves for a few hours before Claire appeared; at night, he still fell asleep within seconds after his mother closed the door. I was the one who lay on the room's second bed with my mind both blank and busy—the insomniac's paradox—tossing and turning my way through the small hours.

Our room looked as though it was used by the owners for houseguests rather than any children of their own. Replica ship wheels and seascape watercolors hung above the two single beds, aggressively anodyne in the moonlight. When I couldn't bear lying awake any longer and stood up to pace the room, I was struck by the indifference of my empty bed, its sheets crisply tucked under the mattress and folded back at the top with military precision. Sometimes I slipped out of the room and prowled around the darkened house. Next to our bedroom was the den with its collection of VHS tapes we never watched and its wall clock that never showed the right time. Upstairs, I looked at framed photographs of the owners' family, freckled redheads of different ages and eras. They smiled out at me from side tables and bookshelves: little children in life jackets, teenagers with tennis racquets, a middle-aged man standing on a dock with a fishing pole. The older photos had a faded, sun-bleached quality that somehow suggested simpler times. Everyone looked like everyone else at a different age. I wished Claire would hide them all away in a drawer somewhere. I did not want to live among the evidence of someone else's memories. Later in the winter, Luke and I took the photographs out to the beach in his backpack and buried them under the sand as if they were real dead people and not just pictures of them.

A month after our arrival on the island, Luke and I were playing together on the beach when we heard the school bus rumble toward us across the sand. On the other side of the dunes, Claire kept an eye on us from the deck of the house. Since dawn I had watched Luke wheel his toy dump truck across the high-tide line and fill its flatbed with pebbles, seaweed, and crab shells, before adding each load to a row of similar deposits. He poked at the mounds of debris, salvaging the most promising objects and cleaning them off on his jeans to bring home to present to Claire. The little school bus now emerged from the mist and bounced along the beach, pulling to a stop fifty feet to the west of us. A small figure with a backpack trotted down the steps leading from the boardwalk to the beach and picked its way carefully across the sand to the waiting bus. The door swung open; the child climbed in; the door swung shut again. Luke put his dump truck down and watched as the bus drove past us, continuing east to the island's single tiny schoolhouse. The children were shapes fluttering behind windows murky with condensation and grit. A patch of bright clothing flashed here and a palm pressed against the inside of the glass there. Red taillights shuddered, the last thing to be swallowed up by the fog.

"My mother says I'm not going back until next fall."

"I heard her."

He stood up, clumps of sand sticking to his jeans. "She says it's better for me to be out here with her now, but I don't know. School wasn't so bad."

I was sick of thinking about it, so I just said, "Let's play a new game." The thought of touching all those strange children, even of sharing a room with them, filled me with nausea. The germs on their wormy little fingers, thick in the saliva of their mewling mouths. Children were repulsive.

I pointed at a tangle of seaweed and driftwood lying thirty feet down the beach. "Last one there and back has to stick his head in the ocean." Luke ignored me and squinted at where the bus had disappeared. Without saying anything more, he turned his back on me and walked toward the house. It squatted among the dune grass, its coat of weather-beaten gray paint the same shade as the mist, a dull chameleon on stilts. Claire waved from her perch on the deck. Luke's pockets bulged with sea glass, green and blue shards rubbed to a milky finish. If she were in a good mood, Claire would pore over these fragments together with him, and the best, carefully sorted by color and size, would take their place in the milk bottles that lined the kitchen windows.

But she was rarely in a good mood, which suited me fine. She mostly just holed up in her bedroom, sleeping, or talking on what I assumed was a telephone, although I never actually found one in the room. I didn't need her around, the way her lip now curled or her brows knit every time Luke mentioned me. I didn't share their sadness either. She and Luke drifted around the house like ghosts, but I felt as strong and alive as I could remember. The island's melancholy air was thick, rich with nourishment. I loved the town's silence; there were so few people to breathe on me with their filthy breath, to rub against me with their greasy bodies. We were alone out there, and Luke turned to me more each day. Our games took on new levels of complexity. The antic world behind the world—with its dinosaurs and wizards, its talking elephants and two-headed tigers—asserted itself with pushy insistency. We found Pygmies crouching in the dune grass and stalked rocs strutting along the shoreline. Under the shadow of a pine tree, whole empires rose and fell in a single afternoon.

Yet when we returned to the house this morning, I could tell something was different. Claire wore jeans and a clean turtleneck instead of her usual sweatpants and flannel shirt. She clapped her hands in front of her smiling face. "Okay! Luke, sweetie, what do you want to do today?"

He sat down at the kitchen table. "I have some sea glass," he said.

Claire pulled up a chair next to her son. "Okay, and then after that we're going to do whatever you want, today and every day. The only rule is it has to be something we can do together, the two of us. That's all."

They settled on a checkers tournament, and then moved on to hangman. They spent hours constructing a Lego castle they found in a musty closet, the set complete with its own moat, drawbridge, and battalion of knights. In the afternoon, when the fog cleared, they put on their rubber boots and left for a walk on the beach. I wasn't invited, and even if I'd wanted to come along, I suddenly felt far too weak to leave the house.

From the upstairs deck, I watched their figures dwindle down to two dots, hemmed in by the ocean on one side and dunes on the other. Luke hadn't spoken to me or even looked at me since breakfast that morning; he'd forgotten all about me. I drifted around the living room, dizzy and weightless. I pressed my back against the kitchen wall, slid down to the floor, and clasped my arms around my knees. The feeling of the tiles beneath my feet became faint and then disappeared altogether; sudden darkness, sickening and absolute, swept over me. I was left floating in the black, the shadowy twin of sleep, until I finally heard the click of the front door opening below, and the patter of Luke's feet running up the stairs. He sprinted to the refrigerator for a glass of apple juice and didn't see me there, hunched into a ball in the kitchen's corner. When he finally noticed me, all he said was, "What are you doing? The floor's dirty," before he ran back downstairs to where I could hear Claire calling his name.

4

THREE AWFUL DAYS later, I sat on the plaid living-room couch and tried to repair my failing health. I thought of the school bus we had seen on the beach, all those solid little children packed together inside. They could take their bodies and lives for granted, while I depended upon the fickle attentions of a six-year-old child. I attempted to explain how I felt to Luke, but it was impossible to prove; he could never see the problem, because to look at it was to solve it.

At the kitchen table, where they sat playing checkers again, Claire pinched her son's arm and said she had a surprise for him.

"What is it?" he asked. "Tell me."

"You'll have to wait and see. Get dressed. We're going to meet the ferry."

"Why? Who's coming?" He bounced in his chair. "Is someone coming to see me?"

"Something like that."

I followed Luke downstairs to our bedroom and sat on my bed as he pulled a sweater over his curly black hair and tightened the Velcro straps on his sneakers. I hated those sneakers; they were toys, with the Velcro and the red lights blinking on each heel, infantile, not something I would ever choose for myself. He glanced over at me. "Who do you think it is?"

"I have no idea. Your father, maybe?" I guessed that's who he wanted it to be.

Luke considered this, then shook his head. "No. He's not coming. My mother said she didn't tell him where we were going." He spoke flatly, as though the subject were neutral. I thought he might have been acting; it seemed strange to me that he could accept such a separation so easily.

He paused in the doorway. Claire already stood out on the porch, holding a bulging envelope stuffed full of manuscript edits and annotated contracts. I had seen her packing it the night before; it was the first work she had done since we arrived on the island. She carefully knotted a plaid scarf around her neck and called over her shoulder, "Luke, let's go, we can't be late." She had been taking greater care with her appearance over the last few days. It was something she must have been doing for herself, because there was no one except Luke and me to notice. He turned around and looked at me. Almost as an afterthought, he said, "You can come with us if you want to."

"Okay," I said, hating how grateful I felt. I stood up unsteadily and followed him out the front door. It seemed I now needed an invitation to accompany him anywhere. We set off down a boardwalk that ran over the marshy and sunken interior of the island. Outside each locked-up house, rusty spokes and handlebars poked out from underneath vinyl tarps. Bamboo stalks leaned in from both sides to form a tunnel through which Claire and Luke briskly walked. When we reached the dock, I could already see the ferry slicing its way through the chop. Sandbars and shrubby islets clotted the Great South Bay, and ropes of seaweed lay slack on its surface. In the misty weather, mainland Long Island, only five miles away, was a smudge on the northern horizon. I watched as the captain cut back on the throttle and the boat slid parallel to the dock. A crewmember looped his line over the pylon, and Luke tried to rush the boat. Claire held him back, laughing as he almost jerked her off her feet. I hung behind them. I didn't trust all this excitement. Nothing good could come of it for me; I only wanted things to remain as they had been when we first arrived.

The ferry drew steady and a crewman rolled open its metal door. First came a pair of workers wearing overalls and carrying landscaping tools, and then off stepped John Bellwether, the permanently sunburned contractor who fixed our broken pipes and leaking ceilings. He nodded toward Claire and Luke. After he passed, Claire whispered, "I don't trust that man. He never looks me in the eye."

Last off the boat was a pasty teenager in khakis and sunglasses, a black Labrador puppy wriggling in his arms. He put the dog down on the dock and wrapped its leash around his wrist before he shook Claire's hand. Luke broke free of his mother and flopped down onto his stomach, poking at the puppy, his hand darting out for quick, tentative pats. The animal lurched at me, and I jerked my leg out of its way. Its face looked damaged and its tongue lolled inanely out of its mouth. "Get away," I hissed. "Don't touch me."

"It's for me," Luke said. "It's for me, right?"

The teenager brought out a clipboard and handed it to Claire. "He's scared of the water, but that shouldn't last."

"He's so *small*," Claire said.

"You'll want to let him run around a lot at first."

"A little piece of midnight."

The kid pointed at the clipboard. "Just sign here, please."

He shook her hand again and gave her the leash before getting back on the boat. Claire handed her envelope of work papers to a crewman to drop into a mainland mailbox, slipping him a twenty-dollar bill underneath the envelope. While his mother loaded the weekly shipment of groceries onto our wagon, Luke tried to scoop up the puppy, but it scrambled out of his grasp. Claire reined the animal in and tucked it under the crook of her arm. She pulled the wagon with her other hand and started off toward home.

"But I want to hold him," Luke said. "He's mine, right?"

"You'll get your chance, honey." The dog squirmed under Claire's grip. "I think he's a little frightened right now, so it's probably best if I carry him."

"But—"

"Luke, don't get greedy, okay? There will be plenty of time to play with him later."

"What do you want with that thing anyway?" I said. "It's just a bundle of fur and spit."

Ahead of us on the boardwalk, Bellwether stood outside the firehouse talking to a pair of cops clustered around one of their red ATVs. The contractor poked at the vehicle's engine, divining its troubles. We approached, and Bellwether looked up. Days could go by before we ran into another person on the island, but as we passed the firehouse Claire put her head down and quickened her pace. When we drew even with them, the puppy slipped out of her grasp and bolted over to the three men. Bellwether ducked out from under the hood and scooped up the dog. "I got you." He held the animal in front of his face and shook it lightly. "Trying to run away from Ms. Nightingale already?" Claire dropped the wagon handle and darted toward the men, but Luke got there first.

"Give him to me," he said. "He's mine."

The three men looked down at the child. Bellwether said, "Nobody's trying to steal anything."

Luke held out his hands. "Give him here. I want him now."

"Luke!" Claire came up behind him. "Have you completely forgotten how to talk to people?"

Luke stared at Bellwether. "I don't trust him either," he said. "And the dog's mine."

Nobody moved for a few seconds, but then Bellwether held the dog out to Luke. The thing kicked at the air, flailing against Luke's chest and trying its best to break free again. Luke staggered under the weight, but he held tight to his gift.

"I'm sorry, John, he didn't mean it like that, I—"

Bellwether brushed away Claire's words. "Don't think about it twice. He's just a kid." The cops' walkie-talkies squawked on their utility belts, and they busied themselves with the dials; I was the only one who noticed the sneer on Bellwether's face. Claire said, "Well, I'm sorry anyway." She took Luke by the arm and led him back to the wagon. The dog panted against his belly, a thrumming black ball of fur. It looked fake, like a wind-up toy slapped together in a factory. I imagined underneath the fur patches of something shiny and synthetic. I bent my head to its chest to listen for the whirring of its machinery. Claire started to pull the wagon again, and Luke and I trailed behind her. "Let me touch it," I said, reaching out my hand.

Luke spun away from me. "Leave him alone. He's mine."

Claire said, "We need to work on sharing."

⊷⊶

Within a few more days, I knew I was dying. Luke hardly even acknowledged me anymore. When he wasn't playing with Claire, he was running around with the dog, this cheap replacement for— who? James? Me? Every morning, he threw a tennis ball from our yard out into the dunes and watched Midnight scramble through the grass to retrieve it. He took the thing into our room at night, and it slept curled up at his feet, entwined in his sheets while I lay sleepless on the second bed. My body began to fall apart. I often lost all feeling in my feet and legs, and when I looked down at my torso I noticed gaps, raw holes through which I could clearly see the floor or the chair in which I sat. Sometimes I was too weak to move at all, and I just lay on the couch for hours. One night, a week after Midnight's arrival, I went into the bathroom while Luke and Claire slept to stare at my reflection in the mirror.

I was old. I was tall and stooped, with sloping shoulders and meaty hands. My face had lines, deep crevices and pockmarks. What I saw had nothing to do with who I believed myself to be. I looked like a distant cousin of Luke's father. Bits and pieces of my face and body had been pilfered from his own— the rigid jawline, the large hands, the recessed brown eyes—but others must have had their origin elsewhere, in the features of an uncle, a family friend, or even a complete stranger. As I stared into the mirror, I wondered if I had always looked like this, or if my appearance changed along with Luke's needs. My face was the shape of Luke's loneliness, but now that shape was disintegrating.

I crept back into our bedroom to make sure Luke was still

sleeping. He was: in the sliver of moonlight slanting across his body, I saw his little hands folded on top of his chest as though in prayer, his chin tucked into the hollow at the base of his neck. I envied him. When was the last time I had spent a night in such peace? I left him there, and prowled the ground floor looking for the dog. It wasn't in the den or sleeping among the dust and silence of the other, unused guest bedroom. I climbed the stairs, listening for the click of its paws on the hardwood floors: nothing. The second floor had an open-plan design that offered few places to hide. The only separate room was Claire's, and that door was closed. Could the animal be sleeping with her? She had never let it into her room at night before, but maybe she had been feeling generous that evening, or lonely. I stepped toward her door, then saw a silver flicker of movement out on the deck. One of the sliding glass doors had been left partially open. A breeze heavy with salt and pine slipped through the open space, and I went to meet it.

Outside, Midnight paced from one end of the deck to the other like a convict, as though someone had wound the animal up with a key and let it go. The dog stopped moving and sniffed the air when I stepped toward it. The wind was cold, the ocean cracked glass under a brilliant half-moon. The Fire Island night sky was huge, vertiginous on a cloudless night in its clarity and depth. Between the moon and its scattered reflection on the ocean, I could see the dog staring at me, perfectly still; it seemed to know what I was there for.

I carefully stepped forward, and the dog stayed where it was, vibrating as though an idling motor were locked up in its stomach. When it was within reach, I lunged at it, all grasping hands, but it skittered under me and shot inside through the open door. Its speed was startling, and I realized this might be more difficult than I had imagined. Inside again, I couldn't find it. I didn't want to turn on the lights, afraid I would alert Claire or Luke, so I had to squint into the darkness and hope the thing's movements would give it away. I was going to use my bare hands; I was going to grab the thing by its neck and squeeze until it stopped breathing. I had been too accepting of my deterioration, too passive. It was time to act. So where was the fucking dog?

A pillow on the couch moved. I quickly went after it, but again the animal was far too fast for me. I banged my toe on the couch's leg and fell face-first into the cushions. My toe felt like it had been pried open by a crowbar. I paused there for a moment, listening to see if I had woken Claire, but I heard nothing except the soft whine of the dog from somewhere behind the couch. Luckily the thing was not a barker.

I chased the animal around the second floor for the rest of the night. It pinballed off walls and pieces of furniture, corkscrewing around chair and table legs, impossible to track, a flashing blur of fur and a wet red mouth. And those paws! The clatter of the thing's nails on the wood floor drove me mad. I tried crouching behind the bookshelf, poised to topple it over as soon as the dog drew near, but it never came within range. I tried herding it like a cow back onto the deck to force it through the railing's slats and over the ledge, but it kept its distance. Finally, at the first sign of dawn, I gave up. I was exhausted. The hunt had drained the last of my energy. I lay down on the couch, defeated, and fell asleep.

Luke shook me awake what felt like minutes later. Sunlight pierced the glass deck doors at that acute early-morning angle. He sat next to me on the couch, bleary-eyed and irritated. "What's going on?" he said.

"What do you mean?" I feigned confusion, looking for the dog out of the corner of my eye.

"Why did I wake up on the couch next to you?"

"You did?" This was not a question I had anticipated.

"I went to sleep downstairs and I woke up here. I'm not sure why, but somehow this is your fault." His big right toe was purple and yellow underneath the nail. He stood up and limped to the windows. The ocean glittered, too bright to look at for more than a second.

I felt awful. I looked down at my body and saw why. I was naked, and my skin provided only patchwork cover for my organs and bones, and even those were riddled with holes. The blue-and-white plaid of the couch showed clearly through my drafty torso. "Luke." He stared out the window, ignoring me. "Luke!"

He wearily turned. "What?"

"Look at me. Help me."

He blinked. "What's the problem?"

"Can't you see? Fix me, please."

"I don't think so, Daniel. I really don't think there's anything I can do."

The dog crouched in the corner, spying on us. "I don't know

what's wrong with Midnight this morning," Luke said, "it's like he's scared of me." He moved toward the animal, and the thing tensed before deciding to accept his stroking hand. The door to Claire's bedroom opened; she smiled at us in the secondhand sunshine. While his mother busied herself with the coffee machine, Luke grabbed a tennis ball and ran outside with the dog. I summoned up all my remaining strength to follow him downstairs, into the pines and sand behind the house. He tossed the ball out onto the carpet of needles and the dog shot off after it. The animal returned with the ball clamped between its teeth, and as Luke pried it out, I said, "Mind if I play too?"

"I'd rather you just watch." Luke flicked the ball out in a high arc beyond the first clump of pines, into the snarl of dune grass near the neighbors' house, which was locked and dark like all the others. The dog knew what was expected of it, and off it went. I stood out there with Luke for what must have been nearly an hour. The animal was tireless and single-minded as it ricocheted through the pines. Luke loosened up, succumbing to the rhythm of the throws. He started talking, and I didn't interrupt. He talked about the cartoon he'd watched, the Connect Four game he'd won, the constellations Claire had pointed out from the deck a few nights before. These were the trivial facts of his new happiness—false, all of them. His memory was truncated, foreshortened; as for a fly, his present situation was his only situation. It was so easy for him now, and I didn't believe it for a second.

Luke threw the ball again, but this time the dog ignored it, distracted by something behind us. We turned to see two deer step in their dainty way across the high ridge of the dunes, pausing to bend their heads and pick at the dune grass as they went. Both had mangy and tattered coats, threadbare like third-hand clothing; they looked diseased, and probably were. These things were all over the place, an infestation. Claire told us that they had walked onto the island hundreds of years ago, when most of the Great South Bay had been filled in with sand. The waters rose, and the deer were cut off, marooned without a single predator, left without the proper fear, to grow fat and diseased and complacent. Now they went wherever they pleased, eating flowers and spreading infections. They regarded us from the crest of the dune: we were nothing to them. Claire stepped out onto the deck and called Luke in for breakfast.

She set a plate of chocolate chip pancakes in front of her son before she drained her cup of coffee and announced that the downstairs deck needed repainting. "As a goodwill gesture to our hosts. So they'll have one less thing to pay John Bellwether for." She put her hand on Luke's forehead. "I'll be down there for a little while, but you have Midnight to keep you company."

"What about me?" I said.

Claire looked down at Luke for a long moment. "It was the right thing to come out here," she said quietly. "The two of us alone. Out here I can keep you safe. I'm sorry about how I . . . disappear sometimes. But you always know how much I love you." Luke nodded but said nothing, and she lifted her palm off his head and went downstairs. I watched through the window as she swept her hair back into a ponytail and dragged a paint bucket out from the empty space underneath the house. The bucket was dented and rust-spotted, as though it had been sitting under there for decades. Claire paused, then rolled up her sleeves to inspect the flaked coat of gray that barely covered the deck's raw wood.

Luke sat at the breakfast table and buried his face in a second helping of pancakes. They were disgusting, a stack of doughy discs soaking in a pool of sugar-larded syrup. *The act of eating reduces people to animals.* I sat across the table watching him and kept my own face neutral. The dog jumped down from the couch, ingratiating itself by pawing at Luke's feet. He gave it a piece of pancake and said, "Don't tell my mother."

I pointed at his plate. "Looks like the dog really loves pancakes."

"Yeah, I give him food when Mom's not looking." He turned conspiratorial. "I think that's why he likes me better."

I looked down at the purple tongue licking Luke's extended fingers. "You might be right. But I know something that will make him like you even more."

"I doubt it."

"I'll show you if you don't believe me." I stood up and walked toward Claire's bedroom. "Come on. Don't you want to see?"

He hopped off his chair and followed me into the dim corner room. We stepped over the scattered manuscripts and books that Claire had dragged onto the ferry in that ancient and gargantuan trunk, books that she hoarded in piles like stolen treasure. Many of the hardbacks bore the Nightingale Press emblem on their spines, a simple tracing of a bird in flight. The manuscripts leaned against the walls and one another, precarious towers of paper. Red pen markings had been scribbled in the margins and all over the typed text, but everything seemed so chaotic it was hard to imagine she had done any useful work. We made our way to the doorway of Claire's bathroom in the far corner. Here Luke stopped and looked nervously back toward the living room. "We aren't supposed to go in there. My mother said."

I peered out the small window above Claire's unmade bed. She was still on the lower deck, dunking a roller into the paint can. I turned back to Luke: "You're not scared, are you?" It was the question he had asked me all winter before sneaking into the crawlspace underneath the house or jumping off the lifeguard stand onto the mound of sand below. Now he responded as I always had.

"No"—he shook his head—"I'm not."

"Good." I stepped into the bathroom and told Luke to open the medicine cabinet. The bottom shelf was crammed with orange plastic pill bottles. I could only read a few phrases of the text printed on their labels: "Three times a day," said one. "Take with food," read another. The rest of the words were beyond me, and I couldn't work out the names of the medicines themselves. I tried to identify the bottle I had seen Claire dip into every night during our first two months in the house, but I couldn't be sure. I narrowed it down to two of the same size and shape and just guessed.

Luke palmed the bottle, and we brought our bounty out to

the kitchen. He had problems opening it, so I pointed out the proper way to depress then twist the lid. He finally pried it off and shook a handful of yellow pills out onto the table. He looked at them blankly. "What are these?"

"These," I said, "are magic pills made from powdered gold and dried sunflowers. It's a medicine that will cure any disease." I frowned at him. "Haven't you noticed that the dog's looked a little sick the last few days?"

"So why doesn't my mother give them to him?"

I shrugged. "Maybe because she doesn't understand the dog as well as you. Or maybe she just wants to keep all the pills for herself. She gets sick too sometimes."

"I know that." He looked at me, then back down at the pills. "I'm not sure about this. Midnight seemed fine earlier this morning."

"Yeah," I said, "but look at him now."

We both turned to observe the thing dozing underneath the kitchen table.

I said, "That's what a sick dog looks like."

"These pills will help?"

"They can help with anything."

"My mother won't be mad?"

"Claire won't be mad because Claire won't know. We'll put the bottle back and we won't tell her. Only the dog will know it was you."

Luke's eyes wandered between the dog, the pills, and my face— what did he see when he looked there?—until he finally nodded.

He swept the pills off the table into his free hand. "We have to mix them with his food," I said. We pulled out the bag of food and filled the dog's bowl in the corner of the kitchen. Luke gave me one last look before he emptied his hand into the bowl and stirred the pills into the dog food. He clapped and called the animal over.

The thing scrambled up to the bowl and ate, not looking up once before the bowl was empty again. It was a slavish, stupid creature. All that was left to do now was wait, but I felt no satisfaction, no sense of accomplishment, just queasiness and a dull dread. Luke, on the other hand, could barely contain his excitement, and he slid on his socks across the tile floor, body-checking the refrigerator at the kitchen's far end.

I wasn't sure how long the pills would take to work. On many nights I had observed Claire take one and then go to bed about half an hour later, but we had given the dog at least fifty, so I guessed the thing had a lot less time left than that. I watched the animal paw its way across the living room to the deck doors, briefly scrabble its claws against the glass, and then pad unsteadily back to the kitchen. Luke asked how we would know when the medicine was working; I told him it would be impossible to miss.

Claire had brought a boom box out onto the lower deck, and strains of acoustic guitar drifted up to the second floor. The dog hiccupped once, violently, and then shook itself from head to tail. Luke said, "What does that mean?" and I didn't answer. I didn't know exactly what was going to happen. I hated a mess, so I had hoped the dog's death would be quiet and neat and somehow dignified, that it would lie down to take a nap and never get up, but things didn't seem to be turning out that way. The animal hiccupped again, and a small stream of bile slid out of its mouth. Luke was silent. A few more convulsions shook the dog, and then it let loose a long torrent of vomit mixed with blood. The shaking died down and the animal slumped to the floor, a puddle spreading out around its body.

I looked at Luke. He backed away and stood in the middle of the living room, his hands on his face, the knuckles of one fist stuffed into his mouth, a perfect caricature of horror. I stood up, unsure of what I was going to do, when I noticed the music had stopped, and in its place Claire's footsteps climbed the stairs to the second floor. When she mounted the last step, we were still frozen in our respective positions, our ridiculous tableau. She saw Luke first, and walked toward him with a puzzled expression until she caught sight of the dog. She gave a single abbreviated shriek before she rushed over to the animal's body.

"My god, what happened to him? Luke? What happened?"

Luke said nothing, just took another step backward. Claire left the dog's body and reached out for her son.

"Luke, are you okay? Please tell me you're okay. What—" She spotted the pill bottle, uncapped and empty on the kitchen table. "Where did . . . Did you give him these? Answer me, did you give him these?" She grabbed the bottle and shook it once, brandishing it in front of her like a weapon.

Luke didn't say anything at first, but then he pointed a finger at me and said, "Daniel told me to do it. Daniel said it was medicine for Midnight."

"Daniel? No. You did this, Luke. How can you blame Daniel? Never lie to me, never."

"I'm not lying, Mom. I'm not."

"You didn't take any of these, did you? Please tell me you didn't."

Luke shook his head and started to cry, great wracking, messy sobs. "Okay." Claire breathed deeply, like a diver coming up for air. "We're okay." She said: "How many times did I tell you to stay out of my bathroom? How many times did I tell you never to touch my medicine?"

Luke sat down on the floor and took big, gasping breaths, opening his mouth wide to draw in lungfuls of air. A few feet away, the corpse lay on the kitchen tiles. I carefully stepped back and retreated to the far corner of the room, my work complete. Luke stared up at me from the floor. He would hate me now, but hate can't be ignored or forgotten. He could not separate me from his guilt, from the grotesque knowledge that together we had removed the bottle from the cabinet, placed the pills into the bowl, mixed them in with the dog food. We were complicit in this crime. The more he tried to rid himself of me, the less possible it would become, and in this way I was saved.

<hr />

The day after Luke and I killed the dog, the three of us took a walk on the beach. They didn't want me there with them, but I didn't care. I felt strong; I could do whatever I liked.

The horseshoe crabs were back. A storm had rolled through overnight, and low clouds like bruised knuckles still scudded across the southern horizon. The Atlantic was roiled up, bands of foam marbling the gray-green chop. A string of dark blobs, hard and shiny, lay along the edge of the high-tide line, helmets looking for heads. Claire picked up a piece of driftwood, wedged it under one of the crabs, and flipped it over: a dozen segmented legs and a fringe of gills. Behind the insect-like appendages, something pulpy and soft. It looked ancient, as though the prehistoric past had washed up on our shores. She and Luke crouched over the exposed undercarriage. The tiny legs batted at the air; the animal was not yet dead. Claire dragged it by its tail to the edge of the water and waited for a wave to wash it away. She said, "Things in our life are going to change." Along the beach in both directions the crabs dotted the sand by the thousands.

A week later we returned to Manhattan for the first time in almost two months. We took the ferry across the bay and then drove the rest of the way in the maroon Saab, our windows rolled down to let the suddenly warm air rush in. I wasn't confined to the trunk this time, but instead sat serenely in the backseat. We were going to the city to see Dr. Claymore, whose office was on the ground floor of a grand apartment building on West Eighty-third Street. During the appointment, Luke drew volcanoes and spaceships on a sketch pad while Claymore, a bald, fuzzy-brained man with gold-rimmed bifocals, asked him questions about his favorite animals. I sat on the corner of Claymore's desk, frowning. "Don't tell him anything, Luke," I said. "I don't trust him."

The interview was a big surprise. I had only known that we were going to see "the doctor," which had previously meant booster shots and tongue depressors, not whatever this was supposed to be.

"Dinosaurs, hmm?" Claymore said.

"Yes," Luke said, "and it's best when they can fly."

The office made me nervous. Childish watercolors of rainbows and balloon-headed stick people crowded Claymore's walls, desperately cheerful, as though painted at gunpoint. The rest of the room was strangely familiar to me: the framed diplomas, the potted plants, the pile of toys in the corner. I felt as though if I did not know this specific room, I knew this kind of room, that it was of a type with which I was intimate. The particulars of this feeling, the how and why, slid off the edges of my thoughts, but this did not make the feeling any less powerful. I began to feel flushed, panicky. I focused on the white splotches on top of Claymore's bald red head, grounding myself in the sun damage and patches of dry skin.

"Would you like to go back to school?" he asked.

Luke frowned and showed us his sketchpad, a crayon moon winking over a waxy black ocean. "Very much," he said.

"That's good," Claymore said. He made a note on his yellow pad. "It will be easy to pick up where you left off. You'll see."

After the inquisition, Claire smiled bravely at us out in the waiting room. "Yes? Yes?" Claymore stuck out a pink hand. "I think that was a solid start, Ms. Nightingale." He handed Claire a slip of watermarked paper. "What we discussed on the phone. We'll see you again in a week."

I felt better as soon as we stepped outside onto the sidewalk. Claire stared at the passing traffic. "We're coming back," she said. "This is home." I wasn't too concerned; Claire said many things she didn't mean.

We walked a few blocks south to the Museum of Natural History, up the marble stairs, past Roosevelt and his entourage. "There's no rush," Claire said, "we have all afternoon." In the Hall of African Mammals, a herd of elephants guarded the middle of the room, the smallest tucked into the middle, surrounded by a ring of outraged adults. We peered down at them from the high balcony, then Claire pointed into the cluster of dusky gray bodies. "See how they protect their young?" She ran her hand through Luke's hair. Across the room, behind a pane of glass, jackals and vultures picked over the corpse of an antelope. The dead playing dead, hides stretched tight over sculpted bodies. Someone had decided on the best way to arrange the limbs, manipulate the postures, construct the scenarios. I preferred these imitations of life to the real thing, each player's role in the drama clearly defined. I slipped through a seam in the glass and crawled to the back of the diorama, where the dirt and trees ended and the painted world, curved and unending, began. Luke looked at me from the other side, his mismatched eyes wide as I reached up and ran my fingers over clouds and distant hills. He insisted that we see the dinosaurs, so we climbed the stairs to the top floor of the museum, where real bones and plaster casts of bones were fixed together and bent into predatory poses. Later, we all three stood in reverence before the grizzly bear drawn up on its hind legs and craned our necks to see the giant blue whale, regal, plastic, and bloated, suspended like a planet far above our heads.

After three more visits to Dr. Claymore and one month of the new pills—tiny sky-blue tablets, like chalky candy—I was banished to the inside of Luke's skull. It wasn't gradual, like my decomposition on Fire Island; it was like a trapdoor unlatched, brutal and abrupt.

We moved into a new apartment on Central Park West, again arranged by Claire at the speed of wealth, and things began to happen to me quickly, one after another. First, Luke packaged me in a taped-up cardboard box that sat in the corner of his new bedroom, but after a few days of struggle, I pushed my way out. Then he dragged me behind him wherever he went, my body bound in steel wire, a metal plate screwed over my mouth and a leash clipped to a collar around my neck, my head bumping along the ground as he walked. After the clip broke one day—sending me rolling across the sidewalk and out into the street, coming to a stop just short of the wheels of a city bus—he stuffed me into a narrow blue bottle, some apothecary antique his mother had bought to add character to his bookshelves. Wadded up like a dirty tissue, my face smashed into the mottled glass, I watched his comings and goings through a blue tint, as though submerged underwater, until the glass cracked and then splintered, spraying shards across the floor and freeing me to fall among them. Finally, on day twenty-one of the pills, he placed me inside the dollhouse, which Claire had retrieved from its storage locker, holding me by the head between his thumb and forefinger like an insect.

The Newport Nightingales welcomed me in their own special way. I stepped into the foyer, where Luke's grandmother Venetia sat reading in a wicker chair. When she saw me, she flung the book down and ran wildly out of the room, banging into walls and furniture before collapsing facedown in the sunroom. I nudged her body with my toe, but she was unresponsive. In the parlor, a hoary old man and his younger opponent played chess. Their porcelain faces were frozen in expressions of mild surprise as they swiveled their heads between me and the chessboard. After an exchange of bishops, the old man sighed. "If you're going to be here for a while, why don't you make yourself useful and check on the baby."

I couldn't think of anything better to do than follow his suggestion. The nursery's crib was empty, and I found baby Claire stuffed into a closet, hidden under a mound of dirty linens. She lay on her back crying, waving her arms and legs like a flipped beetle. I thought about suffocating her beneath the heavy cloth, but I couldn't bring myself to do it; instead I just carried her back to the crib and tucked her in under the sheets.

Luke kept me in the dollhouse for a week. The two men tolerated me, and soon enough they invited me to sit down and play chess with them. It was hard to get used to their unchanging faces, the way their features stayed exactly the same—slightly

parted mouth, smooth cheeks, eyebrows lifted over vacant eyes—
whether they were content or sad or murderously angry. And it
was disconcerting when they sometimes broke off in the middle
of a sentence and then would resume their thought hours later as
though nothing had happened. But they weren't as bad as Venetia, who was terrified of me. She hid in closets and cupboards,
scrunched under tables and behind couches, her pink dress crin-
kling and rustling like dried flowers. She hissed at me as I walked
by, and once she even spit on the back of my neck, her porcelain
face smooth and serene, belying her venom. Every time I tried to
leave the house, all the doors and windows were locked from the
outside.

But then, on the seventh day, a window suddenly opened and
Luke's giant fingertips plucked me out. He dangled me in front
of his massive face, a craterous expanse of white skin, eyebrows
like forests, his nose a mountain. "Maybe I can't get rid of you
completely," he said, "but this is the best I can do for now." He
cocked his head to the side and held me over his left ear. He
forced me into the cavity, mashing me down with his palm. My
body crumpled, and I was enveloped by hot, damp darkness. I
tumbled through some sort of tube until I came to a stop. I
opened my eyes and saw Luke's new bedroom at the far end of a
long tunnel: the low, sleek bed, the cherrywood desk, the Persian
throw rug. But where was Luke? I opened my mouth to speak
and nothing happened. Then I realized I didn't have a mouth; I
didn't have any shape at all. I was an itch tucked away somewhere
at the back of Luke's skull. I saw through his eyes and heard

through his ears. I was a tapeworm, a suckerfish, some unheard-of species of parasite. I thought at Luke, but I was thinking into a void.

I was locked up there for twelve years, and for twelve years I lived Luke's life as a voyeur. I witnessed the banal tragedies of his childhood and adolescence from my perch in the corner of his brain, and I could do nothing about them even if I had wanted to, as though I were watching a tedious film that never ended.

He started going to school again. On the first day of kindergarten, he sat alone with a little windup race car that he cocked back on the carpet and then let go flying into the wall. It ricocheted off the painted brick to land upside down with its wheels still spinning. He did it again and again and again, winding the car back and letting it go, winding it back and letting it go, the car's blue paint chipping away with each collision. After ten minutes of this, a stocky boy with a face like a closed fist reached down and snatched the car mid-run. He held it out to Luke and said, "Once is enough."

But Luke didn't take the car back; instead, he began to moan, softly at first, but then scaling up to a wail, an aggrieved keening. The sound filled the inside of his head, echoing all around me until I was surrounded, and the difference between me and this awful noise was erased. The boy just held out the car and waited. Luke's fingers bunched around the loose fabric of his shirt, twisting it, kneading it like dough, and he rocked back and forth on his knees as though praying. The boy stood patient and still as the teacher rushed over, all jangling jewelry and hushing hands.

After that, the other kids mostly just left Luke alone, as though he were too strange even to tease, but Omar, chubby and patient, gave him his car back and became his friend. He sat cross-legged on the classroom floor and cut snowflakes out of white construction paper, folding each sheet into a tight packet before making crafty incisions along its sides. He unfolded the papers and gravely presented them to Luke in delicate bunches, drifts of discarded snippings piling up all around him. He didn't try to draw Luke out that day, didn't care when he went silent; he was happy to sit there with him and wait for the next thing to happen. Luke was just relieved he had found someone to whom he did not have to explain himself.

This was the first day of school, but it can stand in for the twelve years that followed. As Luke grew older, some things in his life changed and some things didn't. The things that mattered didn't. He did well in his classes and maintained his friendship with Omar; he met with Dr. Claymore and took his medication; he almost never saw his father. He didn't so much live as simply exist. He drifted through his days at school and nights at home with Claire, the weeks and months and years accumulating almost imperceptibly, like snow falling on snow. I pounded myself against the inside of his head, but it was useless. He couldn't hear me; I was trapped. So, like any other prisoner, I waited. I bided my time. I put my faith in the idea that something had to change, and eventually my faith was rewarded.

PART TWO

The Forty Steps

1

I OPENED MY EYES to darkness and the sound of breaking glass. I found myself tangled up in a pile of blankets on the floor at the foot of Luke's bed. The sound came from everywhere at once, a smash and a rain of glass and then another smash. I stood up. I had been given shape again after twelve years, but I didn't have time to wonder why now, why here.

Luke said, "I don't want to go out there." He sat up in his bed, the whites of his eyes bright in the dark room.

"What's going on?" I said, but he didn't answer. We listened together to the shattering.

"Luke!" Claire called out. "Sweetie, wake up."

"Go away," Luke said, too softly for her to hear.

Outside the bedroom windows, Central Park was a hole underneath the orange-black sky. The digital clock on the bedside table read 4:13 A.M. With no warning—she was so slight, after all, nearly weightless—Claire appeared in the room. "Luke, sweetie, please get up. Come help me, there are things to do." Yellow light slanted in from the hallway, casting Claire as a twitchy shadow. I couldn't see her face, but I could see that something wet, something black and slick, covered her hands and forearms. She moved toward the bed and Luke shrank from her outstretched arms.

"Mom, stop it, what are you doing?"

"What's the matter with you? This is important."

"It's four in the morning. What's going on?"

"My own son won't help me when I ask him to." There was a sharpness to her voice, something petulant and resentful. "My only son, when I ask him to come help his mother."

"Don't get up," I said to Luke. "Maybe she'll go away."

"It's not that easy," he said.

Claire shook her head. "I'm tired of seeing my mother in every room of this apartment, staring out at me from every mirror. I'm finally doing something about it, and I want to finish what I started."

She grabbed Luke underneath the armpits, this teenager far heavier than her, and lifted him out of his bed as though he were a sack of feathers. He didn't struggle. He let himself be placed feet-first onto the floor. They stood facing each other, and in the weird light they looked almost like twins, two near-identical profiles at different heights, breathing shallow and fast. I didn't know what to do. What could I do? Twelve years of confinement had corroded my strength; I was still busy shaking off the rust. Claire reached out her hand and touched Luke's face. She spread her fingers across his forehead, and then his cheeks, his nose, his mouth. "My beautiful son," she said. "My baby boy." And then she dropped her hand and guided him toward the doorway, toward the light, and I saw that she had smeared blood across Luke's face, that it was blood covering her hands and running in rivulets over her wrists and forearms, blood from cuts on her palms and the backs of her hands. It was seeping out of her wounds, and it was not stopping.

Luke didn't try to fight her, and she took us into her bathroom. "See," she said. "See, I tried to smash it, but after the foyer I couldn't manage." The bathroom's mirrored cabinet was fractured and spiderwebbed, but it stubbornly clung together. Claire looked down at her blouse, at its stained and sticky white silk, and at the black leggings she wore underneath. She twisted a thick rope of pearls around her neck. "My hands started to hurt too much," she said.

"Why are you doing this?" Luke said. "What's happening to you?"

"Who needs all these mirrors?" Claire said. "Who needs these mirrors when I can just look at you instead?"

Luke gently tried to take his mother's wrist to lead her out of the bathroom, but something inside her that had gone dormant for a moment woke up. She jerked out of his grip and said, "I've had enough of that woman," and smashed her fist into the middle of the cabinet door. The glass panel fell away and collapsed into the sink below. I heard the breaking as if had been inside my head. I had never seen her spin this far out before; the violence of it, the ferocity, were new to me, and to Luke as well. Shards of glass protruded from her knuckles and bristled in the webbing between her fingers. She smiled and said, "Guess I didn't need your help after all," and then she sat cross-legged on the cold marble floor and began to cry.

"Mom, Mom." Luke tried to take hold of her arms to pull her up, but she slapped at his hands and curled up into a ball in the corner of the bathroom between the toilet and the white marble walls.

"Mom, you have to get up, please." He reached toward her again, and she lashed out, scratching at his face and grabbing onto his arm. Her grip ground tiny pieces of glass into his skin, pieces too small to be visible until pinpricks of blood marked their presence. She pulled him down toward her, then changed her mind and shoved him away again.

I finally spoke. "We need to get out of here," I said. "Call somebody, call James, call the police, and then let's go while we can."

Luke looked at me. "This is nobody else's business but ours, and I'm not leaving her." There was something so calm in his eyes, some quiet purpose he had found at the center of all this. I don't think he could have found that purpose without me there to see him do it; I had been released to be his witness. Claire folded in on herself until only the crown of her dark head and her black leggings were visible. She spoke quietly: "I've broken all her hiding places."

Luke touched his cheek where a thin sliver of glass stuck to his skin. "Mom," he said, "I won't let you stay here like this."

She raised her head and her eyes were black holes. "You won't *let* me?" She barked out a laugh. "You won't let me. Okay. Well, I'm not staying anyway." She picked up a jagged triangle of glass and slashed at her right wrist. "I'm leaving this place. I'm done with it." The glass was sharp enough to tear her skin but not sharp enough to slash the veins. Even so, blood flowed thicker now, until it coated her arm up to the elbow.

"She's going to die," I said. What did I feel? I still don't know. I didn't want to stop her, but I couldn't watch it happen either. I covered my eyes and turned toward the wall. "Let her do it," I said into my hands.

Luke stood still for a few moments. I didn't know what he would decide to do. What would his life be like without her? "I can't," he finally said. He tried to grab Claire's arm, but she thrashed away from him and screamed, a sound inhuman and without any meaning. Luke picked up another, larger, shard of glass and held it to his own throat. "Look," he said. "Look at me."

Claire bent herself around the toilet, contorting her body into an impossibly small space between the porcelain bowl and the wall. She glared at Luke from behind a curtain of dark hair.

"Look at me," he said. He pressed the glass against his throat, against the pulse that beat wildly in the hollow of his neck. "If you're going, I'm coming with you."

I peeked out at him between my fingers. "What are you doing? Put that down."

He ignored me. "I'm ready," he said.

Claire held the triangle of glass in her left hand and looked at it carefully. She turned the shard over and examined it from every angle as though it were something to be studied, something from which she could learn. The deepest gash on her wrist, raw and unstanched, continued to empty itself in time with her pulse. She looked at Luke and untangled herself from the toilet. Again they stood facing each other, their bodies inches apart. Luke was shirtless in his cotton pajama pants, and streaks of Claire's blood shone wetly across his pale face and hollow chest. The hand that held the glass to his neck was the only part of his body that did not tremble. Claire raised her own shard to her neck in a mirror image of her son. They stood like that for a long time, and then Luke pressed down with his fragment and drew a trickle of blood, and Claire cried out like a wounded animal, throwing her shard of glass to the floor to embrace her son.

I realized I had been holding my breath the entire time, and then quickly remembered I could hold my breath for hours and it wouldn't matter. But I felt ill anyway. I did not know if Luke had actually been prepared to slit his own throat; worse, I did not know what would happen to me if he did. It was likely our bond ran that deep, that we were entwined together that tightly. The thought of such dependence enraged me and made me feel weak, drained. Who was Luke to make these decisions for me, to have such control? How had I let myself fall into such a position? I sagged against the wall and said, "Luke, what the fuck was that?" but he wasn't paying any attention to me. They stood in the center of the bathroom, wrapped tightly into each other. Slowly, Luke unraveled himself from his mother's arms and opened the ruined door of the medicine cabinet.

"Show me what will help you now."

Claire trembled violently, and I saw that it was only with the greatest effort that she held herself from exploding in all directions at once. The sick energy still flowed through her veins, but she was fighting it now as best she could. She bit down on her lip so hard she drew blood there, too, and then she pointed at a bottle of pills on the bottom shelf.

"I'm trusting you, okay?" Luke said. He was eighteen years old. "I'm trusting that this isn't going to kill you." He tapped out a pill into Claire's outstretched hand, but she shook her head and said, "Another." He did as she asked.

Claire closed her eyes and swallowed the pills without water. "It's not right. This is not her place. She should be far away from here."

"She's seeing ghosts," Luke whispered.

"No," I said. "She's seeing herself and she's scared."

Claire said, "I think I'm going to lie down."

She'd lost a dangerous amount of blood, and she was deathly

pale, far beyond her usual pallor. Luke helped her to the bed and finally called for an ambulance. After he hung up the phone Claire shook her head. She tried twice to sit up before succeeding. "They are not coming up here. We will go downstairs to meet them."

"Just lie down," Luke said. "Just rest."

Claire staggered to her feet. "Nobody will see my apartment like this. I don't care who they are. We are going downstairs."

Claire ran hot water over her arms and face in the bathroom sink, wrapped herself in a floor-length overcoat, and pulled on a pair of leather boots. We took the elevator down in silence. Covered by the overcoat and with her face freshly scrubbed, Claire still looked ill, but no longer half dead. Luke, too, had hidden his wounds beneath a ski jacket and jeans. They both presented themselves to Victor, who was watching a tiny portable television by the lobby door, with something close to a picture of normalcy.

Outside on the sidewalk, Claire said, "As soon as we see the ambulance coming, I want you to run back inside and get upstairs. I don't want you to come with me, and I don't know what they will do with you if they know you're here alone. After I'm gone, call your father. He'll take care of you."

"I'm coming with you," Luke said.

Claire shivered in the early April chill. The faintest hint of purple dawn touched the sky above the park. She didn't say anything. Victor stood on the other side of the front door, pretending not to watch us as Claire leaned against the side of the building and closed her eyes.

"Luke," I said, "she's right. We have to stay."

Soon the garish lights of an approaching ambulance lit up the deserted street. Claire opened one eye. "Get inside the building. Now."

Luke gave his mother an anguished look, and for a moment I thought he might stay with her, but as the ambulance sped up the block, he darted inside the building without looking back. I followed close behind. At the threshold of the lobby, I glanced over my shoulder and saw Claire slowly walk toward the curb with her arms spread wide as though stepping off a cliff. Upstairs, Luke stood in the shower under scalding hot water and scrubbed at his skin until it tore.

· · ·

We sat together in Luke's bedroom and waited for the sun to rise. I could tell he wished I would go away again, but I just sat there on the leather chair opposite his bed, watching him watch me. At eight o'clock, Luke stood up, packed his book bag, and walked to high school like it was any other Friday.

I was disoriented to be on the outside again, scoured by the harsh air and buffeted by light and sound. The day went by in the fog of a dream; one moment stumbled into the next. I felt vulnerable, exposed. Even Omar's smiling face loomed like a menacing planet; I wanted to take a pin and pop it like a balloon. But within the disorientation beat a steady pulse of euphoria: I was out. I was free. My true work could begin again.

After school let out, Cassie, the eighteen-year-old daughter of James's second wife, plucked us from the crowd of eleventh graders smoking and boasting out on the sidewalk. She smiled at Luke—a real smile, full of surprise and care and pity—and hefted their two backpacks, declaring his the winner. "James couldn't leave the office yet," she said. "I got to cut last-period gym so I could come tell you, but I'm not going to make up for it by carrying this bag of bricks."

Luke just looked at her. "What do you want?"

Cassie flinched, but her smile didn't slip. "I don't want anything. We're going to your apartment, so you can get what you need. You're going to stay with us for a while."

"I want to be by myself."

"It's been decided," Cassie said. "You can argue with your father later if you want to."

"How does he know anything? I never called him."

"Well, somebody did. Let's go."

Luke was too exhausted to fight. We stopped on our way to the apartment so Cassie could sit on a Central Park West bench and smoke a cigarette. She stubbed it out on the cobblestones after two drags because she saw somebody who looked like her mother in the back of a passing taxi. "Spies!" she coughed. "Spies, everywhere." She took off her clogs and tugged at the navy knee-socks she wore with a pale blue skirt and white Oxford shirt as part of the uniform of her all-girls school across town, where she was a senior. She wiggled her bare toes and sighed, producing a pair of flip-flops from her bag. " 'Man is free at the moment he wishes to be.' Woman, too. Have you gotten to Voltaire yet?"

I remembered Luke shying away from Cassie the handful of times they had met. I didn't know whether he was intimidated by her—she was only six months older than him, but had always seemed far wiser and more mature—or if he just didn't like her. Neither made sense, because she was lovely, with thick auburn hair pinned up by chopsticks into a complex knot and wide blue eyes untouched by either Claire's fever or James's calculation. I imagined underneath her uniform a body strong and smooth as marble.

Five blocks north, we waited for the elevator. I reached out to touch Cassie's cheek, but my arms were roughly pinned down to my sides. Burlap straps cut into my skin. Luke had wrapped me up in a straitjacket, and I stumbled crazily between the two of them. "Luke, this is stupid. Let me out of this thing." He glared at me, and I felt my lips seal shut.

"Why are you looking at me like that?" Cassie said.

Luke shook his head. "I'm sorry," he said, "I was thinking about someone else."

Inside the elevator, polished brass outshone varnished walnut. It smelled like Lysol and Chanel No. 5. The doors opened; 3F was the last unit on the left. Luke unlocked the door, and I saw the apartment as if for the first time. All the objects were the same, but everything seemed sharper and more vivid when viewed from without Luke's head than from within. The five rooms were aggressively neat and austere. Claire had stripped away the encrusted glitz of the old Fifth Avenue penthouse, where Cassie now lived with James and the rest of his new family, and replaced it with low-slung modern furniture and cryptic photographs of flowers and guns. A framed charcoal tracing of the Nightingale Press bird in flight hung alone on the wall opposite the front door and a quartet of Noh masks held court in the hallway, but there were few other remainders of the old apartment.

Luke and I went into his bedroom to pack his duffel while Cassie wandered around the rest of the apartment. I felt the seal over my mouth loosen. "Why don't you like her?" I said. He ignored me. "Is it because she's smarter than you? She is, I can tell. You get slow when I'm not around. Slow and soft." He stuck his head under the bed and pulled out a math textbook that went straight into the bag. He opened a desk drawer and considered a row of orange plastic pill bottles. He looked at me, then back at the bottles, before leaving them undisturbed and closing the drawer. He zipped up the duffel and walked over to the window, where Central Park appeared bucolic in the late-afternoon light. "But it doesn't matter what you think of her anyway," I said, "because she'll figure you out soon enough. She'll find out everything about Claire. She'll see how weak you are, what kind of problems you have." He wouldn't turn to look at me, so I shuffled toward him. "Pay attention. You should start to listen more closely to what I have to say." Leg restraints materialized around my thighs and calves, but I kicked my knees up and snapped them easily. "Come on, Luke, give it up." I strained my arms against the straitjacket, shaking myself from side to side, and in my thrashings I tripped over the duffel and fell on my face. Luke finally turned to look down at me on the floor. "You stay out of this." He yanked the duffle from under my body, slung it over his shoulder, and walked out of the room calling Cassie's name. I staggered to my feet and followed him into the hallway, where Cassie leaned against the wall outside Claire's bedroom with studied casualness.

"What were you doing in there?" Luke said.

She widened her blue eyes and popped a stick of gum into her mouth. "What? Where?"

"Nobody's cleaned it up," Luke said. "She didn't want anybody to see the apartment, what she'd done to it. But now you have. Does that make you happy? You can tell your friends all about it."

"But how could you just go to school and pretend nothing had happened?"

I could see it was the question she had wanted to ask all afternoon, ever since James had assigned her the task of picking us up. I looked behind her into the bedroom. Shards of glass spilled out of the corner bathroom onto the mahogany floor. Dried blood streaked the bed's white sheets. Luke turned to leave, and all he said was, "It will be taken care of by the time she comes back, so get a good look while you can."

❦

They welcomed Luke that night with cartons of Chinese food. Five plastic-and-tin containers, three white cardboard boxes: a

89

feast. James opened four cans of soda and poured himself some wine while Molly, his second wife, shoveled the moo shu pork and sesame chicken and garlic prawns out onto white china, where the food sat in steaming lumps. Cassie upended a carton of vegetable fried rice into a bowl, and the rice retained its container's shape, a greasy geometry lesson. "Volume equals height times length times depth," she said brightly. "A times B times C." James poked the tower with a fork, and it fell apart. "S stands for entropy," he said.

We ate in the kitchen of what used to be the Nightingale penthouse. It had been James's home for twelve years now. The wooden table was gone, and we sat on precarious leather stools around a high marble island, the kitchen gleaming with chrome and brushed steel. They squeezed the baby into a high chair even though it was two years old and barely fit. The smells were ferocious. I had forgotten how disgusting I found food, with its oily glisten and unclean origins.

"The pullout couch in the TV room is very comfortable," Molly said. "Don't listen to Cassie, you won't have to share a room with James Junior."

"But you were so looking forward to it, weren't you, Jimmy?" Cassie sang. She pinched the toddler's stomach, ruffled the hair of this late addition to her patchwork family. "Your very own big brother, poof, like magic."

"I can stay at home," Luke said. "It really would be fine."

"Oh, stop, please." Molly reached out to flick James's tie over his shoulder as its tip dipped dangerously close to his plate. He looked up, startled, before leaning down into his food again. "We can't have you all alone in that apartment, with nobody to keep you company or look after you. You're still in high school, for God's sake."

"But I'd be there, Luke," I said. He still had me bound in the straitjacket, and I felt clumsy and unbalanced. "I'd keep you company."

"What I really like," Cassie said, "are the crunchy little pieces. They're like popcorn." She speared a nugget of sesame chicken with a chopstick and dropped the specimen into her mouth. "Perfect. Did you hear the crunch?"

"Don't talk with your mouth full, honey," Molly said. She was a blond woman just shy of forty, full and healthy without being fat, the kind of woman whose impossible reserves of energy and good cheer are distressing to people like Luke and Claire. Cassie shared her mother's figure and blue eyes, but her absent father must have donated the reddish-brown hair and a few extra inches of height to his daughter before fleeing the scene. Molly still wore her makeup and work clothes—a lime-green skirt and blouse—and looked fresh enough for this to be breakfast instead of dinner, as though the day hadn't already happened. Pink elephants marched across James's baby-blue tie as it slid off his shoulder and grazed his fried rice. This scene was so absurd, so unreal, that I burst out laughing. Who were these bright people? This was a set and they were actors hired to confuse us, to dazzle our eyes with bone-white china and guileless smiles.

"We want to make you comfortable," Molly said.

"I'll be fine." Luke flashed the sheepish half-smile I hated, the one that got him things he didn't deserve. "It won't be the first night I've spent in this apartment." I watched for a response, but not even James, silent and tense at the head of the table, seemed embarrassed by this statement.

"Tomorrow's Saturday," Molly said. "Why don't we all do something together, maybe go to a movie or, I don't know . . . What do you like to do, Luke?"

"Actually, I have football tomorrow." Luke inspected a prawn, then glanced up. "Spring league. In the Bronx." The second family looked at him blankly. "School doesn't have a team, so I play up there. The van comes by my building at nine. I haven't told them I'm staying here, and my gear is still in my room anyway."

James frowned. "Football?"

Cassie said, "In the Bronx?"

Molly laid her chopsticks neatly along the edge of her plate. "We can be in a taxi at eight-thirty."

"Thanks, but it's no big deal. I'd rather go alone."

James and Molly glanced at each other. "I don't think your mother would like that," James said.

"I don't think you know what she would or wouldn't like," Luke said. Then he smiled again. "But you can wait for the van with me anyway if you really want to. Just to see that I'm not making any of this up."

92

After an uncomfortable night spent wedged against the foot of the sofa bed, I woke up to find Luke tying his sneakers and watching muted sports highlights on the giant television. The slow-motion buckle of a football player's knee was replayed from three different angles; a baseball star in a pinstripe suit exited the courtroom into a fusillade of flashbulbs. I staggered to my feet, my arms pinioned so tightly to my torso by the straitjacket that I thought my shoulders might dislocate. Molly sat in the kitchen with the baby, eating brioche smeared with blackberry jam. She gave Luke a wide smile as he passed by the doorway. "Be safe," she said. "Sorry!" the baby yelled, its mouth full of cereal. "Sorry, sorry!" James appeared, wearing khakis and a baseball cap with the slogan *Parallax Capital,* which I assumed was the name of his current company. From the little I'd heard from Claire over the years, I knew he raised money for ventures related in some way to Russia; the names of the companies kept changing and the details remained hazy to me, but the money seemed real enough. As we left, the door to Cassie's room remained closed, and I imagined her still sleeping, the rise and fall of her breathing body outlined by silk sheets.

I sat in the backseat during the taxi ride across the park, squeezed between Luke and James as they discussed pro football games neither of them fully recalled. Ever since Cassie had delivered Luke to the apartment, they had all vigorously avoided the only topic any of them could be thinking about. When mentioned at all, Claire was spoken about in passing, neutrally, as though she were on vacation, or dead. If any of them knew exactly where she was, or when she was coming back, I hadn't heard it.

James waited downstairs while Luke packed up his gear; into another duffel went helmet, pads, cleats, jersey.

"Not giving up yet?" I said.

"I just like it," he said. "I don't have to be good at it."

"Nobody really feels that way about anything they do."

The three of us waited outside the building. James studied the traffic and said, "I thought your mother wouldn't let you play football."

"It's been four years already," Luke said. "Catch her at the right time and she'll agree to almost anything. But you know all about that."

A white van pulled up in front of the building and honked once. Luke ran toward it without looking back. Inside was only the driver, who said, "Buckle up, *chico*" over his shoulder and gunned the engine the second Luke touched the seat. On the route north, we made stops at 135th and Amsterdam, 156th and Covenant, Dyckman and Broadway. Kids—black, white, Dominican, almost all bigger than Luke—filled up the van. A lanky one lurched into the seat next to us as we made a hard left. He rapped Luke's skull. "Watch that play-action today, man. Get your head out of the backfield."

We sped over the Henry Hudson Bridge high above the river, the Palisades standing sheer and dark against the water. Van Cortlandt Park's fields lay soggy and rutted. Pizza parlors, bodegas, and sporting goods stores hid their faces underneath the elevated train tracks. The morning intrasquad scrimmage ended when Luke took a knee to the head while filling the gap on a draw play. Inside the pizza parlor, he picked at his calzone with a dazed look in his eyes. Bruises mottled his shins, and he ran his fingers back and forth over the purple-and-yellow lumps. The lanky kid from the van walked by and touched his head. "Chin up, bro."

The afternoon game against a neighborhood team from Tremont was a blowout from the beginning. On the opening kickoff, a flanker clotheslined the Wildcats' return man. The Tremont tailback blew through tacklers as if they were made of wet paper, while the Wildcats quarterback was forced to scramble almost every time he dropped back to pass. Tremont ran a halfback option for their first score and quickly recovered a Wildcat fumble on the next drive. Luke subbed in at free safety and got flattened by a pulling tackle twice his size. On the sidelines, he sat on his helmet with his head between his knees.

At halftime the Wildcats were down 14–0, but during the third quarter I noticed a pattern. Whenever Tremont lined up in an offset-I, two times out of three their quarterback tossed a swing pass out wide right to the tailback after a three-step drop. Their offensive line walled off the linebackers, and the tailback was free to get around the corner. When the Wildcats next had the ball, I sidled up to Luke as he waited on the sidelines. "Next time they line up in that offset-I," I said, "blitz around the right tackle and step in front of the swing pass." He gave me a blank look. "The swing pass," I said impatiently. "That kid throws it every time without even looking." On Tremont's next possession, they broke the huddle on a second and two and lined up in the offset-I. I ran onto the field, stumbling in the straitjacket, yelling at Luke, "Get up on the line! Blitz, you fucker!"

Why did I want him to succeed? Earning back his trust was part of it; I realized my hostility was only going to get me locked up again unless I tempered it with craft and restraint. But I also couldn't stand to let the stupidity of the Tremont strategy go unpunished, and I couldn't exactly intercept the pass myself. As the quarterback started his snap count, Luke inched up to the line of scrimmage. Tremont snapped the ball and Luke shot around the right side of their line. The quarterback faked a look downfield and then flicked the swing pass out to the right without checking for a blitz. Luke was there. He tipped the pass up with one outstretched hand and then brought the carom down into his chest, returning the interception twenty-five yards before he was dragged down from behind. I weaved through the scattered bodies, hopping from one foot to the other: "I told you! I told you!"

It didn't change the game, though. Tremont ground the Wildcats down during the fourth quarter, but Luke never quit, fighting off tough blocks, giving good pursuit. I was almost proud, even though it was a dumb idea to play in the first place. Sometime near the end of the game, Tremont ran a reverse and Luke changed direction at full speed to track it down. Tremont's biggest player threw a vicious blindside block and leveled Luke with a shoulder pad to the helmet. Luke was lifted up into the air, his feet parallel with his head as though he were levitating.

He landed flat on his back, and the play moved down the field without him. I stood over him, looking down at his face nestled within the oversized helmet. His eyes were closed, but the eyelids trembled delicately, frantically, as if there were two tiny creatures underneath struggling to escape. "Luke?" He moved his arms and legs as though making a snow angel. "Luke?" He opened his eyes one at a time, first green, then brown, the pupils glazed and unfocused. A slug of blood crawled out of one nostril. He stared up at my face, at the sun behind my head, and then he started to smile.

2

ON MONDAY WE went back to school. As a reward for my advice on the football field, I wore some sort of shabby business suit instead of the straitjacket. It was apparently Luke's idea of a smart outfit. The cuffs were too short and the knees had been worn to a shine, but it wasn't yet the right time to complain. I didn't like the face I had been given, either—it was too similar to Luke's own, with only its fleshier features offering any differences. It needed to be changed to something that better represented my idea of myself, but that too would have to wait until I grew stronger.

Omar stood on the corner of West Ninety-first Street, bouncing a handball against the school's brick wall. His low-slung backpack swung from side to side as he played, and he nodded his giant square head to kids as they passed by. He palmed the ball and pointed at Luke. "What was up with you Friday? You looked half dead."

"I haven't been sleeping well. You know that."

"And then nobody answers the phone all weekend."

"Oh," Luke said vaguely. "There's some problem with the service. It might not be fixed for a while."

The tide of arriving students pulled us through the open doors and into the echoing lobby.

"Don't lie to me," Omar said. "What did your mom do this time?"

"She didn't do anything. We're fine."

Omar cornered Luke against the lockers outside assembly. "You're allowed to ask for help. You don't have to do everything alone."

Luke glanced at me. "I'm not alone." He couldn't look Omar in the face. "She'll be all right."

"It's not her I'm worried about."

Morning began with Latin class. Mr. Doyle, the teacher, was a gaunt man in his forties with a face draped in sagging, pockmarked skin and ornamented by thick black-framed glasses decades out of style. A bird's nest of scraggly brown hair topped his head, and his shirt and tie were already rumpled even though it was only nine in the morning. Such disorder, such slovenliness. It was disgraceful; how were these teenagers supposed to learn the value of discipline and rigor—the things that mattered—under such an example? He passed out marked-up exams and said, "Do you know what it is like to grade fifteen tests that don't show the slightest respect for a language that was good enough for Virgil and Ovid but apparently isn't good enough for any of you?" Fifteen eleventh graders stared at him blankly. The students passed the tests around, muttering as they read the circled number scribbled in red pen at the top right corner of each exam. I peered over Luke's shoulder. "Seventy-seven percent. C-plus. You're smarter than that." I'd noticed from my perch inside his skull that his normally high grades had deteriorated over the last few months; the problem had to be distraction or indifference rather than any lack of intelligence. I hadn't particularly cared then, but now I saw an opportunity. "It's not easy," he whispered. "Just wait," I said. On the open page of Luke's *Metamorphoses* was a line drawing of four men in robes walking under a colonnade, their heads bent together in some deep discussion. Somebody had drawn an arrow through one of their stomachs and accented it with gushes of inky blood; a cartoon penis protruded from the forehead of the man leading the discussion.

Doyle wrote this phrase on the blackboard: *"Interea niveum mira feliciter arte sculpsit ebur formamque dedit."* "In English, please."

A frantic-looking girl in the front row blurted out, "Meanwhile, with wonderful skill, he luckily carved snow-white ivory and gave it a shape."

"Clunky, but gets the point across. Thank you, Sarah."

Luke stared at the back of Sarah's head with something like longing, while I looked over her shoulder at her paper and saw that this translation was the second question on the test. Luke's own version read: "Meanwhile, he brilliantly gave a form to a snowy ivory sculpture with talent."

"Most of you will notice that this sentence looks familiar," Doyle said. "What won't be familiar is the answer to my next question, since only one person got it right." Doyle circled *arte*. "Case and reason. Somebody other than Sarah, please." Luke had no clue, and Sarah zealously shielded her test from the class. "Nobody knows? Surely somebody can tell me just the case."

I stood up from my squat beside Luke's chair to get a better look at Sarah's paper. She let her arm slip for just a second, but it was enough. "It's ablative," I said to Luke. "Manner."

"Nobody?"

Sarah pressed her hands over her mouth, as though she had to physically obstruct the answer from popping out like a jack-in-a-box. Luke raised a hand.

"Luke! I've missed the sound of your voice." Doyle pushed his glasses up on his nose. "Can you help us out here?"

Luke was red-cheeked, tapping his foot nervously on the floor. I couldn't understand his anxiety. It was all just another game, hermetic, without true consequence.

Luke said, "Ablative of manner."

"Right." Doyle seemed surprised. "Why?"

Luke looked over at me. I frowned. Sarah's paper didn't offer any more clues. "It's the way in which he carved the statue," I said. "Just tell him that." Luke took a deep, rather melodramatic breath: "It tells us that he made the statue with craft, with great talent."

"That's exactly right. *Mira arte*—with wonderful skill. No *arte*, no *amore*, *capice*?"

Fuck this dead language, I thought. Its decadence, its preciousness. Old things should stay where they belong, buried in the ground.

In the hallway after class, Luke pulled me aside. "I don't cheat, Daniel."

I brushed his hands off the lapels of my suit. "You got it right, didn't you?"

Students flowed around us under the flat fluorescent light. I heard the glass tubes buzzing behind their plastic covers and felt the phosphors pelting my skin. This light left no room for shadows. It stripped away pretense and lies, which was the purpose of anything useful. Luke spun his locker combination. Inside, on the top shelf, were rows of prescription pill bottles, most of them full, with expiration dates stretching back six months, nine months, sometimes more. Luke pushed them aside to make room for his textbooks. I watched the students meld and splinter into clusters and momentary cliques, the rules of their fusion as complex as those of any chemistry experiment; yet, just as in science, there was an underlying logic, an airtight chain of equations. It was part of my job to peel back this busy skin—the pushing and teasing and shrieking—to show Luke the simple order underneath, how to manipulate it, how not to be so detached and ineffectual. The trick was to show him enough so that he trusted me, but not so much that he didn't continue to need my advice.

The second-period bell rang, sudden and shrill. Wads of dried gum dotted the gray industrial carpet and bars guarded the ground-floor windows. James and Molly were already deliberating whether to enroll James Jr. here in four years; there was talk of hiring an interview coach before they made the preschool rounds the following fall. Cassie tapped her little brother's skull, called him the six-million-dollar baby. "We can rebuild him," she whispered in an awed voice. "We can make him . . . *better* than he was before." In the hallway outside history class, I studied my palms and forearms and reviewed the notes I'd scrawled there the previous evening. The lines of ink were tightly packed across my skin, a dozen bullet-pointed key concepts and an alphabetized glossary. I was going to play this game as long as I needed to. I was sure there were gaps in my preparation, but for now it was the best I could do.

After school, we walked to Luke's weekly meeting with Dr. Claymore, where Luke said nothing about what Claire had done to herself or where she was now. This was not unexpected; he had years ago developed a habit of omission in his sessions with Claymore, first in regard to me and then later in response to any questions the doctor tried to direct toward the topic of his mother. All Claymore knew of me were the handful of inaccuracies Claire had mentioned during those first few sessions over ten years ago. Of Claire herself, he knew only whatever she chose to tell him in their private monthly conferences, which, since she had her own shrink, were supposed to be about her son; nothing of significance ever came out of Luke's mouth.

Small deceptions were second nature for Luke. Just that morning he had informed Molly of his after-school commitment to the Chess Club, which of course met during the same hour as this session with Claymore. It's not that he thought his time with the doctor was in any way essential, or even useful, but Luke believed in involving the least number of people possible in his life and its problems. Complications and discrepancies brought questions, and there was nothing he hated more. His face had been blank when he spoke to Molly, one hand on the door frame, the other fiddling with the strap on his backpack. She had smiled, said something about commitment. Aside from Omar and his mother, I was the only one who ever knew when Luke was lying, and there wasn't any way I could tell anybody about it.

Today Claymore seemed unsettled. His questions about classes and sports and books were unfocused, and he seemed barely to be listening to Luke's answers. He rubbed his shiny head with first one hand, then the other, his eyes roaming the room from behind his bifocals; then suddenly he snapped his attention together, and said, "And how are your friends?"

Luke paused. He had been talking about football. "My friends?" he said cautiously. "Omar's fine."

"Yes," Claymore said, folding hands as pink and hairless as a baby's. "And Omar is as good a friend as anyone could ask for. But I don't believe he's the only one you've ever had."

I turned away from the window, where I had been peering through a slit in the blinds at a group of high school girls flitting by in a blur of baby-blue skirts and bared knees. Luke glanced at me and then looked away. "Everybody's fine."

Claymore paused, then said, "Do you remember why you came to see me that very first time? Twelve years ago?"

Luke's face went still. "What about it?"

"You were a very scared little boy then, Luke. But we were able to help you, your mother and I."

I stood at Claymore's shoulder, my hands clasped behind my back, trying not to betray the anxiety that suddenly possessed me. I looked at Luke again, but he wouldn't meet my eye. "I guess so," he said.

"This, ah, friend—you called him Daniel—who was troubling you then, you would tell me if he ever came back."

Claymore made me sound like a disease, or an infestation. "Our relationship is none of his business," I said. "He has no idea what's best for you."

Luke looked at Claymore calmly. "I'm not sure what you mean."

"What I mean is that if you ever see or hear things that you shouldn't be seeing or hearing, you need to tell me. We can make the necessary adjustments."

"To my medication, you mean."

Claymore spread his pink hands across the desk. "To your

medication, to your life. Whatever is necessary. You have a friend here, too, Luke." He tapped his chest. "I'm not going anywhere."

Luke tightened his mouth. I could see he was holding back a smirk, and I felt relief sweep through me. Luke was beyond such facile manipulations. Claymore was not a real problem; as always, it was Claire with whom I needed to be concerned.

Tuesday night, James knocked on the door of the television room and delivered his report: "The clinic says another four days until she's allowed to use the phone. Something she signed." He shrugged, absolving himself. James had first mentioned "the clinic" at dinner on Sunday; when I pressed Luke all he said was, "It's where my mother is recovering," as though I couldn't figure that part out for myself. James was in contact with this place, wherever it was, and he relayed the pieces of information he received from it stingily, with little elaboration. In this and all other matters, he now appeared committed to remaining as phlegmatic as possible; it was as though any show of emotion would prove that he had been dragged back into the middle of something he thought he had left far behind.

I stood at the window. The setting sun, sliced into ribbons by the towers across the park, caught the windshield of a passing taxi and splintered brilliantly into my eyes. I turned around and could barely see Luke and James behind a screen of floating spots, little glitches that ducked and dove across my field of vision.

Without looking up from his homework, Luke said, "What about visitors?"

"I'm not sure. They didn't say."

"You didn't ask."

"I figured one thing at a time."

Luke nodded but still didn't look up. The spots faded, and I saw James standing in the doorway, rubbing at his recessed eyes with a bony finger. "Don't you want to hear how she is? What they told me on the phone?"

Luke finally closed his binder and looked up. "I guess I'd rather wait until she can tell me herself."

James frowned at his son. "Don't be so stubborn. None of us wanted to be in this situation. I'm just trying to help as best I can."

His words sounded canned, rehearsed. But the more I thought about them, the more I felt he was speaking honestly: of course he didn't want to be in this situation, and of course he was trying to help, because what was the alternative? A moral sense might have influenced him, but love did not. I watched the two of them blink at each other in the failing light. I waited for some current of feeling to surge between them, but nothing moved underneath the silence.

"Thanks," Luke finally said. "I'll take your word on it."

James shook his head and left the room, pulling the door shut behind him.

The next morning Cassie leaned against the brushed-steel refrigerator and ate a waffle with her fingers, cradling a jar of blackberry jam. She wore her school uniform, book bag slung over one shoulder, poised to sprint out the door. She leaned and chewed and eyed Luke, who poked mechanically at a bowl of cereal. I could see her appraisal of him constantly shifting, each individual piece of new information altering the whole, like the way a single brushstroke changes the entire composition of a painting. I wondered what James had told her about him. It didn't seem like much.

"You don't have to pretend to like that," she said, "just because James remembers you ate it when you were, like, six."

Luke shrugged. "It's cereal. Who cares?"

"We could go to the grocery store tonight and get stuff you really want. We might as well stock up, since you're going to be here awhile, right?"

Luke didn't take the bait. "I don't know. It depends."

"On what?"

"What do you think?"

Cassie opened the refrigerator, rattling some cans around in search of a Diet Coke. "I mean, have you . . ." She paused, her face hidden behind the refrigerator door. "Have you heard anything? Is there any news?"

Luke slid the morning's *Times* across the marble island. "Here's the news. I have to catch a bus."

Luke managed to avoid any more time alone with Cassie and her questions until Sunday morning, when the three of us walked nineteen blocks down Fifth Avenue to buy some music. We had been told Claire would call that evening, and Luke was too anxious to just sit around the house and wait. We walked past the Conservatory Garden's gates, glazed by another April rain squall, past the Cooper-Hewitt and its schizophrenic's lawn of modernist furniture, past one after another prewar building, each replete with a crisp hunter-green awning and brass-buttoned doormen. The park glistened on our right, drops of water like marbles weighing down the leaves, the smell of damp soil primal and incongruous in the thick of Manhattan. We turned left on Eighty-sixth Street and the smell was replaced by bus exhaust. Lexington Avenue lay sodden and trash-plastered after the rain. The record store abutted a subway entrance, so Luke and Cassie were forced to ford a stream of people rushing up from underground to the bus stop twenty yards down the sidewalk. While the two of them dodged and weaved, I walked calmly through the middle of the crowd, letting all of them flow around me, these ugly, bulky, sweaty people. They lurched and stumbled, clutching purses and plastic shopping bags, leaning on canes and umbrellas. One bus took off, filled to the brim, while the stragglers queued up impatiently for the second, a puddle of lumpy flesh stuffed into ill-fitting clothes. In the midst of it all, I was untouched, inviolate. Unsullied. At the store's entrance, I waited for Luke and Cassie to run the gauntlet. I drew my fingers through the part in my hair. I may have been saddled with an unfortunate approximation of Luke's body and face, but I could still take better care of them than he did. The thought that this vanity was for my and Luke's benefit alone bothered me for only a brief moment. I looked at the line of people waiting for the bus, and I was glad to be something different, something apart. It didn't matter that I was more proud of myself for what I was not than for what I was.

Inside the store, garish spotlights pinned shoppers to the industrial carpeting as though they were actors in some dire, tedious play. We split up from Cassie and found the classical section sequestered downstairs in its own glass-walled compound, as though it required protection from the gauche world beyond its doors. Here Luke could locate works by the composers Claire embraced as a counterpoint to the Janis Joplin and Jefferson Airplane that dominated the summer months, when she flung open the apartment's windows and let the sunshine, humid air, and rock 'n' roll stick together into one gummy ball. Luke saved his love for the winter's dizzying Minimalist compositions, thick music constructed out of a dense, spiraling architecture that only occasionally opened up into moments of hard-earned release.

I remembered Claire one night, green eyes shining, take Luke by the shoulders, sit him down in her desk chair, and place her giant freestanding speakers on either side of him. "Listen," she said. She waved the LP cover in his face. "This was composed for people like us, for people who would understand what is being said." The sound that poured out of the speakers was impossibly dense, colossal and like a Möbius strip in its circularity: no entry, no exit. "Do you hear?" Claire said, turning the volume knob farther to the right. "Listen closely, and you'll hear what I do." Stuffed inside Luke's head, I had felt dizzy, giddy, deprived of oxygen. Luke had been playing their music during the last week as well—Philip Glass, Terry Riley, Steve Reich, these rigorous, peculiar men—their CDs smuggled over from the Central Park West apartment in his book bag and listened to surreptitiously on headphones. I preferred silence; all of it made me queasy. Beneath the cleverness I sensed something earnest; optimism, maybe, or something equally naïve.

Luke picked through the racks. The department was softly lit, and the few salesmen minced around the space like mimes. "Look at this." Luke held up a set of Philip Glass's *Music in Twelve Parts*, six discs packaged in a glossy box. The price sticker said eighty-five dollars. "I don't have that much money."

"It's an import, isn't it?" I said. "I have an idea."

The bargain bins sat on tables outside the classical sanctuary, cardboard boxes tightly packed with orphaned albums. The price stickers had been affixed one on top of another as the CDs' value had decreased, so that on the very cheapest, pink $1.99 stickers crowned a welter of other abandoned price points. I gestured at one of these sad albums. "Take that and follow me." I picked a lonely section of the store full of comedy cassettes and guitar tablature books. "Listen," I said, "since it's an import, that box set doesn't have the right kind of barcode. They'll just have to go with the price on the sticker." There was no one around; I had chosen an aisle almost entirely blocked from view, a corner hemmed in by walls and high shelves. "Pull a sticker switch. The cashiers won't care enough to check up on it."

Luke frowned at me. "That's stealing. I don't steal."

"They're basically taxing you for liking difficult music," I said.

"Why should you have to be deprived because of everyone else's poor taste?"

He licked his lips and nodded. He glanced around him, saw nobody, then turned away from me, scraping at the stickers in the concealed space between his body and the wall. I peered over his shoulder. "Careful. Don't tear it." We were standing like that, both facing the wall, oblivious to what was behind us, when the kid prodded the small of Luke's back.

"Let me ask you a favor."

Luke flinched and turned around, hiding the CDs behind his back, but it wasn't a salesman or a security guard. It was a high school kid, about Luke's age, his lanky body almost lost inside a puffy ski jacket, his pale face long, rawboned.

"Let me ask you a favor."

"What is it?"

"Let me borrow twenty dollars."

"What?"

"Let me borrow twenty dollars. I know you got twenty bucks on you."

"I don't have anything."

The kid stepped closer, trapping Luke in the corner. "Bullshit. What were you going to do, steal those CDs? Let me get twenty dollars."

I checked down the aisle over his shoulder, but there was nobody. Luke looked at me pleadingly. "Don't give him any-thing," I said. "What's he going to do to you here in the store?" This was easy to say when I wasn't the target. The kid moved his hand around inside his jacket pocket. He said, "You don't want me to bring out this knife." "He's bluffing," I said. Luke took all his money, thirteen dollars, out of his pocket and handed it over to the kid, the outside world exacting its toll. "Coward," I said.

Shaking his head, the kid took the crumpled bills and stuffed them into his jeans. "That's all you got?" He was turning to go when we heard Cassie's voice, loud and querulous: "Luke, what are you doing?" She stood at the end of the aisle, a stack of CDs in her hands. The kid's eyes bugged, and he bowled right by her to get to the escalator, taking it three steps at a time. Cassie stood openmouthed. "What the hell was that?"

Luke trembled in the corner, all sick adrenaline. Cassie frowned. "What have you been doing? It's been half an hour already." "Go on," I said, "tell her how you just got used." He opened his mouth, but before he could speak, a security guard came down the escalator holding a badge in one hand and the kid's puffy jacket in the other. "Mind coming with me?"

And so Luke was quickly revealed to be a victim, and all three of us were marched through an unmarked metal door into a kind of observation chamber, something like the combination of an air traffic control tower and a television editing room. I saw banks of grainy black-and-white monitors; inside the screens, ghostly customers drifted around the store. Two bored-looking men split their attention between the cameras and the tabloids. One looked up to wink at Cassie and then turned back to the sports pages. "We saw what happened on the camera. We grabbed him at the door, but he slipped out of the jacket and got away. Kid's fast, but that's not going to help him much." The guard pulled a sheet of paper out of the jacket's pocket and placed it on a table, smoothing out the wrinkles. It was a test, a chemistry exam. "Let's just say he's not the sharpest tool in the box." The guard pointed at the D+ written in red ink at the top of the page, and then the name scrawled on the left.

It took half an hour for a police officer—round, young, also bored—to arrive, and another twenty minutes for Luke to give a statement and sign a pile of forms. Through it all, Cassie sat there smirking and chewing gum, while Luke sweated and stewed. His anxiety was so obvious that at one point the security guard touched his arm and said, "I know you're spooked, but you're safe now, so just calm down for Christ's sake." But I knew Luke's nervousness had little to do with the mugging itself and everything to do with the fact that if they had seen the mugging, then they could very easily also have seen our price sticker scam, the evidence of which—Philip Glass's *Music in Twelve Parts,* retailing for $1.99, and some bargain-bin garbage, price defaced—sat on the table, as incriminating in Luke's eyes as any blood-spattered knife or smoking gun. Had they seen it? Did they know, and were now just toying with him, waiting until he was about to leave before laying a hand on his shoulder and saying, "There's just one more thing . . ."? But apparently they hadn't, because they didn't, and finally we were told we could go.

Out on the street, Cassie shook her head and laughed. "It may seem bad now, but getting mugged is part of growing up in New York, right? It's like getting new teeth." She nudged Luke with a friendly elbow. "Don't worry, I won't embarrass you by telling James or my mom. I can keep a secret."

⋘⋙

At the bottom of Luke's duffel bag were two books that bore the Nightingale Press emblem, two books Luke had grabbed off his mother's shelves and stuffed into the bag while neither Cassie nor I was paying attention. One was something called *A Flower of Evil*, which seemed to be about a female serial killer and the detective who becomes aware, absurdly, that this same woman has been the object of his romantic and professional pursuits both. Luke read this ridiculous book late at night, propped up in the sofa bed after finishing his homework. I stood by the window as he read, watching the shifting pattern of bright and dim windows across the black wound of the park. I wasn't going to waste my mind on such garbage. But on Sunday night, when Luke lay down on the sofa bed and opened the second Nightingale Press book, I took a greater interest in what he was reading.

It had been an uncomfortable afternoon and evening. Luke sulked around during the hours between lunch and dinner, carrying with him the limp tension of someone waiting for an event beyond his control. When dinnertime came and went without a call from the clinic, and when James's own call was answered by a brusque statement that telephone hours were over, Luke locked the door to the television room and refused to speak. The plasma screen hung Cyclops-like on the white wall. I sat on the floor with my back against the sofa bed, staring into the blank screen as Luke took the tattered hardcover out of his bag. I ignored him, letting his anger burn itself out. On the book's worn jacket, a silhouette of Manhattan's skyline—the classic version, with the Chrysler, Empire State, and Flatiron buildings at its center—cast a reflection that cleverly formed the words *Shadow Life: A Novel.* Below, in blood-red Courier font: *Alexandra Tithe.* The edges of the pages were dyed the same deep red, and the whole package— the lettering, the graphics, the red pages—screamed 1970s.

"What do you have there?" I asked, more out of boredom than anything else. Luke glanced at me over the top of the book, but said nothing. "This is stupid. You're not going to talk to me?"

"It's one of my mother's books. You probably could have figured that out on your own, though."

"Is it better than *A Flower of Evil?* Because that was a real piece of shit."

"You're a snob."

"If that's what you want to call it. What's the deal with this one?"

"I don't know. It's older, from my grandmother's time at the press." He bent the spine backward and it gave out a very human creak, the sound of muscles and tendons that haven't been stretched in months. He flipped through the pages. "Somebody's written all over this thing."

I stood up and looked over his shoulder. On almost every page were scribbled notes and comments, both in the margins and over the printed text itself, in a variety of different pens and what looked like two different hands. I pointed to a block of blue-inked writing that ran vertically down the side of one page. "That's your mother's handwriting." "But that's not," Luke said, pointing to some seemingly random phrases jotted in red at the bottom of the same page.

"No. Your grandmother's? That would make the most sense, wouldn't it?"

"I don't know. None of the other books were like this."

I sat down on the edge of the bed and studied the notes. "But I don't believe it is entirely accurate to call it a haunting," Claire had written. Then, a few paragraphs later: "Perhaps she hides in the blood instead." Her mother, presumably, had written on the same page: "There cannot be a price too high for such an escape. Nothing is too much to give."

I frowned down into the book. "I don't understand. The novel was already published, it's not as though these are edits." Luke turned the page. Claire had written in the top margin, "I don't believe a word of it, but will that make any difference in the end?" "I don't have much time," her mother had written at the bottom. "I must act soon."

Luke said, "I'm going to have to start at the beginning."

There was no author photograph and the entirety of the bio was the terse "Alexandra Tithe lives in New York City. This is her first novel." What this faceless woman had created was an odd, claustrophobic version of mid-twentieth-century Manhattan, a patchwork city assembled out of crumbling tenements, dead-end alleys, and trigger-happy thieves. She pushed her men to the margins, these effeminate incompetents or thick-brained dupes, either way easy prey for the mysterious women who glide through the smoky bars and dank streets like piranhas in a muddy river. Juliet, Tithe's protagonist, is not at first one of these women. Stuck in a secretarial job she loathes, subject to the lascivious attentions of her repulsive boss, eking out an existence in a Lower East Side studio apartment, she drifts through her days in a strange fugue, never quite certain of what she's doing, where she is, or, later, who she is.

Venetia's and Claire's comments on these early pages were minimal until Venetia used a seemingly tossed-off line about the Hudson River—"mottled with moonlight like a wet log with moss"—as the starting point for an inquisition into the nature of drowning: what it might feel like; similar methods of death ("Suffocation?" in big loopy letters); famous historical drowning victims (she mentions Virginia Woolf, as well as Percy Bysshe Shelley and the passengers of the *Titanic*); and an anecdote about once, as a child, finding a body washed up on a Rhode Island beach after a winter storm, its skin seeped of color, a ball of snarled seaweed stuffed into its open mouth like a gag. These musings had been written with a red editing pencil directly over the top of the novel's printed text, which made reading the next few pages nearly impossible. Luke squinted in the lamplight. "It's something about Juliet's apartment," he said. "She feels the locks on her door are insufficient, I think." On the next page, in what seemed like a response to something, Claire had written: "No, 'inevitability' just means you gave up."

Sometime after midnight, Luke yawned and said he was having trouble keeping his eyes open. We had reached the midway point in the novel. Juliet has for a few chapters been spotting a woman who looks, dresses, and walks exactly like herself. The woman skulks around the city, drifting among the racks of an Orchard Street wholesale clothing store, ducking into a Washington Square bar, darting by Juliet on Madison Avenue in the early-morning Midtown rush. Late one night, as Juliet sits on her fire escape smoking a cigarette, she sees the woman strolling down Clinton Street, framed between Juliet's dangling feet. The unknown woman keeps her head low, but it is she—that is, it both is and is not Juliet, in the same way the woman has both been and not been Juliet each time Juliet has seen her. "Hey," Juliet calls out with stifled urgency, afraid to wake her neighbors. "Hey!" The woman turns, looks up, her face caught momentarily in a streetlamp's glow, and it is Juliet's face, but wearing a sneer Juliet incorrectly imagines has never gripped her own features. And then, before Juliet can do any-thing except stub her cigarette out in a flowerpot and untangle her legs from the slats of the fire escape, the woman turns down Rivington Street and is gone.

"That's enough for now," Luke said. "I'm exhausted, and I don't understand this."

"The novel or the notes?"

"Both. Neither."

"I think I'll keep going."

"If you want to." He slumped back against the pillows. "I remember my mother reading this book just last year. Grandma had already been dead for over a decade."

I moved closer to him on the bed, and laid my left hand over his right along the edge of the book. For a moment we touched, near-twins, almost-brothers, and then he handed over the book and closed his eyes to go to sleep.

I stayed up all night and finished the novel. I decoded the scribbling of the Nightingale women as best I could, trying to untangle a very strange commentary by Claire on what was already a very strange commentary by Venetia, at the center of which stood the book itself, an ingrown, paranoid knot of a thriller. Juliet witnesses her double commit a murder, slashing the throat of a drunken gambler she lures out of a bar into a garbage-choked Chinatown alley, but when she runs home she sees it is her own hands that are covered with blood, her own skirt and heels that are blackened and tacky with the stuff. Venetia wrote in the margin, "She has lost any control she once had over the thing," while Claire, in her tighter, neater hand, added, "It is herself she must learn to control."

Madness, all of it. But I could not stop reading. Juliet became in those few hours as familiar to me as anyone except Luke himself. I felt as if I knew what she would do next—or rather, I had to keep reminding myself, what Alexandra Tithe made her do—before she did it. I believed in her terror as she sees someone who both is and is not her do awful, awful things, and I believed equally in the appalling, hidden sense of pride she takes in these crimes, as the victims—drunks, mobsters, rapists—keep piling up. I could smell the stale, smoky air of her tenement studio, the grease frying on the stove's single burner, the hot summer breeze carrying its taste of trash and despair. Behind her secretarial desk, she forgets who she is and sneaks glimpses at her compact mirror, which does nothing to help. I felt that as I read about her she somehow took me into her skin, inside her body, that I settled down somewhere behind her eyes and among her bones. Her damp panic as the web grows tighter around her became my own.

Juliet soon fears she is losing her mind. She sees a psychiatrist she cannot afford and begins to tell him her story before she stops, afraid of the look gathering on his face, afraid of where he might send her. She tapers off, mumbling something about not being able to sleep, palms his prescription for Seconal, and never returns. She attempts to confront her twin among the oil-drum fires of 2:00 A.M. Tompkins Square Park, but her strange sister disappears into the shadows without saying a word. Yet Juliet does not stop searching for help, and one day she finds it in an old book left on the sidewalk outside her tenement, stacked alongside garbage bags, a broken toaster, and a mangled vinyl chair. It is a volume of folklore from every remote corner of the world, a giant, musty, falling-apart thing, the kind of book forgotten for decades in an attic or moldy basement. Juliet doesn't know why she takes the book back upstairs to her apartment, but she does, and she begins to read.

At first she finds the stories dull, sunken under leaden morals, or else trite, peopled by talking animals and plucky heroes. But then she reads a tale from a cold northern country. A village suffers a rash of murders during the months after a fisherman, grieving over his wife's death in childbirth, throws himself into the sea. There is arson, a throat-slitting, a pair of poisonings, but there is no explanation for the murders, no motive, no suspects. It is a small village; no one can believe that any one of their neighbors is capable of these crimes. Baffled, the village council sends a messenger to a hermit, a supposed wise man, who explains that the spirit of the dead fisherman has remained behind to trouble those still living. This spirit found the saddest man in the village, and now walks by his side dressed in the shape of a dead relative or lover, or perhaps in the shape of the sad man himself. The hermit says the spirit will walk alongside this man and speak into his ear and continue to make him do these evil things, until finally he will slip underneath the weakened man's skin and there will be no difference anymore between the man and the spirit. Only if the sad man also takes his own life will he spare the village and what is left of his soul. The man must raise his knife with a peaceful and empty mind, the hermit says, and when the first drop of his blood touches the dirt, the spirit will flee to search elsewhere for its new home. The messenger thanks the hermit and returns to the village, where, in front of the village council, he recounts the hermit's words, takes his knife from his belt, and cuts his own throat.

Juliet puts down the book. She thinks of the boarded-up windows on the fifth floor of her own tenement, the scene of a suicide six months before. The police cordons, the wailing mother, the tarp thrown carelessly over the body on the sidewalk, a bare foot poking out from underneath like a misplaced comma. She thinks of the recent murders and the rancid pride coiled within her fear. Then she stands up and goes out to the fire escape to smoke a cigarette, formulating a plan with as clear a head and light a heart as she has felt in months.

I read Claire and Venetia's comments on all of this too, and I found myself muttering my own responses to these madwomen, to the digressions and theories and rants that spread like ivy over every page of the novel. Next to the final paragraph—in which Juliet finally corners her doppelganger on an abandoned Hudson River pier from which they both fall, intertwined, into the cold water and are swept beneath New York Harbor—Venetia wrote, "Easier written than done, perhaps," to which her daughter replied, "If only that had been true."

My hands shook even as Luke snored peacefully at my side. What had come over me? I felt as though I had seen the inside of Claire's mind, and it was familiar and disorienting all at once. I felt, too, as though the plot of the novel had slipped inside of me to hide behind each of my thoughts like a bad memory. It was only early the next morning when, still unable to sleep, I realized what I had been reading was also Venetia's suicide note, that her annotations were an explanation of why and how she had chosen to end her life.

Luke finally woke up and I waved the book in his sleepy face. "We have to get rid of this."

"Why?" He yawned. "And anyway, it's not ours to get rid of."

"It's dangerous."

"What are you talking about?"

"It's not safe for Claire to ever read this again. She's fragile. Whenever she comes back, it will only upset her."

I knew how to get his attention. He turned to me, and his face took on sharper edges, shedding any last traces of sleep. "How do you know that?"

"I finished it while you were sleeping. Venetia wrote some horrible things in here, things Claire should never read again." He stared at the book for a minute, and then nodded without opening it; anything for his mother. Of course, concern for Claire had nothing to do with my real reasons. Reading it had frightened me—because Venetia and Claire's ramblings began to make an awful kind of sense, because I found myself convinced by their most paranoid points, because the novel's characters had climbed into my head and refused to leave. I felt the book was trying to tell me something about myself I did not want to know, and that I did not want Luke to know either. We were the ones who should never read it again.

We slipped out of the apartment that night after dinner, receiving sideways looks from the doormen. We crossed the street and vaulted a locked side gate into the Conservatory Garden. The wide central lawn was patchy, its grand fountain dry, and the flower plots that ran along its sides filled only with dirt. It had been a cold winter; the flowers were late to bloom. We'd brought a garden spade, and Luke dug shallow holes in the plots, uncovering bulbs seeded like mines. He tore *Shadow Life* apart. He ripped clutches of pages from the spine, and then tore the pages themselves into smaller scraps. He sprinkled the paper into the holes. The spine went last, into the largest hole, and then he filled them all up with dirt. We were back inside the apartment in less than half an hour. Nobody noticed we had been gone.

<hr />

When Claire finally called the following evening, eleven days after she had left us, I was lying on the couch in the TV room beside Cassie, pressed tightly against her, grafting my body onto hers. Luke sat in the chair beside the couch, trying to ignore us, red spots rising on his cheeks, while Cassie stretched out, languid, her head cradled in her hand. I worked my body in against hers until our faces touched, until my nose rested against her cheek and our mouths breathed the same air. She wore sweatpants with the cuffs cut off and a yellow tank top with rainbows and fluffy clouds flanking the words *I hate myself and want to die*. She was soft and warm as I pressed against her, and I allowed myself to sink deeper into the feeling of her shape, into her curves and hollows. As I listened to the television with one ear—we were watching something about a civil war somewhere, and the sound of artillery rattled around the room—my hands cupped her breasts, which pushed, braless and heavy, against the faded tank top, and then I strayed down to the waistband of her sweatpants. I slid my hand into the space between her thighs and then moved it up into the warmth above, pressing my fingers against the cotton and the unfamiliar form underneath. She felt nothing, of course, saw nothing, and I could not get closer without entering her body, without becoming a part of her. Her skin was the boundary I could not cross.

Luke answered the phone on the side table before its second ring; it wasn't his place, but he was too anxious to care. "Mom," he said. Cassie tilted her head to look at him, and I matched her movement with my own. "How could you even ask me that?" My entire field of vision was taken up by Cassie's gigantic blue eye, flecked with tiny pieces of black like flakes of ash, the pupil enormous and wet. She wrinkled her brow, and the perfect oval collapsed, crumpling from the top. Luke said, "Of course we'll come get you," and Cassie blinked and shifted, pressing her thighs together, and my hand was consumed by fire.

And so on the following morning we skipped school and I sat in the backseat of James's BMW, flying down the left lane of the Long Island Expressway at eighty-five miles per hour. We drove an hour out of the city before turning off the main highway onto a two-lane road and then a smaller country lane, the interchangeable strip malls giving way first to equally interchangeable leafy towns, and then to row after row of mansions set back from the road and guarded by acres of landscaped lawns. Suddenly we burst out of a copse of oaks, and there was the Long Island Sound, glittering and placid, sailboats floating on the water like toys in a bathtub. I pressed my face up to the window as the road swung hard to the right and hugged the shore the rest of the way to the clinic.

Molly had rushed around the kitchen before we left, pressing plastic bags full of tuna salad sandwiches and apples into Luke's hands, babbling about what a beautiful day it was going to be, what a nice drive we were going to have, how happy Luke's mother would be to see him. I couldn't figure out what she was so nervous about. Maybe she was afraid some authority had decided Claire was no longer fit to take care of Luke, and that she, Molly, would have a new stepson to watch over for the year until he became a legal adult. Or maybe it was the opposite, that she was afraid for Luke to return to his mother's apartment. There was no place in my universe for such altruism, but perhaps it existed here, sloshing around inside Molly's chest. Whatever it was, she took Luke's cheeks between her hands and held his face in front of hers for a few long seconds. Cassie, too, hugged Luke too tightly and for too long, and I sensed a new emotion—jealousy, I thought, that's jealousy—as I remembered how she had felt pressed against me on the couch, and I stood there by the front door, wanting that feeling back.

The look Molly and James shared as we waited for the elevator was too complex for Luke to understand. "She's scared," I explained to him in the lobby. "She's scared that James used to love Claire, and she's scared that he might again." "And James?" "James just wants to pretend he never did." This was the principle around which he had organized the last twelve years of his life; he wanted to erase his time with Claire, which meant erasing Luke from his life as well. I told Luke this, and he nodded. "Of course, but you say it like I should care. Why would I want things to be different? He's boring, an ordinary person. He's not like us." It took me a moment to realize "us" meant him and Claire; even after I did, I wasn't sure I believed his indifference.

The clinic was called Shady Bay, but I didn't see much shade, just a broad, treeless lawn stretching out beyond low redbrick walls and a wrought-iron gate. The clinic itself was also low and redbrick, two stories of gabled windows and limestone trim, and at one end of the lawn a seawall held back the lazy Sound. It looked more like a resort than a hospital, but that was probably the point. The reception area was done in shades of peach and tan and smelled like eucalyptus and sea salt; I couldn't tell if these odors were part of the designed atmosphere or just happened to drift in through the open bay windows. The receptionists and nurses and orderlies who rustled by on the lawn or in the lobby were dressed not in lab coats or scrubs but beige uniforms that made them look like flight attendants or Third World dictators. A tinkling sound trickled out of the wall-mounted speakers, and it took a moment for me to realize it was the recording of a flowing stream, even though there was real, wet water making its own noise less than a hundred yards away.

They took our names, and Luke and James sat down to wait in molded teak chairs. I was restless, and paced around the room. James had driven here without directions or a map, and there was something about the way he now sat, some slackness in his pose, that suggested he was familiar with this place. On the lawn outside the window, a young woman in white pajamas spread out a sky-blue beach towel and lay down on her stomach with a book in her hands. She looked like an office worker stealing her lunch hour in Central Park or a teenager lolling around her parents' backyard.

"Mr. Tomasi?" It was a doctor, I supposed, who spoke, or maybe some sort of administrator, with his houndstooth sport jacket and gold tie clip. But who cared about him when Claire stood by his side, dressed not, as I had assumed, in some cheap bathrobe or hospital-issue paper gown, but in a crisp navy blue pantsuit and cream blouse. Her dark hair was straightened and combed carefully to the side in a tidy wave, and her face was relaxed and smiling. I had forgotten not only how tiny she was— how compactly and efficiently her body presented itself, as if she had sloughed off all the unnecessary layers everybody else carried around—but also how composed and flawless was the shell she tried to show the world. Even here, where these doctors and nurses had seen her at her worst; even now, when her son and ex-husband were prepared for anything, when bandages crept out from underneath the cuffs of her suit jacket and covered her palms in a patchwork of tape and gauze. It's a lie, I thought. Don't believe it. But I didn't say this out loud, because my response would seem so shrilly Pavlovian to Luke, so stupidly predictable. That's not really her, I wanted to say, but I could already picture him twist his lip at me in disgust, so I just kept my mouth shut and watched the happy reunion.

3

LIFE WITH CLAIRE began again. By the time we moved back in a few days later, the apartment had been cleaned up and all the mirrors replaced. The place looked immaculate, as though I had imagined everything that had happened in those rooms, as though our two weeks away had been some garish dream. Someone had called and arranged everything; Claire had paid from a distance.

After her return, certain rules became more clearly defined.

Objects were useless without Luke's permission. Sometimes when we were alone, he let me read my own books, and often he had me hold the pen during homework and exams. But whenever I tried to do anything without his approval—hurl a soda can at some student; pinch a magazine from the newsstand near school—my touch lost its persuasiveness. The soda can slipped through my fingers; the magazine became heavier than a lead brick. This had all been true before, when I first met Luke, but there had been exceptions; now there were none. People were both simpler and more complicated, as they had always been: I could touch them, but they could not feel me. I traced the lines of their bodies and faces, and they never knew.

As Luke moved through the last few months of his junior year of high school, little between us changed. I guided him through classes and football and the rare party, nudging him forward when he stepped back. I helped him with his photography, a new obsession he nurtured in the high school's basement darkroom. My patience during these months was immense, like a silent, forgotten creature spread across the ocean's floor. The first time I acted hastily had led to twelve years of imprisonment, so there could be no lapse in self-discipline. Still, I welcomed when Luke's clamping down was balanced by a small freedom: my shape, the form I presented to Luke and to myself. Before, I had little control over what I looked like. My ridiculous clothes, my scrawny body, my almost-Luke face: I chose none of these, and the best I could do was polish my shoes or comb my hair. But Luke loosened up and let me play around with my appearance so that by summer I had the jaw, cheekbones, and fluorescent teeth of a movie star; the ropy body of a surfer; the spotless voice of a politician; and the tailored wardrobe of a dandy. It was all a better fit for who I was; even Luke admitted that.

I also became freer with some of my opinions, and I certainly did not censor myself on the topic of his new "girlfriend," Sarah Wise, the spastic girl from Latin class, whom I considered to be dull, prissy, and only moderately attractive. They had gone to school together for eight years, and Luke had cultivated a crush on her for the last two. I didn't understand why, because Sarah was above all a grade-grubber. She hovered on the periphery of the popular cliques, redeemed at least in part by her parents' house on the East End, to which she was always inviting gaggles of her female classmates. Yet it seemed she lived for nothing more than her teachers' approval. She studied constantly, feverishly, but without any apparent love or even interest for what she was learning. History, literature, chemistry: these were no more than hurdles to be cleared on the track to a pat on the head, a clean report card, and admission to a suitably impressive college. I hated the idea of learning for its own sake—the reverence with which teachers treated the dead languages of Latin and Ancient Greek especially repulsed me—but sycophancy was even more disgusting. A bad grade sent Sarah into a fit of rage, which it was apparently now Luke's job to soothe, and for all her supposed intelligence, she was incapable of extending any academic discussion beyond the exact parameters of what she had been taught in class. "She's not smart enough for you," I told Luke, but what I really meant is that she was not smart enough for me.

We spent most of that summer before Luke's senior year of high school holed up in the air-conditioned Central Park West apartment or hanging around the Nightingale Press offices, hostages to the absurd Manhattan heat. Omar disappeared below Fourteenth Street with his skateboard and a bag of marijuana, seeking grittier thrills, and sometime around the middle of August, when the sky looked bruised and the air tasted poisoned, we began to spend a lot of time hiding out in Sarah's apartment, lounging away the afternoons in her frigid bedroom. In that first week, they barely touched; Luke would sprawl over her gray flannel couch, while Sarah would lie across the bed on her stomach, cradling her head in her hands. I sat at the window, bored. I wasn't interested in her at all. The television would be on the entire time, although its primary function seemed to be to give the two of them something to look at besides each other. On the screen, somebody famous would do something stupid, and Luke would look at Sarah and ask, "Why would anybody want to be like *her*?" and Sarah would roll her eyes and say, "Totally," and then they'd both look back at the TV, inexplicably embarrassed.

But by the end of the month, they were lying together on the bed, their fingers and legs entwined. This was when she became more interesting to me, because sex was something in which I was interested no matter with whom. Two weeks of living with Cassie had stirred up these feelings inside of me. Since then, Luke had kept me away from his step-sister as much as he could, afraid of the things I would do. It didn't matter. After those two weeks, I looked at all girls and women in a new way, and I tested how their bodies felt, stroking and palming them on the subway or in line at the movie theater. It was all incomplete and rather pointless, though, like palpating a fruit without eating it. I often thought of the couple we had stumbled upon in the park when Luke was little; that was what I wanted, that rawness, that blunt currency of lust.

Finally, one afternoon, watching television again on Sarah's bed, Luke broke off in the middle of a sentence and leaned over to kiss her. He caught her by surprise, and his tongue ran up against her teeth until she parted her mouth to let him in. It didn't go beyond that, but it was all he would talk about for days. Luke's first kiss had been three years before, with the bossy, brassy daughter of a Nightingale family friend, behind a clump of elms on a miserable Adirondack camping trip—I had peered out from his skull and noted that the puckered-up girl looked like a blind fish—and there had been a few awkward encounters since, but he hadn't particularly cared about any of those girls. They had all pursued him. I suppose they thought of him as mysterious or aloof or intriguing—cute but damaged, a reclamation project—when he was really just shy. (And, of course, they had all compared poorly with his beautiful, brilliant version of Claire.) But he treated Sarah differently, and I didn't like it. She simply wasn't worth our time.

"There are too many other girls," I said. We sat together on a shaded bench in the Conservatory Garden on the last day of August.

"What are you talking about?"

"Sarah's dull. You need to find somebody like Cassie, an adult. Look over there." I nodded toward two girls who sat on a bench on the other side of the lily pond. They looked to be eighteen or nineteen, and they wore sundresses, one patterned with tiny elephants, the other navy blue with white polka dots. "That's the kind of girl we need to go after." The girls sat in front of an explosion of flowers, a hallucinogenic palette of electric purples, candy-cane reds, and neon pinks that seemed to have been created for the sole purpose of framing these wonderful creatures. Both were tan, as if they had spent most of the summer somewhere else, somewhere with sand and yachts. I hadn't seen a beach since that dismal winter in Fire Island over a decade before, and Claire had made it clear we were never going back.

"Look at them." I stood up and walked toward the girls. In the center of the pond, the statue of a child held aloft a bowl of water in which bronze sparrows were harassed by their flesh-and-blood counterparts. On the far side of the pond, I stroked the hair of the taller, prettier of the pair, its light brown streaked with strands of gold. I leaned over and smelled her neck. "She's wearing perfume," I called over to Luke. "It smells like vanilla. Sarah never wears perfume."

My face was inches away from the tops of her breasts, and I flicked out my tongue and pressed it against her skin. She was very warm, the sun's heat layered on top of her own, and I ran my tongue down to the edge of the dress and back up to her jaw. She tossed her head, and her hair swept across my face. Although she was probably only two years older than Sarah, there was something entirely more adult about the way she carried herself, the way she spoke and gestured with her friend. I decided it was because she'd had sex; she knew something about which Sarah, Luke, and I could only imagine. She uncrossed and recrossed her legs, leaving a slight space between her thighs. I put my hand on her knee and began to slide it up her leg until Luke shouted, "That's enough!"

Both girls flinched and stared across the pond. I jumped back. "Luke! What's your problem?" Luke covered his face and stood up to leave. He stalked out of the garden, his eyes fixed on the ground and the bright blush returning to his cheeks. The two girls watched him go. "How creepy," my girl said. I looked at her beautiful hair, the crossed thighs, the tan cleavage, and then I looked at Luke's receding back. I cursed and followed him up the stairs and out to the street.

"You're sick," he said to me as we walked through the Vanderbilt Gate.

I shrugged. "I only do it because you won't."

<hr />

We left for Sarah's family beach house the next morning. On the 9:15 to Montauk, Luke squeezed into a seat next to a fat man with a bad comb-over. I perched myself on the empty overhead luggage rack. The train was full, and there was nobody in the car on whose lap I would even consider sitting, so this was the next-best thing. Long Island sped by outside the windows, a blur of highways, strip malls, and marshes, and the ride passed quickly.

Sarah waited at the East Hampton station. She wore turquoise shorts and a white polo shirt, and squinted behind white-rimmed glasses. She looked well put together, prim and studious, which was just about right. She smiled when Luke stepped out onto the platform, but restrained herself to a chaste peck on the cheek. Her father didn't get out of the car—Sarah couldn't drive—and he offered Luke a listless half-smile in the rearview mirror as he shifted the Mercedes station wagon into gear. They had met many times over the years, but never before had Luke been trying to fuck his daughter. The Wises' ludicrously large house sat at the end of a quiet lane. Sarah pointed at a golf course from the back deck. "The beach is just on the other side," she said. "We can walk across after dark."

But we didn't do that until Sunday night, our second and last. On Saturday we went out to a sushi dinner in some town that wasn't East Hampton. Again, there was nowhere to sit, so I stood at Luke's shoulder inspecting the cubes and strips of fish-flesh rotting on pillows of white rice. The various cuts had been arranged artfully on the plates, but no amount of ritual could camouflage the grotesque act of putting dead things into one's mouth. Mr. Wise drank *sake* and talked about golf. Sarah's brother muttered curses at a cell phone he hid under the table, his face pinched and mean, while her mother smiled benevolently at Luke, then said she had received a call from Claire a few days ago. "She does worry about you a lot, doesn't she?" I wondered how much she knew, then I wondered if she knew anything at all. I thought few did. Sarah and Luke sent each other secret smiles until I grew bored and spent the second half of dinner sitting on top of Mr. Wise's head, my legs dangling over his shoulders.

They stuck us on the ground floor directly underneath Sarah's bedroom. Luke pulled Sarah into a corner and spoke urgently into her ear. "I'm going to sneak up later. What time is best?"

She laughed. "Don't even think about it. The stairs creak like crazy."

"It doesn't matter," Luke said.

She made sure nobody was listening and touched Luke's chest. "No way. I promise we'll figure out something tomorrow. Now go to bed and be patient."

Luke sat up reading while I paced the room. "This is ridiculous. I told you she's a waste of time."

"She's a sweet girl," Luke said, "and that's not all I'm here for."

"That's gallant of you, but if I were in charge of things, we'd be upstairs fucking her right now." As soon as the words left my mouth, I was afraid I had gone too far.

Luke shut his book and stared at me. "Well, you're never going to be, so don't waste your time thinking about it." He held his eyes on mine for what he intended to be a pregnant moment. Finally, he returned to his book, then jerked his head back up a second later: "What do you mean 'we'?"

After a second day of lying around all afternoon under the angry sun—an activity I loathed, it was so utterly pointless—Sarah suggested taking a walk across the golf course to the dunes. We stood on the back porch watching shadows advance across the tenth green, and before Luke could answer, Sarah's brother wandered out with a beer. He finished it and waved the empty can at us. "Now that one won't go in Mom's official tally," he said and walked back inside. Sarah turned to Luke. "We have an hour before we need to be back for dinner. What do you think?"

They went barefoot across the dirt path to the golf course, but I followed in my tan summer suit and loafers because I didn't think proximity to the ocean was an excuse for slovenliness. Sarah carried a beach towel under her arm. Dew had already settled on the grass and salt-heavy air blew in off the Atlantic. Everything was damp. Sarah took Luke's hand. "Hurry," she said. "They turn on the sprinklers at sunset."

At the far edge of the course, the manicured greens gave way to stiff tawny weeds and dune grass. A track had been worn into the brush, and we followed it though a cut in the first line of dunes. The sand rose far above our heads on either side to create a sheltered hollow from which both the ocean and golf course were hidden. A main path led through the second line of dunes and out to the beach, but Sarah turned onto a fainter trail off to the side. The low sun streaked the hollow with gold, and Sarah spread out the towel in a pool of shade. She sat down, crossing her legs underneath her, and patted the space at her side. Luke sat where she wanted him to, while I sat on her other side, half on the towel, half on the cool sand. She wore a light cotton skirt she kept pulling down over her thighs and a ribbed tank top over which she had draped a baby-blue cable-knit sweater. Goose bumps stood up along her arms and calves, and I watched them rise and fall with the breeze.

They spoke for a few minutes about nothing, as usual. "What are you doing?" I whispered. "We haven't got much time." At last, Luke leaned over to kiss her, and she leaned into him, and they sank back onto the towel. I got up onto my knees and hovered over them. Luke had his left arm pinned under Sarah's back, while his right hand gripped her left shoulder. The breeze lifted an edge of her skirt, and she broke the kiss. "I'm so happy you came out here. You're not bored of me yet, are you?"

"Yes," I said.

Luke shook his head. "Of course not. Why would I be?"

She smiled at him. "Just asking. I worry about how you feel sometimes. Only because I can't always figure it out."

What did she want, to "lower his defenses"? To "connect with his true self," or some other pop-psychology excreta, like something straight out of the mouth of Dr. Claymore? All these girls who wanted to rescue him. Cassie would never say such an asinine thing.

He leaned in to kiss her again, and this time he let go of her arm and slid his hand under the tank top, letting his fingers play over her breasts and ribs. She arched into his touch, and my curiosity was enormous. "Make her touch you," I said. Luke shifted his hips so his crotch pressed against her thigh. She stiffened and then relaxed again. "She wants this," I said. "Why else would she bring you out here?" Luke slid his hand down to her thighs and tried to work his fingers up into the space between her legs. She pulled back again. "Luke, stop."

Luke flushed. "I'm sorry."

"No!" I shook my finger at him. "Never apologize."

Her glasses were smudged and crooked on her face, and she took them off and lay them beside her head. "Just go slowly, okay?" She blinked her unfocused eyes. "We have plenty of time."

"Only seventeen minutes, actually," I said.

Luke twisted his arm to reach into his pocket. "I brought one of these." He held up a condom in its wrinkled turquoise wrapper.

"Luke!" She laughed out of surprise, not because she thought it was funny. "I'm not going to do that!" She stopped laughing and looked annoyed. "Did you really think this soon—and out here?"

Luke's attempt was clumsy, but it turned out to be an effective gambit anyway: she offers nothing, he offers sex, and they meet somewhere in the middle. Too bad he was telling the truth when he said to her, "I thought it would make you happy": it wasn't a conscious strategy at all. She touched his face. "You're so odd," she said, but she made it sound like a compliment. "I think it might make me happy, but just not yet."

"Jesus Christ!" I said, my exasperation getting the best of me. "Are you completely useless?" I was talking to Luke, but could just as well have meant Sarah. He shifted his hips again until his erection brushed against her hand. "Maybe it's not too soon for everything." Her fingers danced around the fly of his khakis. "Maybe not," she said.

She unzipped his pants and curled her fingers around his

penis. I leaned in to get a closer look. She started moving her hand, and I could tell from Luke's expression that it did not feel very good. "This is it?" I said. "But you can do this at home." He reached out and grabbed her wrist. "I was thinking of something else, maybe." He gave her his attempt at a meaningful look.

She said, "I don't do that."

"Why not?" I said.

"Why not?" Luke said.

"Because I don't want to."

"Do it anyway!" I snapped. She blinked as though she had heard me.

Luke put his hands on her shoulders and eased her down. I had never seen him be so bold. She resisted at first, but he kept up the pressure, and she gave in. She put his penis inside her mouth and lay there. I heard a family calling to its dog on the other side of the dunes, the white-noise roar of the ocean somewhere beyond them. "Isn't she supposed to do something?" I said. I was speaking on the basis of locker-room hearsay and stolen glances of pornographic magazines in the senior lounge at school. Luke put his hand on top of her head and forced it in closer. She began moving her mouth up and down. Her eyes were closed and her brow pinched, as though she were solving a math problem. Luke made a noise, and suddenly I was insanely jealous. I wanted to feel everything, and I felt nothing. I deserved this, not him.

"She's a worthless slut," I said. I had lost control. "I bet she would do this to anybody who asked." Luke opened his eyes and looked up at me with a confused expression. "You heard me," I said. "She's just a dumb, overachieving slut."

He opened his mouth to speak, but then his whole body spasmed and he arched his pelvis off the towel. Sarah pulled away from him and spit onto the sand. A strand hung across her chin and she wiped it away with the back of her hand. Her face was tight, furious.

"I didn't want to do that," she said, "and you made me."

Luke quickly tucked his penis back into his pants. "I'm sorry. I'm sorry. I didn't mean it."

"I don't even know what that means," she said. She looked at her watch. "Shit. We have to get back." She stood and tugged at the towel. "Get up."

Luke scrambled to his feet, reached out for her, then thought better of it. She turned and marched back toward the main path, and Luke began to follow. The sun had set and the sky was deep purple laced with low streaks of orange. I couldn't see well in the weak light, but I noticed Sarah's glasses half-buried in the sand. Luke hadn't seen them, and I decided not to say anything.

We were halfway across the golf course when the sprinklers sputtered to life. By the time we got back to the house, Luke and Sarah were soaked to the bone, but my suit remained spotless.

<hr />

Ten days later, on the third morning of the new school year, the principal plucked Luke out of calculus. I saw the little man standing outside the door checking his watch as Luke gathered up his books. Two students in the back rows whispered and pointed until Omar glared at them and drew a finger across his throat. "I got you covered," he told Luke. "Just remember, you can say no sometimes."

"Your mother," the principal said. "Perhaps she should consider offering you a salary." We took a taxi down Columbus and then Ninth Avenue before the driver cut east across Twenty-second Street and pulled up in front of a grimy old office building. Nightingale Press was on the fourth floor, which they shared with a personal-injury law firm and a meditation center. Luke pushed open the double glass doors and waved to Claire, who spotted him from across the large room. "Sweetie! Finally! We've been waiting for hours. Your talents are urgently required."

Claire strode across the raw wood floor, which was scattered with discarded printouts, towers of galleys, and a few threadbare throw rugs. The chaos of the press offices reflected the chaos of Claire's home study, just on a larger scale and with twelve employees to contribute to the mess. The office was open-plan, and all the editors, designers, publicists, and salespeople sat on top of each other, everybody talking at once, phones ringing insistently, ancient fax machines spewing out contracts and correspondence on crinkly, scroll-like paper. What Claire prized above all else in her company was an antiquated, probably apocryphal sort of literary authenticity. This was the meaning of the gigantic, scarred wooden meeting table in the center of the room, the green banker's lamp on every desk, the unbelievable quantity of books,

books, everywhere, stacked on every surface and crammed into every free space. She had tried in her fifteen years as publisher and editor-in-chief to modernize the imprint's list, but the aesthetics of the office itself—both the way it looked and the way in which she and her staff conducted business—were a deliberate holdover from Venetia's days. It was an idealized vision of how publishing books should be, and it was also nonsense, a quaint myth, just another thing she had inherited from her mother.

Claire stood on her toes to kiss her son's forehead. "I have lunch with an author at one, and I need your opinion on his manuscript before I go."

Luke shifted his backpack from one shoulder to the other. "You want me to read a manuscript in an hour and fifteen minutes?"

"No, no, no, of course not, sweetie." Claire clasped Luke's face between her hands. "Just the first chapter. You can tell everything about these sorts of books from the first chapter."

Luke followed his mother to the meeting table, and we all walked by a giant bookshelf that seemed to contain one copy of every Nightingale Press publication. I scanned the spines to see if *Shadow Life* was among them. I didn't spot it at first, and I didn't want to draw Luke's attention by looking any more closely. A muscular young man with a shaved head sat at the table, his black T-shirt tucked into black jeans, which were in turn tucked into black combat boots. He drew a cigarette from a pack of Marlboro Reds and pinched at the pink skin between his eyebrows as if removing a splinter. This was Gregory Herzen, Nightingale Press's senior editor. He liked to announce that the only reason he worked here was because Claire let him do things like wear T-shirts and smoke cigarettes in the office, yet two minutes after I first met him, I knew he was almost as deeply under Claire's spell as Luke himself. They all were, everybody who worked at the press, or else they wouldn't have been there in that battered office, breathing that stale air, producing those stale books.

"Luke." Gregory nodded at us and spoke around his lit cigarette. "I was told you'll be my stand-in this afternoon. Thank God. I might have made that poor bastard choke on his gazpacho."

"Sit, read." Claire pushed Luke into a chair and handed him a thick manuscript.

Luke brushed her hands away. "I'm going to lunch? With an author?" He seemed unsure whether to be flattered or annoyed.

"Yes, of course. Why not?" Claire patted the manuscript and looked at her watch. "No time for questions." She walked away, pausing to let her fingers graze the stubble on the top of Herzen's head and trail down the back of his neck. He didn't acknowledge her; he just smoked his cigarette.

Lunch was at a French place on Eighth Avenue. We sat in the "garden," the blank backs of buildings walling us in on four sides, a spare square of sky floating far above our heads. The simple fact that we were eating outside seemed to warrant five minutes of chatter about the lovely clay flowerpots and mild September weather. The small talk didn't seem to set the author any more at ease, though, and he laughed too loudly when Claire joked about firing Herzen and replacing him with Luke. I studied the man across the white tablecloth. He was pale and gawky,

146

with rimless glasses and razor nicks on his neck. His Adam's apple, a massive lump of cartilage, bobbed up and down with every swallow of water. The brawny, trigger-happy hero of his thrillers was such an obvious projection of the kind of man he wished he could be. Could it all be any more pathetic?

The first courses came, three different types of salads, Luke's topped with a poached egg and globules of pork fat. I watched the three of them eat like pigs at the trough, ruled by these nauseating impulses, this repulsive cycle of consumption and excretion. My own position was the more evolved. Just watching Luke bite into a cherry tomato—the way the juice splurted all over his chin and onto the collar of his white shirt—was proof enough.

Claire laid her knife along the edge of her plate. "You've taken Pollard in a rather interesting direction in this volume. I hadn't expected him to turn quite so . . . brutish."

The author nodded vigorously, his Adam's apple bobbing along with his head. "That's right. I wanted to show the way anger and revenge can blind anyone, even someone like him. When and why is he willing to compromise his morals? Is it right, or does that even matter?"

I said, "A terribly written potboiler is not the best vehicle for these questions."

"But the opening torture scene . . ." Claire paused. "He's as vicious as the people he's supposed to be fighting." She turned to her son. "Luke, you had some ideas about the opening. Won't you share them with us?"

This man was a bad writer, but he had sold nearly forty thousand copies of the previous Pollard thriller, and now he had to listen to a nineteen-year-old's ill-informed critique of his work. Luke faked a cough and looked embarrassed. "You should be embarrassed," I said. "You won't get any help from me on this one." I needed him to see that it was Claire who put him in such an uncomfortable situation, that this was her fault.

"Um," Luke said. "I think we should get Natalie's kidnapping first. Before the torture scene."

"Natalie's kidnapping first." The author flicked his eyes back and forth between Luke and Claire, who was smiling blissfully at her son. "Okay. Why?"

"Um." Luke took a swallow of water. "So that when we see Pollard with the pliers and the electrodes we know why he's doing all of this awful stuff. Instead of finding out after." Nobody said anything, and Luke flushed again. "I mean, so that we know he's doing it because he thinks he can save her life."

"Just listen to yourself," I said.

The author squirmed in his seat. "Don't you think, Claire, that the power of the first scene lies exactly in this not-knowing? Readers will wonder if Pollard has flipped out, gone insane. They will wonder what, exactly, is going on here."

Claire cracked her knuckles. "I'm too intimate with your work to be useful here. What Luke thinks is more important."

The author blinked rapidly behind his little glasses as he tried to adjust to this new information. "Well, then, Luke, what about in the third chapter, when Natalie gets killed? When the readers learn that Pollard was on the right track from the start, and that his mistake was not being too ruthless but being not ruthless *enough*? Doesn't it make you go back and remember how *appalled* you were by that first scene, by the torture? And then you realize he didn't go far enough." He was getting angry. Tiny beads of sweat clustered around his eyebrows and the outsize Adam's apple vibrated. "Wouldn't that tension be lost if you switched the order of the scenes? If the torture was obviously *justified*"—he spit out the word—"from the start?"

"Um." Luke glanced at his mother. "I didn't actually get that far. I actually—well, I actually only read the first chapter."

The author fell back into his chair. "The first chapter? The first chapter? Claire, this is absurd."

"Do you see how your mother humiliates you?" I said. "It's not right."

"Luke is a natural." Claire flashed the author a beatific smile, bright white teeth pushed forward. "He sees what everybody else misses. The first chapter was all that was necessary."

"But, Claire, he's only . . ."

She laid a hand on Luke's shoulder. "I trust his judgment better than I trust my own."

Luke twisted away from his mother's touch, but underneath his discomfort hid a greasy sort of pride it made me ill to see.

Later that evening, Luke read in bed and I assumed my familiar position at the east-facing window. I could now identify the old

Fifth Avenue apartment on the other side of the park. I could even tell which window belonged to Cassie's bedroom, although now that window was dark, and had been ever since she had left for college a month before. She was at school in Rhode Island, and suddenly absent from our lives. She had called once to check up on Luke, to ask how Claire was doing, displaying a kind of detached sisterly concern. This was enough for Luke, but my relationship with her was going to be different. We would be equals; we would behave as two adults. Looking across the park, I felt a strange sensation unfold at the base of my throat. I realized I missed her. The feeling was new, and I rolled it around inside my mouth, sampling it, trying to determine if it were good or bad. I thought it was a bit of both, and I decided we would go visit her.

By the time we got up for school the next morning, Claire was already gone. She left a note saying she had headed in to work early and would be home late, but when we came back from school that afternoon, we heard muffled thumps behind the door of her study. "What is your mother doing now?" I said.

Luke let the front door slam and marched into the foyer, opening the door to the study with a sullen tug. The room was in total disarray. Claire had attacked the floor-to-ceiling book-shelves and scattered their contents across the floor. Books lay in drifts like shoveled snow. She stood at the center of the mess, hands on her hips, panting from the effort. She wore a black cocktail dress and a diamond-encrusted silver rope. The clothes and jewelry were her mother's, taken from a large closet she used to store Venetia's things. She jerked her eyes toward us, and they were vacuums, dead stars.

"Why can't I find anything in this apartment?" she snapped. "Nothing is ever where I left it last. So everybody wants to play a trick on me? Move Claire's stuff around and see her go crazy? Well, congratulations, very funny."

"Don't yell at me," Luke said.

"I'm not yelling," she hissed. "I'm just a little frustrated. Maybe you can explain things to me."

"I don't know what you're looking for."

Claire tugged at her necklace and noosed it tightly around her neck. "You did this, didn't you?" Suddenly her voice grew sly. "I bet you think it's a big joke, to take a Nabokov and put it in the middle of my Hemingways, to mix the Fitzgeralds with the Faulkners. Very clever. And the Noh masks in the hallway: you switched the Fierce God and the Old Man, didn't you?"

"What would be the point?"

"The point?" Claire kicked over a pile of Raymond Chandler first editions. "*This* is the point. Me, right now. I'm the fucking point."

Luke forced Claire's hands down from her neck and held them in his own. "Why don't you tell me what you're looking for?" As always, he grew calm in the face of her fury, as though together they were a closed system, with only a finite amount of anger to share between them.

Claire threw Luke's hands back at him. "Don't talk to me like I'm a child."

"Then stop acting like a child," I said.

"I'm trying to help," Luke said. "If you don't want my help, I'll just leave."

Claire rubbed at the purple scars twisting across her wrists and hands. "I'm looking for a book."

Luke glanced at the empty shelves. "I guessed that."

"It's one of ours, one of the press's."

"So what's wrong? Don't you have copies of all of those at the office anyway?"

"You don't understand," she said. "This one is different. It's unique."

"I know what she's looking for," I said. "You're in trouble."

"Why?" Luke asked.

"Because it's not the book," Claire said, "it's what your grandmother and I wrote in it."

"What did you write?"

But Luke could not lie to his mother, and Claire sensed he was concealing something. She narrowed her eyes. "Where is it?"

"Shredded, defaced, lost!" I cried joyously. I couldn't help myself. "Dead and buried!"

"I don't even know what you're talking about."

"Luke, it's extremely important that you give me that book right now."

Luke folded his arms across his chest. "Why, so you can kill yourself like your mother did?"

"What?" Claire stepped back and stumbled over a stack of Virginia Woolfs. "Why would you say that?"

"Because that's what Grandma did. She drowned herself when I was two years old. Why? How?"

"Then you read the book." Claire's voice was lifeless.

"How did she do it?"

"If you read it, you should be able to guess."

"She jumped in the Hudson River," I said. "Like those women in the novel."

"Why did you lie to me about her? Brain cancer? That whole elaborate story?"

"A child doesn't need to know everything about his family," Claire said. But she was lying again; Claire had never protected Luke from knowing too much too young. She looked at him for a moment, and then said, "She's everywhere inside of me. She's inside of you, too. I'm afraid for myself, but I'm more afraid for you."

"Just please don't lie to me again."

"I could say the same to you." Claire bent down, picked up a book, and replaced it on the shelf. "I need the book to show me where my mother went wrong. I need to see her notes. I need to read her mistakes again so I don't make them. Now can you please give it to me?"

But we couldn't, because of course it was gone. It had been April when we buried the novel. By now, the dirt had absorbed Claire and Venetia's words, and then given them over to the plants and air. There was nowhere to look for them except inside the stems of flowers, and above, in the empty sky.

4

A

FTER LUKE ADMITTED he had lost the book, Claire retreated into a quiet mood for the rest of the evening. All the fury drained out of her. She didn't yell or throw things; instead, she replaced the books on her shelves, smoothing their bent pages and straightening their dust jackets. Luke watched nervously from the doorway. A few times he seemed about to speak, only to shake his head and keep silent. Later, as Claire chopped vegetables for a salad, her knife thudding against the cutting board like a metronome at the far end of the hall, Luke blamed me for getting rid of the novel, as though any of this were my fault.

"Stop making excuses for her," I said. "That's not your job anymore."

When we sat down for dinner, Claire apologized to her son. "I wasn't fair," she said. "You couldn't have known how important it was." I noticed she still wore her mother's dress and necklace.

Luke probably shouldn't have left Claire alone two days later, but he did it anyway. At my suggestion he pitched our weekend visit to Rhode Island as college research; Claire conceded its necessity, and Cassie was happy to play host. She met us at the train station in downtown Providence on Saturday morning. It was raining when we arrived, and she wore a yellow slicker without the hood, letting her hair get wet and stringy. She had grown it out since we had last seen her at a coffee shop on Madison Avenue in August, and it spilled down her back, twisting and knotting in on itself. Her tan corduroys hugged her hips but the cuffs flared out like bell-bottoms and dragged in the puddles, collecting grime. Her face, though—her face was fresh and clean and apple-cheeked. A wholesome New England face.

She hugged Luke. "My almost-brother," she said. "Welcome to Providence."

Her station wagon appeared clean on the outside, but inside, soda cans, magazines, and clothing—thrift-store chic, all flimsy fabrics and dated designs—coated the floor. Twine-wrapped bundles of newspapers were stacked across the backseat. "Our alternative weekly. Unfortunately, delivery girl is the fastest way to join the team." She swept sketch pads off the passenger seat, then left the car in neutral while she rolled a cigarette. "Still smoking, yes. But at least since I got up here I take the thrifty approach. James the businessman would approve." I stretched across the newspapers like a dog and stared at the back of her head, wondering if she actually cared what James thought about her. I doubted it; from what I could tell, he seemed to have given up on his stepdaughter as well, focusing all of his molding efforts on James Jr. Cassie lit the cigarette and turned to Luke, her profile outlined in gray-blue smoke. "You look good," she said. "Healthy." Luke looked out the window, smiling slightly. "No reason you shouldn't," she continued quickly. She put the car into gear, and we lurched forward.

"Don't worry." Luke patted her knee. "I never refuse a compliment." He seemed comfortable here with Cassie in a way he never was with Sarah, or even Claire. I thought it might be because neither Luke nor Cassie held any serious expectations for their relationship. Within the context of their occasional meetings, Luke was free to reinvent himself as witty and confident, a competent teenager. But his attitude was a mistake; Cassie was too important to me to be treated with such insincerity.

The antiseptic downtown gave way to old, crooked streets and patrician redbrick buildings. We drove up a comically steep hill, and then we were there, parked outside a house—Cassie had never even considered living in a dormitory—painted an optimistic robin's-egg blue. Cassie had eight housemates whose names

Luke didn't bother to remember because he knew I would do it for him. She had placed her mattress on top of an Oriental carpet in the exact center of her bedroom for "compositional" reasons. Luke was to sleep on a futon in the crusty living room. "There can be some late-night traffic," Cassie said, "but we'll get you drunk enough you won't notice." Luke told her that alcohol didn't really agree with him, but this was a lie. He'd never had a drink in his life; Dr. Claymore had warned that it would interact "drastically" with his medication, and it was one of the few pieces of the shrink's advice he ever followed. Yet Luke was barely using the blue pills any more, so I suggested perhaps now he could give drinking a try. He frowned at me, but I wasn't concerned; the idea had been planted in his head.

We spent the afternoon wandering around the campus, its endless procession of quadrangles and redbrick. I don't know what we were supposed to learn from this tour. Young people hurried around in the rain under hoods and umbrellas. Many rode bicycles. Some gathered in front of a campus laboratory and held up signs that read "We are all animals." Soggy leaves clumped together in dispirited piles. Cassie took us to the music library, a place of fluorescent lights and dozens of little booths equipped with headphones and computers. Luke logged onto the database and found things that appeared to interest him, probably some baffling Minimalist compositions. Then she took us to the actual library, which was dimmer and smelled of formaldehyde; we surveyed the lobby and left. In her painting studio, she showed us canvases of bug-eyed girls ensnared in evil-looking

157

vines and weeds. She painted in a slick, hyperrealist style that made her work look like stills from horror movies yet to be made; it was what she had come to this school to do. In an unfinished piece, a dead unicorn was strapped on top of a Jeep, hunted for its horn. "It's about sex," she said. The rain stopped, and we walked along Thayer Street, past head shops, pizza parlors, and vintage clothing stores, Cassie smoking cigarettes as fast as she could roll them. Back on campus, guys in kneesocks and headbands emerged to whip Frisbees around the lawn.

The party that night was at an upperclassman's house on the other side of campus. We sat on Cassie's bed and did shots of clear tequila before we went. Luke looked at me and gave a small shrug before he threw his first shot back. Sometimes one of her housemates would come in and do a shot with us. A kid with a red beard fiddled with Cassie's stereo, putting on funk at an aggressive volume, then asked Luke if he had any pot. "He's my almost-brother," Cassie yelled over the music. The bass popped like a tendon. "What?" "He's my step-brother. He's just visiting." The guy gave us a thumbs-up and left the room. I watched Luke struggle with the tequila. He fought the taste, but he was swallowing.

Cassie wore one of her high school dress shirts with the sleeves cut off at the elbows and the top two buttons open. She leaned back and laughed at something, and her breasts rattled around underneath the shirt. She had changed into tight jeans that rode low on her hips, and when she leaned forward again, I could see the top of her underwear and the curve of her ass. I wondered if Luke noticed. He probably didn't care even if he did; he couldn't recognize a worthwhile girl when he saw one. They clinked shot glasses and sucked the tequila down.

"That's number three," Cassie said. "Keep track. I'm your chaperone tonight, and I don't want your mother pissed at me because the campus cops found you facedown in a gutter."

"Christ," I said, "does Claire have to follow us everywhere?"

Suddenly, Cassie's blue eyes burst wide open. "I love this song." The stereo played something warm and electronic, full of sleepy clicks and clacks. A female voice floated on top, singing in a foreign language. "It's Icelandic," Cassie said. She leaned back on the pillows and closed her eyes. "It's beautiful, isn't it?" She lay between Luke and me, her arm less than an inch from mine, close enough that I could see each fine white hair. I lifted my own arm and reached over her head, over the auburn hair pinned up in its high knot. I let my hand rest on her far shoulder. My fingers wavered above the curve of her collarbone. She shifted slightly, her eyes still closed. I traced the line of her jaw with my index finger and stroked the soft flap of her earlobe. I slid my touch down along her neck toward the hollow at the base of her throat and the V of her open shirt. Luke looked at me with something close to horror, but he did nothing. Suddenly, Cassie opened her eyes and saw Luke's expression.

"What's wrong?"

Luke started. "What?"

She touched her nose, patted her cheek. "Is there something on my face?"

"No, no, you're fine. I was just spacing out."

She looked at him for a long moment, then smiled. "That's allowed." She stood up and went into the bathroom, turning down the volume on the stereo as she went. Luke glared at me. "Cut it out," he whispered fiercely. "Leave her alone." His breath smelled like gasoline and baking pavement. I shrugged. "No harm done, right?"

The party was loud, and the wet warmth of human bodies filled the house, which listed to one side like a sinking ship. Cassie threw her jacket on top of a pile in the corner and hugged a busty girl who wore a black halter top and silver glitter around her eyes. "This is Luke," Cassie said. "My little step-brother." Something knowing passed through the girl's eyes and then disappeared. She pinched Luke's cheek. "Make yourself at home, cutie pie." A drunk, panting kid grabbed Luke's hand. "This is the next four years of your life." He gestured toward the living room, cleared of furniture and packed with people dancing, drinking, shouting to be heard. A lean boy in his underwear and aviator sunglasses struck poses on the stairway landing. There were stains in the armpits of the pale kid's tan sport coat, and as he leaned in close to Luke, his shirt billowed out and I saw his sweat-slicked scrawny chest covered with tattoos. Cassie pried Luke away and led us to the back of the room. His unfocused eyes searched somewhere to the left of my head. I signaled at him. "I'm over here." "Sure, sure," he said vaguely, trailing Cassie into the crowd. She made him a Tequila Sunrise from the sticky bar in the kitchen and pointed out people worth knowing. I felt claustrophobic and loosened the knot of my tie. In the living room, somebody rolled a giant disco ball across the floor, shouting, "Glammer than thou!" Cassie disappeared somewhere, and Luke stood by himself, leaning against the wall and frowning into the bottom of his cup. I asked how he was feeling.

"How am I feeling?" He looked up at me and smirked. "I'm feeling like I wish you would leave me alone every once in a while. Why don't you go follow Cassie around. See how far that gets you." He raised the cup to his lips with a smug look on his face.

"You little brat," I said. Where had this attitude come from? Without thinking, I reached out and flicked the bottom of his cup. Orange juice and grenadine splattered across his face and sweater, and the cup fell to the floor. Luke slowly wiped his mouth. I don't know which of us was more surprised, but when he looked at me again, I composed my own face carefully, as though I had expected this result.

"There you are!" Cassie burst out of the crowd laughing. "What happened to your sweater?"

Luke looked down at the garish splotches. "I seem to have had an accident."

"That's it." She wagged her finger at him. "No more drinks for you."

He flushed, and then swayed a bit, reaching out to steady himself on the wall. "I'm fine. Can you get me one more?"

Cassie stepped away and quickly returned with a Screwdriver. "Last one."

When Cassie went outside five minutes later to smoke a cigarette, Luke poured himself a cup of gin out of a plastic bottle and
downed it in one gulp. I was not going to stop him. Drinking was
making him weak and sloppy, but I felt fine. When all the alcohol
finally hit him with one sick punch, I followed him to the upstairs
bathroom, guiding him through clutches of chattering girls and
sweaty boys. "You need some water," I whispered into his ear. "You
need to get away for a minute." His skin was feverish beneath my
hand on his back and he fumbled with the bathroom lock. Patterns of tiny black and white tiles ran across the floor and walls,
and a framed poster of Gandhi hung above the toilet, the man sitting cross-legged and emaciated with a white towel draped over
his head. Luke leaned into the toilet and vomited a reddish-
orange liquid that looked like fruit punch and smelled like disease.
He sank to his knees, flushed the toilet, and then did it again. "It's
okay," I said. "Let it all out." Luke flushed a second time, and I
pushed his head down into the bowl. I couldn't help it; he deserved it for his comment about Cassie, and I didn't know when I
would again find him so defenseless. I jerked him up by the hair
and looked at his sputtering face. Snot bubbled out of one nostril
and his dark hair was plastered over his eyes. He coughed and another small stream of vomit trickled out of the corner of his
mouth. "Stop it," he said. The words were wet and useless.

"We need to get you cleaned up," I said, "and the toilet's not
going to do the trick." I dragged him to his feet. He felt dense
and limp, like a sandbag. The shower was small and mildewy,
with colorful bottles of hygienic products lining the rim of the

tub. Luke kicked them aside as I shoved him in. I turned the water to scalding hot, and steam began to fill the small room. Luke wiped his hair away from his eyes, lurching under the water. Somebody pounded on the door; I ignored it and wiped the mucus from Luke's face. "There," I said. "This is disgusting, all these fluids. You should be ashamed of yourself." His sweater and jeans sagged and bulged under the weight of the water. His sneakers squelched obscenely as he shuffled back and forth.

"I feel heavy," he said. "I want to sit down."

"No. You're still dirty."

He pulled at his sweater. "These clothes," he said, "they weigh too much."

"Then take them off. They're probably filthy too."

He tugged his sweater and shirt over his head. They stuck there, a dumb lump, glued to his face and head like a leech. He staggered into the wall and almost fell over. I caught him and pulled the clothes free. He sat on the edge of the tub to take off his sneakers, and then I helped him yank off his jeans and boxers. I felt vicious, sharp, alive. He stood under the shower, naked, his pale skin flushed angry pink. His penis curled up into his crotch and his thin arms hung slack at his sides. The water beat into the back of his skull. He shivered and worked his mouth silently, as though he had forgotten how to speak. This is what people are so easily reduced to, these ludicrous, inefficient bodies. You turn water on them to blast away the grime and taint and filth of living in the world, but what's left underneath is worse, just a naked, confused animal.

The pounding came at the door again. This time I heard Cassie's voice: "Luke, are you in there?"

"Go away," he called out. "I'm fine."

"Luke, please let me in." The doorknob rattled. "I just want to make sure you're all right."

"No more hiding," I said. "I want Cassie to see you now. I want her to know who you are." I pushed Luke to the door, and forced him to unlock it and turn the knob.

Cassie stood in the hallway gaping at us, a small group of her friends—the glitter girl, the tan sport coat, the red beard—clustered behind her. The bathroom was a foggy mess, and Luke slouched naked in the middle of it with his head down, water pooling around his feet. I swept my arm toward him like a carnival barker, and invited them all to enjoy the show.

An hour later, Cassie tucked Luke into her bed. She fed him water, toast, chamomile tea. Each time he passed out, she shook him awake to force more water down his throat. She finally let him drift off only when she was satisfied he wasn't going to die in his sleep. While she smoked cigarettes and played nurse, I raged around her room. My intrusion on the physical world had been unbearably brief. I had flitted mothlike around the margins of the crisis as Cassie bundled Luke up in borrowed clothes and hustled him into the backseat of a friend's car. She helped him into her bed, stroked his forehead, told him he was going to be okay. This was apparently the way the world worked: weakness and failure rewarded, and strength ignored.

When we went downstairs in the morning, her housemates joked around, called Luke a lightweight. "I think you missed a spot," one said, "there's a shower in the back if you need it." We ate breakfast at a diner where Luke stuffed his face with a runny omelet and hash browns. He couldn't look me in the eye; he knew something terrible had happened the night before, but he couldn't remember how much was my doing and how much his. He didn't know how wary of me he needed to be; meanwhile, I remembered everything, and I didn't know either.

Cassie drove us straight to the train station from the diner. One night of playing babysitter had been enough for her. I wanted to tell her I would never embarrass her as Luke had. I knew how to behave myself; I had discipline. We pulled out of the station, and I stared at her through the window. She stood on the platform looking somewhere above the train. Her expression was indecipherable, her features refusing to relate to each other in a meaningful way. It didn't matter. She was beautiful anyway. Someday I would make myself known to her. Someday she would know me, and what would happen after that I couldn't say. On the half-empty train, Luke pressed his forehead against the window and closed his eyes. I wondered how soon I could get him drunk again, and whether he would become so pleasingly weak each time. I wanted him to recognize that without my help, without drawing me closer to him, he would only continue to humiliate himself.

I thought we were going home, but at the first stop, only twenty minutes into the trip, Luke jumped up and bolted out through the open doors. I ran after him, shouting, "What's the deal?" He didn't answer, he just kept walking, down into the tunnel that ran underneath the tracks and back up to the other side, then through the crummy stationhouse and out to the parking lot, where a grimy bus sat shuddering. We climbed aboard, and I saw we shared our ride with only three other passengers, each traveling alone. I asked Luke where we were going, but still he gave no answer.

The road curved tightly under a bleached sky before we came to a bridge that arched over a wide inlet. Black rocks and small islands interrupted the water. A candy-cane lighthouse squatted on one; what was left of a wood house and its rotting private dock on another. The bus descended to briefly touch dry land again, and then swooped higher over a second arching bridge, tankers and sailboats passing beneath us. This time I recognized the steep bluffs and scattered wharves on the far side from the photography books Claire kept in a stack beneath her desk. "Newport," I said, and Luke did not have to answer.

We got off the bus outside the grim visitors' center, in the middle of a vast parking lot. We stood there for a minute, inhaling the fumes, before I realized Luke had no idea where he was going. I was tempted to let him wander around until he got discouraged, but I was just as curious as he was. Something had always been wrong with the way Claire talked about the family's old house. It was the same way she talked about her mother: mutably, as though these subjects were holographic, their contours liable to change in the shifting angles of memory and retelling. She had lived in the house as a child and the family, which at this point meant her, no longer owned the property; nothing remained consistent beyond these two details.

We looked at a map of the town pinned behind salt-spotted Plexiglas. "The house is on the southeast side," I said. "Down by the ocean."

"How do you know?" Luke said.

"The address is on the dollhouse."

I saw it clearly in my head, the metal numbers and street name nailed to a post on the front porch. We walked south from the bus station past rows of clapboard houses, baby blue, pink, tan, brick red; past the cramped Jewish cemetery, its Egyptian gates and gap-toothed rows of obelisks; down Bellevue Avenue to the wider boulevards, the high walls and hedges, and the mansions they protected. Out at the end of Narragansett, the paved street stopped, and still we had not found the right address. The avenue gave way to dirt, and suddenly we were at the edge of the ocean, at the top of a cliff onto which had been grafted forty stone steps. The steps curved left, turning in on the face of the cliff and depositing us onto a shelf of pockmarked rocks ten feet above the level of the water. I imagined stepping off the ledge, feeling the ocean pull me under and away from land, the salt water penetrating my throat and lungs, occupying me as the Hudson had Venetia. Across the wide bay, small houses stacked up along a curving spit of land, a four-cornered church tower capping the highest hill. The Atlantic had hollowed out a cave shaped like the top half of an hourglass into the cliff near us; the water rushed greedily into the opening and then retreated reluctantly like fluid drained from a wound. At the curve of the bluff, thick mats of yellow-brown kelp tugged at the stunned rocks, while up above, the Breakers mansion hulked ridiculously, improbably, as though it had been flung from the sky. "This is where it ends," Luke said. "Now what?"

But when we climbed the steps and started back up the street, the breeze lifted the sagging branch of a copper beech to expose four steel numbers hammered into a wood fence. This was the address we had been looking for, but the fence and the shaded glimpse of house beyond were unfamiliar. It was one of the cottages tucked between the mansions like weeds among overgrown flowers; I couldn't see anything more through the thick-leaved beeches. I stepped toward an opening in the fence, but Luke wouldn't move. "We shouldn't go any closer," he said. "It's not our place anymore." I moved near enough to the house to see it was painted a deep red, with a reptilian tiled roof and hexagonal chimney. It did not bear the slightest resemblance to the dollhouse. The new owners must have torn the old house down and rebuilt on the plot. Any evidence of the original had been entirely erased, as though it had never been there at all. "Daniel," Luke said. I could not guess if anybody was watching us from behind the mute windows. "Daniel." I paused, wavering at the edge of the lawn before I rejoined him on Narragansett, where we began to trace our steps back to town.

We made it to the railroad station by late afternoon to board our second train of the day, and this time we took it all the way to Penn Station. The rancid smell of pretzels and burnt coffee floated through the air, and the light Sunday-night crowds milled about like stunned animals. People looked sallow, their faces drippy like melted wax. A soldier in full fatigues leaned against the side of a magazine kiosk and dug a quarter into his lotto ticket. At the taxi stand outside, two women fought over a cab until one slammed her rolling bag down on the other's foot. "There," she said, "you got what you asked for."

Uptown, Victor let us into the lobby and said he hadn't seen Claire since Friday, and was she out of town? We didn't know. The elevator crawled upstairs. Luke unlocked the front door and we walked into the dim foyer. All the lights were off and the shades were drawn. "Mom?" he called out. The foyer and kitchen were silent and tidy, revealing nothing. In Claire's study everything was in order, except the shelf that normally held the Nightingale Press books was empty. The Noh masks lay in a pile on the floor in the long hallway, their bulging white eyes and curling green lips glistening in the poor light. The walls of the hallway seemed to be covered with some kind of paper. Luke turned on the lights. The paper was pages torn from books and glued to the walls; there was not an inch of uncovered space. I looked closer at one of the pages. In the top right corner was printed *The Trial of Alison Warner*. A Nightingale Press book. The pages surrounding it on all four sides were from four different books, all published by the press. The loose corners of pages affixed to the ceiling fluttered above our heads.

"Turn that light off."

Claire's voice slid out from underneath the door at the end of the hallway, curling up on the floor at our feet and lying there, wounded. "Mom," Luke said. He opened the door to her room. She lay in her bed, tiny among great drifts of comforters and pillows. She turned her head toward us, and her face was luminous, ghostly, her huge green eyes burning some fuel stored deep inside her skull.

"So you're home," she said. Her face looked not quite her own.

"I was only gone for one night."

I peered deeper into the room. Shimmering ball gowns and cocktail dresses lay strewn on the floor, across the love seat, on the foot of the bed. Some still had the tags on them. Shopping bags from expensive Madison Avenue stores disgorged more piles of precious cloth. She said, "I was trying on new outfits for the ball."

"What ball?"

She was wearing the black cocktail dress I recognized as her mother's. The door was open to the walk-in closet devoted to Venetia's grand old clothes: velvet sheaths, silk suits, mink coats.

"Never mind that," she said. "Have you looked in on the baby?"

"I don't know what you're talking about."

"Baby Claire, of course. The poor thing was crying earlier."

She blinked at us and hooked her hair behind her ears in a coquettish gesture I had never seen before. Some subtle shift seemed to have taken place in the arrangement of her bones, in her posture and bearing.

"Mom—" Luke began.

"Please," she interrupted, "look in on Claire for me." She gestured at the piles of clothes. "There is so much to do, I don't have the time." We turned away from her. "And switch that light off as you go."

Luke went back into the hallway to do as he was told. The pages on the walls ruffled and sighed as he walked past. He looked at me, his hand on the switch. "This is not something anybody needs to know about." A page worked itself loose from the ceiling and drifted to the floor in a lazy, liquid motion, then Luke turned off the lights and I couldn't see anything more.

⚯

We looked in on Claire the next morning. She was asleep, lying on her back with her arms folded across her chest, still wearing the black dress. Luke stood at the side of the bed for a moment, then left the room without disturbing her. We kept up appearances at school; Luke fixed his face into an alert expression while I took notes, and even Omar was fooled. But I knew Luke had left his mind back at the apartment, and as soon as the final bell rang, he ran down the back stairs and out the side entrance on Columbus, sprinting the short distance home. He stopped just outside the lobby and waited for his breathing to slow, straightening his collar and brushing back his hair, erasing any traces of hurry. Upstairs, he knocked on the closed door to Claire's bedroom. There was no answer, and he slowly pushed the door open.

Claire was propped up in bed, awake now, a silver box open in her lap. Inside the box were antique brooches, pendants, bracelets, watches. More were spread around her on the bed, and she wore a string of black pearls over her nightgown. She looked up at us, and I saw she was entirely in possession of her own face again, the bones and muscles fallen back into their familiar positions.

"Are you all right?" Luke said. It was such a limp, empty question, but what else could he say?

"I'm going to have to sell all of this," Claire said. "It's so sad. My mother would be furious."

"Have you called Dr. Eulberg?" This was her current psychiatrist, whom Luke and I had never met; Claire collected and discarded shrinks at a rate impossible to keep up with.

She didn't answer for a moment. She gathered up the rubies and silver and platinum, the gold fish with its emerald eye. She placed them all in the box, shut the lid, and turned the latch. "I don't think that's necessary."

We stood there in the doorway for a moment in silence. "You scared me yesterday," Luke said finally, his voice low and scrubbed clean of emotion. Claire looked over at us and then quickly looked away again. "Do you hear me?" he said. She bit her lip and nodded, suddenly appearing less than half her age, a bashful teenager. Luke said, "Okay," as though something had been accomplished, then left the room and closed the door behind him.

Claire had still not emerged by dinnertime, so Luke scrambled three eggs and microwaved some green beans; the food looked plastic, fake. He brought the plate into her room, and we found her as we had left her, staring down at her rippled reflection in the lid of the box. Luke placed the food on her night table and tapped the plate. "Eat something."

"Yes, yes," she said, glancing at the congealing eggs. When Luke didn't move, she gave him a crooked smile. "What, are you going to stand here and watch me?"

Tuesday was more of the same: Claire asleep when we left, the school day a tense blur, Claire dozing in bed when we returned. Luke stood in his bedroom rolling a quarter across his knuckles. "I have to do something. I have to call somebody."

I shook my head. "Don't indulge her." I liked the idea of Claire permanently shut up in her room, hidden away like a shameful secret; I wanted this situation to go on for as long as she would let it.

"If you planned this, if you knew what destroying that book would do to her . . ."

I was flattered—it would have been an excellent idea—but of course I hadn't known anything, and I told him so.

"I can't just let her lie in there forever."

"Maybe not," I agreed reluctantly. "But it's only been two days. No use panicking yet."

But two days quickly became four, and still Claire would not leave her room, no matter how often Luke pleaded with her. "Because I'm tired," is the only reason she would give, and after yet another repetition of these three unimpeachable words, Luke finally snapped: "You sound like a two-year-old. At least pretend you're an adult for a minute."

She propped herself up on one elbow to consider her son. "Nobody is making you stay here. Would you like to go live with James again for a while? Why don't you give him a call and see what he says."

"That's not fair."

"No, it's not. But neither is how you're treating me. All I'm asking is to be left alone for a while. Is that so impossible?"

I tugged on Luke's sleeve. "Come on. Let's go."

He shook me off. "I don't deserve this. I do everything you ask of me."

Claire rolled over and showed us her back. Her voice became muffled, distant. "Yes, and now I'm asking you to leave me alone. Why can't you do that, too?"

Luke paused for a moment, then said, "I understand why James left you. I never did before, but I do now."

Claire's voice followed us out of the room: "Don't forget he left you, too."

Luke grabbed his camera—a battered, brick-heavy Pentax that had once belonged to Venetia—and stalked out of the apartment. Photography was his central passion now, after a string of concussions the previous spring had stopped him from playing any more football; the high school darkroom had replaced Van Cortlandt's fields as his favored place of retreat. We headed up Central Park West and then east across the northern edge of the park. Luke paused to take photographs of elms, their knotty, muscular roots pushing up through the cobblestones. The late-afternoon light was fading as we turned up Lenox Avenue. He took photographs of redbrick facades stretching above 99-cent stores and delis on one side of the street, then turned to the project complexes and handball courts on the other. He took photographs of fire escapes, parking meters, a passing bus. I knew he also wanted to take photographs of the people we passed—an old lady in a screaming-pink pillbox hat, two Con Ed workers eating sandwiches over an open manhole—but he was afraid of offending anyone. I kept quiet. He didn't need me to see his mother's cruelty; my silent presence by his side was a contrast clear enough.

A few blocks above the park, the buildings ended, and a chain-link fence separated a vacant lot from the sidewalk. Debris cluttered most of the lot, leaving a narrow patch of dirt running along the fence. Luke stopped to point his lens at the ruined space. He had snapped only one photo when the thing hurled itself from behind a pile of shattered concrete into the fence, slamming its body against the pliant metal. Luke jumped back and almost dropped the camera, then focused his lens on the raging animal. The Rottweiler raised itself up onto its hind legs, swatting at the fence with its front paws and jamming its jaw into one of the diamond-shaped holes. The dog wore a studded leather collar, but no one appeared to claim it. Its barking carried above the rumble of the street, calling attention to our little scene.

"We should leave now," I said.

"In a minute." Luke's lens tracked the movements of the dog as it disengaged from the fence and spun around in a tight circle, its black-and-tan head swinging heavily from side to side like a sack of bones, flecks of spittle gathering in the corners of its mouth. Luke's focus was absolute, almost grim in its intensity, as though missing the shot would be immoral, a personal failure. He took a dozen more pictures, the dog still deeply into its frenzy, then said, "We can go. I have what I need."

Gregory Herzen called later that evening, as he had every night that week. Claire wouldn't talk to him, so he told Luke about her missed meetings and impending deadlines. "She'll be back soon," Luke said. "She's really sick right now." An hour later, he showed up at the apartment. "Gregory is here again," Victor said over the intercom. "Should I send him up?"

Luke met him at the front door. "I'm sorry, Gregory, but you can't come in."

Herzen rubbed his shaved scalp. "I need to see her for myself. I'm worried about her."

"I'm handling it. She's just sick right now."

"I know she's sick. This isn't the first time."

"She'll be fine. She wants to be alone."

"I'm going to come in and see her."

"You can't do that."

The two stared at each other, the front door held half open between them. Herzen's thick muscles tensed; the veins on his forearms popped, then settled. He rubbed his head again. For a moment I thought he was going to push his way through, but he just sighed. "Tell her I stopped by."

At midnight, Luke closed his chemistry textbook and turned

off the light. I sat on the chair opposite his bed, listening to his breathing. I could tell he wasn't going to fall asleep anytime soon, and he didn't, instead getting up after a few minutes to turn on the light and grab his camera. "What are you doing?" I said, but he didn't answer. The camera secure around his neck, he turned off the light again and moved down the darkened hallway to Claire's door. He listened for a moment, his ear close to the frame, then turned the knob. He eased the door open and paused. Orange street light seeped around the edges of the blinds; black clumps indicated love seat, dresser, bed, and there, in the middle of the bed, a ridge that was Claire. We waited; nothing happened. "She won't wake up," Luke whispered. "She's been taking sleeping pills again, I saw them." He pointed the camera at the love seat. The flashbulb illuminated dresses and gowns slumped like drunks over its back and arms. He turned the camera to the clothes on the floor, and a tangle of silk burst into being for an instant, rippled and milky. He catalogued the two ransacked closets, the disordered bathroom, the stack of dishes he had brought full of food to Claire each night, but which he had not removed or cleaned. Finally, he turned his camera on Claire herself. In discrete, brutal bursts of light, I saw a snarl of black hair, a crooked elbow, a hand balled up into an indignant fist. She lay facedown, her head angled just enough to one side to allow her to breathe, her arms stretched and bent above her head as though she were being dragged. She didn't move beneath this assault, not a twitch. Finally, Luke was done. Back in his bedroom, he put the camera down and looked at me.

"Evidence," he said. "So she can't pretend things were some other way."

───━━◦ꔛ◦━━───

Claire was up the next morning before we were, in the kitchen making coffee, the phone cradled against her shoulder. She smiled at us, testing her face for outside. "I feel rested," she said into the phone, as though the last five days had been a choice, some kind of sabbatical. We waited in the doorway until she hung up and turned away from us, busying herself with the coffee machine.

"Gregory came by last night," Luke said. "I didn't know what to say."

"I thought he might."

"I told him to leave. I thought you wouldn't want him to see you like that."

Claire turned to us. Her hair was pulled back into a ponytail so tight it stretched her skin flat against the bones of her face, as though the ponytail's tautness was the only thing preventing the skin from sliding out of place. She wore black slacks, a black blouse, and not a single piece of jewelry. "No," she said. "You're right. I wouldn't." She stepped toward Luke and reached out to touch his wrist, his shoulder, his cheek, her fingers tentative, probing, like blind animals. "Thank you," she said, and with that I saw her debt had been canceled: she was forgiven. It was that effortless, that simple, and it made me furious.

At school, I brooded through the first three periods until we went down to the basement for photography class. I, too, loved the weird red-black tint of the darkroom, the alchemic tang of the developing fluids, the ritualistic steps of dipping the paper into the developer, the stop bath, the fixer, and the wash. Our teacher played classical cassettes on a paint-spattered boom box while we worked, and I drifted around the room peering over students' shoulders as they squinted into their enlargers, the machines' lights shining down through the negatives and onto the blank easels below. The kids fiddled with their apertures, making their images of park benches, graffiti, taxis, and sky-scrapers woozily drift in and out of focus. These were their fantasies of what the city looked like. When everything was how they thought it should be, they fit a sheet of developing paper into the easel and exposed the image. All the students were focused, private. Their bodies were reduced to busy shadows in the dim red light, their pimples and grease and rank humanness concealed. They were something less than people here, and better because of it.

Luke worked on a photograph of the snarling Rottweiler. He approached his prints with a meticulousness verging on the obsessive. Within the borders of the photograph, his decisions of excision, inclusion, and proportion were final, and he seemed to find the thought of this both intoxicating and torturous. The dog's snapping jaws and rolling, crazy eyes throbbed in sharp focus while the rest of the picture—fence, weeds, cement—was a smeared blur. I noticed Sarah at her enlarger in the far corner.

She wore a pleated skirt and tank top, their colors leached out by the sullen darkroom glow. She fidgeted, scratching at the back of one bare leg with the other foot, frowning up at the ceiling. As Luke walked around the room to clear his head, I caught a glimpse of her work: a little girl standing astride an elaborate sandcastle, tiny and imperious with her ruffled bathing suit and lopsided grin.

One by one, students finished their work and left the darkroom. Luke developed some prints of the Rottweiler, but he was unhappy with the framing, the proportions; he didn't know how the photograph should look, only how it shouldn't. "What about the pictures of your mother?" I said. "Why don't you develop those?" He frowned at me and said, "Now is not the time." The teacher left, and soon it was just Luke and Sarah bent over their enlargers on opposite sides of the room. The developing counter, with its trays of fluid, jutted out between them. I leaned over the fixing bath and inhaled. It smelled powerful, toxic. I thought if I were a person this would be my food. It would make me stronger.

"Luke," I said. "Sarah is standing right there. Are you not going to say anything at all?"

He ignored me. They had not exchanged more than a few words in almost three weeks. People were so cowardly, so ashamed. And for once Luke had nothing to be ashamed of. He had exercised his power over Sarah and she had submitted to it; it was that simple, although his embarrassment afterward had almost negated the entire exchange. Despite my distaste for the girl, I had argued for spending more time with her, just to see how far we could push things. But Luke was afraid, and he had not called her once since we had left the Hamptons. Now she turned around, a piece of developing paper dangling from her fingers, and stopped when she saw Luke's hunched back. She stood there, her head cocked to the side, her skin spectral. She seemed to be considering if she should say something, but Luke spoke first: "Who's the little girl?"

"What?"

He turned to face her. "In your photo."

"Oh." Sarah looked at the undeveloped print in her hand as though she had no idea where it had come from. "My little cousin."

Luke glanced at me, and I motioned for him to continue. "She's adorable."

"Yeah. She is." Sarah stepped toward us. "Where have you been, Luke? I've been trying to talk to you."

What was she saying? We'd been in school every day.

"I've been here," Luke said. "Where else?"

"That's not what I mean." Sarah dropped her print in the developer and tilted the pan. "Listen. I wanted to tell you that maybe I overreacted. Maybe I was also mad at myself for letting things go further than I wanted them to. But you've been acting so strangely I couldn't even get that far."

I shook my head. "You don't need her forgiveness."

"Be quiet," Luke said.

Sarah looked up from her work. "What?"

181

"Nothing," Luke said quickly. "I just . . . I didn't mean for things to happen how they did at the beach."

"No," I said. "This is wrong. You have nothing to apologize for."

"I think it's okay," she said. "You were so, I don't know, *scared* the rest of that night, it freaked me out even more." She transferred her print from the developer to the stop bath with a pair of plastic tongs. I saw the little cousin and her little castle bleed into view.

"I wasn't scared," Luke said.

"Then what was it? You could barely even look at me."

"I was embarrassed. That wasn't me out there."

"Stop," I said. "Don't be weak."

"Then who was it?"

Luke said nothing, looked at the floor.

"Luke." Sarah touched his arm. "You know I care about you. You know that. But I don't understand you, and you won't even let me try. I have no idea how you're going to act toward me from one day to the next. And to avoid me for three weeks? How am I supposed to feel about that?"

Luke looked up at her, his hands clenched by his sides. "I'm sorry," he said. It was the worst thing that could have come out of his mouth.

"It's okay." Sarah squeezed his arm and moved as though she were going to hug him, but didn't. "I want to be friends," she said, "but we can't be whatever we were this summer." She waited for Luke to say something, but he just blinked at her. She stood there awkwardly for a moment, then said, "Will you talk to me? I can't stand it when you don't talk to me."

"I don't have anything to say right now."

"I can see that. Later, I guess." She leaned in and kissed him on the cheek, then hurried out of the darkroom. Luke turned back to his easel and the stupidly snarling Rottweiler.

"Do you see now?" I said.

"Shut up, Daniel."

"You see it. That's what your humility gets you: pity and a kiss on the cheek."

<hr />

The first Friday night in October. Cool, damp weather squatted over the city. Luke and Omar sat on the steps of the Metropolitan Museum in sweatshirts and fleeces, drinking forty-ounce bottles of malt liquor Omar had stolen from a deli. This was the new improved Omar, the cocky punk from the East Village whose parents were leftist NYU professors from Lebanon and France. The Omar I remembered had been shy and obliging, obsessed with origami and martial arts. But as he started senior year, his personality grew bigger, and he cast it outward like a grasping, laughing net, his voice and his body becoming huge, sprawling things. He had started hanging with kids from public schools in his neighborhood, skateboarders and graffiti artists; he liked to keep Luke around as a keepsake from a doubtful past life.

The two of them were quiet in the way of old friends with a

shared past but little common future. I leaned forward from my perch on the step above to check Luke's progress on his bottle; it was the first time he had drank any alcohol since Providence, and I was anxious to see what would happen. Omar's moon-face caught the headlights of a passing taxi and lit up like a paper lantern. "Fuck Sarah," he said. "You'll go away to college and forget about her by the end of your first weekend." Luke nodded, even though I could see his sentimental heart didn't agree. Omar took a call on his new cell phone. "People down by Alice. Drink up." Luke tilted the bottle upside down, and I greedily watched the liquid disappear.

We stood and the Metropolitan Museum loomed, a bloated sarcophagus. We walked down Fifth Avenue, ducking into the park at Seventy-ninth Street. Omar meant the sculptures down by the Boat Pond: Alice, the Cheshire Cat, the March Hare, the Mad Hatter, and the Dormouse, the five posed among bronze toadstools. Luke and I used to climb all over them for entire afternoons when he was younger. They spoke to us then, back when I participated in Luke's febrile childhood fantasies, Alice with her calm vacancy and Cheshire his spastic cheerfulness. The Hare was charming and polite, the Hatter caustic and threatening; the Dormouse always appeared to be dead. We had walked by them once this fall already, and it had been almost sad to see them for what they were: mute bronze statues, no more animate than a rock or a tree.

Tonight, Alice and her friends were swallowed up by a group of lolling teenage boys. They wore hooded sweatshirts and heavy parkas, chunky sneakers and sagging jeans. Crisp baseball caps tilted up and away from their faces like cockeyed crowns. Omar stepped into the group and dispensed complex handshakes while I loomed in close to read their cagey faces.

"Luke," Omar boomed, "you've met these dudes before, right?"

Luke glanced around, screwing his face into what was meant to be a tough look. "I don't know. Maybe." They looked back at him as though he were a piece of boring art on the wall of a museum, something to be absorbed and then left behind. "'Sup," one offered. They talked about the graffiti work of which they were proudest, pieces thrown up on water towers, train tunnels, delivery trucks. They discussed new strategies, fresh ways of avoiding the police or executing technically tricky feats. They passed around a bottle of dark rum, and I encouraged Luke to drink double when it was his turn. He leaned against the March Hare's cold flank and let the talk roll over him. A thin, watchful kid sat in Alice's lap, slitting a cigar down the middle with a switchblade. Luke's attention drifted over to the knife and then drifted away again. Mine didn't waver. With a flick, the kid made the blade disappear. He tapped the cigar's innards onto the ground, brought out a bag of marijuana, and began stuffing the cigar full of crumbled buds.

"Take the knife," I said. Luke frowned at me. "The knife," I said. "Ask if you can hold it."

Luke shrugged and nodded toward the switchblade. "Can I see that?"

The kid slowly licked the length of the cigar and sealed it shut. "If you wait a minute, maybe."

Omar said, "Where are those famous Nightingale manners?" and then he laughed, a dumb sound, like what an animal gives out when hit by a stick. The kid lit the blunt, and a curtain of smoke hid his face. He passed it to Omar, and then handed the knife to Luke, its blade tucked away. "Don't be stupid and cut your finger off."

Luke held the thing loosely in his open palm. He looked at it as though it were alive and hostile. I leaned in close. "You should learn how to use one of these." He shook his head. "Yes," I said. "Think of that kid in the record store. You never know when you might need to." Omar closed his eyes and expelled colossal billows of smoke. The thin kid watched Luke, but few of the others paid attention. I ran my fingers along the handle, the smooth pearl and the raised steel button. It was cool and compact, and radiated bad intentions. I curled my hand over Luke's. We pressed the button; the blade sprung out. We slid the button back; the blade disappeared. I laughed. "See?" I said. "It's not that hard." Click, in. Click, out.

"Man, what is wrong with you?" Omar said.

The thin kid coughed and spit. "You better give that thing back before you slice your own motherfucking face open."

Luke paused, the knife's blade extended. "They shouldn't talk to you like that," I said. "Like you're a child, or an idiot." Luke turned the blade this way and that, the metal catching quick licks of streetlamp light.

Omar passed the blunt off and reached out his hand. "Give it here, you crazy bastard. Joke's over."

"What a condescending piece of shit," I said, and Luke grinned. He feinted at Omar, and his friend's eyes retreated, frightened little creatures. They were all paying attention now, a tight scrum of wonder, weed smoke curling and drifting above their heads. "Stupid drunk fuck," the thin kid said. "Give the knife back to the big boys and run home to Mommy." I waited for Omar to defend Luke, but he didn't say anything. "He's out of line," I said. "You should teach him a lesson." Luke hesitated, and I tried to guide his knife hand forward. He resisted me, his wrist holding firm. I pushed harder, but I couldn't force it; he was still too strong. All of us stood poised and frozen for a moment until the tension abruptly rushed out of Luke, and he handed the knife over to Omar with a limp smile. "I was just fucking with you," he said, and everybody laughed as though they'd known it the whole time.

"Here," Omar said, handing Luke the bottle of rum. "I'll trade you." Luke took a big slug and looked at me over the rim. I knew he liked how it felt for Omar—for all of them—to be afraid of him; it almost didn't matter that in the end he had given in. I wanted him to remember this feeling, and I wanted him to remember that I could help him to feel it again, whenever he wanted.

They passed around the bottle until it was finished, and then someone brought out another. Sometime later, the two of us staggered across the hushed park and up Central Park West. At the corner of our block, Luke stumbled, and he would have fallen if I hadn't grabbed his arm and held him steady. We stood together, swaying under a busted streetlamp. After a minute, he straightened and tried to push me away until he realized he couldn't stand without my help.

PART THREE

A Closed World

1

BUT THAT PROMISING, exhilarating night in the park turned out, over the next eleven months, to be an anomaly rather than any real sign of change. Luke renounced alcohol all over again; Claire, suddenly purposeful, attacked her work at the press and when she was home shone the full glare of her affection onto her son. Winter came, and the two of them sat together at the kitchen table each night working on his college applications, leaning their heads together in an attempt to craft on the page the best possible Luke Nightingale. (For this was now his legal as well as practical name. "Luke Tomasi-Nightingale" had always carried within it a hint of the inappropriate, the fiction that Luke had inherited anything more from his father than sarcasm and a single brown eye; on his nineteenth birthday, the state made official what was already obvious, and the Tomasi half was excised.) I watched them working at the table, and the puzzle of college sat in the middle of my mind, a locked box. How would this place function? What were its rules? The answers mattered, because it was there, finally free of Claire, that I would be able to influence Luke more than I ever had before. How pathetic, though, that I was still confined to things like influence and persuasion. My patience, enormous though it was, had started to erode.

Luke's senior year of high school proved to be full of false gains for me, false hope. By the time he graduated, my purchase on the world was still as tenuous as it had been from the moment he hurled me out of his skull and into the middle of Claire's night of madness. The whole school year I continued to help him with his classes when he asked me to. The problem was his focus; often, he simply couldn't be bothered to pay any attention to whatever he was meant to be learning, spending his time instead on photography, Nightingale Press manuscripts, televised football games. He would waste entire evenings after school sitting in the Conservatory Garden while he was supposed to be studying, his eyes closed and headphones on, hunched within a navy peacoat, listening to classical music in the dead of winter. We took the board exams together in January; I worked on one question while he worked on the next. We finished in half the time and missed three questions—all Luke's—on the entire test. Along with his photography portfolio, it got us into the college that, of all those acceptable, Luke wanted not to go to the least. In September, Claire said good-bye to us in front of the apartment building, too upset to make the trip, and James drove us down instead. He told Luke he was proud of him, but it was just something to say. His life had moved on; Luke and Claire were part of the past.

Our dorm room was small and disgusting. It was stuck in the top corner of a Gothic monstrosity that belonged in medieval Germany rather than suburban New Jersey. Dust balls collected in the corners and grime streaked the windows. We shared it with a fool named Nate, who was soft in both body and mind. He tacked up posters of cars and half-naked pop singers on his half of the room. Luke countered with two of the Noh masks, a laughing old man and a ferocious ancestor spirit with goat horns and mad, frightened eyes. They hung above his desk like trophies from a massacre. Nate said he couldn't sleep sometimes because he was sure they were staring at him, while our new friend Richard declared them wonderfully disturbing. He stood in the room one September evening, running his hands over the old man's face, and looked at Luke. "You're a pretty fucked-up kid, aren't you?"

But Richard was pretty fucked up too. He was a twenty-one-year-old senior who regarded college as a kind of sociological experiment in which he was both lab rat and observer. Personal interactions were an arena for testing hypotheses about human nature; people's feelings were an interesting manifestation of chemical disturbances in the brain. He had many acquaintances but few friends; he liked to bait people until they either snapped back or ran away. He had been raised in both London and Los Angeles, and he turned his British accent on and off as he saw fit. Girls he wanted to sleep with and professors he wanted to impress got the Queen's English, while everybody else got a flat trans-Atlantic deadpan. Once, when someone called him Richie, probably without knowing any better, he threw a soda in the offender's face and said if he ever disrespected him again he'd set fire to his dorm room.

And he talked. All the time. Stories and anecdotes and theories flew out of his mouth like startled bats, blindly knocking into each other in the bright air. Everything he said seemed to contain a little bit of truth and a little bit of falsehood. His parents were British nobility; no, they were in the movie business. Well, actually, the truth was they were minor aristocrats who dabbled in film production. And so on. I soon began to regard his words as no more than intricate little figurines: well crafted, aesthetically pleasing, and an accurate representation of nothing. I knew that Luke, on the other hand, was flattered to be the object of Richard's vigorous attention, but even I didn't suspect this attention to be part of a premeditated plan.

We met him our third night on campus, in the upstairs room of a creaking house filled with chatter and smoke. Student artwork, drippy and overwrought, hung at drunken angles on walls painted a deep, swollen red. "If you're lost," he said to us, balanced on the edge of a pool table, his words like change tossed to a beggar, "that's a good start."

"I'm not lost," Luke said. "I'm just bored."

In truth, we were lost. We had gone out for the night with a group of other freshmen from our dormitory, and had ended up here, alone. But there was no reason to admit this.

"Boredom is a plague." Richard slid off the pool table and stretched like a lazy housecat, his frosted blond hair prickling the air above his head. "But it's difficult to be bored if you don't have any idea where you are." On the wall hung a crude painting of a dissected frog, its skin pinned back with what looked like metal chopsticks. I was quiet, drawn inside myself, watching flushed faces rush by shouting about things I didn't understand.

"I know where I am," Luke said, "I just wish I were somewhere else."

"Quite." Richard reached out his hand. "My name is Richard, and I'm the most interesting person you'll meet at this school."

He led us to a dark room with shaggy black carpeting, beanbags, and an enormous television playing a surfing film on mute. Dim figures sat in the gloom smoking cigarettes. On the screen, churning blue cylinders chewed up and spat out muscular little men. Richard brought out a vial of cocaine and snorted bumps off a gold collar stay. He offered some to Luke, who considered it briefly before declining.

"I don't drink, because alcohol's an anesthetic," Richard said. "I want to feel more, not less. So I do this instead."

Luke glanced at me. "I just choose my moments. And to-night's not one of them."

"Tonight you just want to be yourself, is that it?" Richard inserted the stay back into the collar of his starched dress shirt; the vial disappeared elsewhere.

"Something like that."

Richard looked at Luke for a long time, an angry vein throbbing in his forehead. "There's something about you," he finally said. He noisily sniffed and then swallowed it down. "I imagine we'll get along quite well, Luke."

It wasn't long before we spent part of nearly every evening sitting in Richard's austere single room with the blinds drawn, watching him snort gigantic lines off a gold-rimmed makeup mirror. He would talk clever nonsense at us for hours, and there was something charming about him to which even I was sometimes susceptible. He gave you the sense that the most important thing in the world was that you listen to him and become a convert to his point of view. Luke was the perfect target, shy and homesick, sheltering his private constellation of pain and guilt. Richard had sensed this constellation immediately, and beneath all his busy talk hid an unwavering purpose: to expose and explore it.

⚬

One morning three weeks after we had arrived on campus, I woke up to see Luke sitting cross-legged on the floor of our dorm room, one of the Noh masks hiding his face. It was the ancestor spirit, made of light tan wood with a red-painted mouth and two short black horns. In the middle of its wild white eyes were small holes where the pupils should have been. Blades of sunlight sliced up the room, and Luke sat perfectly still in half light and half shadow. He was naked besides the mask, and he barely seemed to breathe. I uncurled myself from my awkward position underneath the window. "What are you doing?" I said.

He didn't answer. He didn't move. It was 9:00 A.M.; Nate softly snored on the top bunk. I brushed dust from my suit and stood up. Luke's hands rested on his knees in an unintentional approximation of a yoga pose. The spirit mask stared at me. I looked closely at the eyeholes but couldn't see anything move. Tightly curled black hair covered Luke's skinny legs. The tip of his penis touched the grimy floor, and the soles of his feet were black with filth. His chest was hollow, the nipples wide and flat, encircled with isolated tufts of dark hair that emphasized the funereal white of his skin. The mask grinned or grimaced, I had never been able to tell which. I walked in a circle around Luke, but he gave no sign that he knew I was there.

Nate's alarm clock went off, loud as a bomb. I flinched, but Luke still didn't move. Nate raised his bovine head and blinked into the light. "Luke," I whispered urgently. "Get up." This was not the kind of trouble I was looking for. The ancestor spirit stared into space. Nate mumbled something and then scanned the room. His cow-eyes blinked, and for a second he didn't seem to believe he was awake yet. "Is this a joke?" he said. When Luke didn't respond, Nate pushed aside his blankets and tumbled to the floor. He saw what I saw: a naked boy in a horned mask. He tossed a towel onto Luke's lap. "Cover yourself up, you freak."

Nate dressed and packed his bag, glancing sidelong at Luke the whole time. Sweat ran down Luke's neck; the wire strung across the back of the mask bit into his skin. "This isn't funny," Nate said. He was right, it wasn't funny, but his own skittish reaction was, tiptoeing around Luke like a thief around a sleeping guard dog. "I should go to the dean," he said over his shoulder, and I wondered if he would. Luke sat like that for three more hours. The sunlight crept across the floor and up the wall. I stood by the window and watched the morning go by. Without word or warning, Luke stood up, took off the mask, and hung it back up on its nail on the wall. He would not look me in the eye. He showered and dressed, and then we went to his freshman writing class.

A week or so later, we sat in the basement taproom of a dilapidated social club, perched on stools at the long, battered bar. It was late on a Tuesday night, and the room was empty except for five kids sharing a pitcher of beer at a table behind us. The ceiling was low and painted black. Neither Richard nor Luke was drinking, but Richard had chopped out three bumps of cocaine onto a compact mirror. He snorted the first one; the kids looked up and glared. He ignored them, and continued to shuffle through Luke's first batch of prints from photography class. They were close-ups of test tubes and microscopes, bubbling solutions and blue flames, taken while he was a guest at chemistry laboratory sessions. A digital camera had given the pictures a cold-blooded aspect; the colors were artificial, gleaming silvers and crackling greens. I had advised Luke to crop the photographs to remove all human hands and bodies, leaving only the instruments in their clean isolation. They were smart, strange pictures; with my help, I thought Luke might make a decent photographer.

"These aren't terrible," Richard said, "but they're quite bland."

"Bland? How?" Luke was concerned, which irritated me. What did he care what Richard thought?

"They're technically sound, but they have no teeth. You want to take memorable photos? Get your camera and let me show you something." He paused to snort the second bump off the mirror. "We'll need a car, though. And I don't know how to drive. Wrong side of the road and all that." He bent his head to take the third bump.

"I can drive," Luke said. I raised my eyebrows. This wasn't really true. He had been behind the wheel of Claire's Saab twice and both instances had quickly ended in ugly arguments. I could see now just how much he didn't want to disappoint Richard.

Nate had a car, a beat-up Toyota with rust spots and Pennsylvania license plates. It was impossible to think he would lend it to Luke, so we were forced to borrow it without his knowledge. When we got back to the dorms, he and two of his slovenly friends were sitting on the floor playing video games. "Evening, gentlemen," Richard said. "Yeah," Nate said, and then he returned to the chattering machine-gun fire. His two friends held their eyes on Richard in his tie and blazer for a moment longer. Luke's hand hesitated over the small digital camera on his desk, but then he settled on Venetia's Pentax instead. "Nailed the motherfucker," Nate murmured. The sound of explosions was constant and shrill. The three buffoons were so transfixed by their fake war that they did not notice when Richard slipped behind them and pocketed the car keys off the top of Nate's desk.

We walked down campus to the student parking lot, out of the shadows of the old Gothic buildings and toward the brutal modern structures. We passed the wide glass wall of the workout room. On the other side, tight rows of girls climbed StairMasters and manipulated ellipticals, dozens of pairs of skinny legs in gym shorts pumping and cycling. They held their heads erect, pointed at the massive TV screens hanging from the back wall. The whole setup looked like some kind of fascist behavioral experiment. "Gerbils," Richard muttered. In the sudden light of a streetlamp, his face looked old and ugly. But then we were in the dark again, and his smile glowed like foxfire. "I can't argue with the results, though," he said.

Richard led us across a wide field, past a giant new dormitory complex. Inside its hundreds of rooms, students studied and argued and fucked and smoked and slept. Behind each window was a student like a tiny cell performing its one dumb function; yet taken together, they formed a complete organism, operative and purposeful. Luke and I had not yet found our function. We stood outside the organism, circling it like flies. I followed Richard's white-blond hair as it bobbed across the field. *Ignis fatuus,* I thought.

It took us fifteen minutes to find the Toyota among the gleaming rows of the student lot. Luke unlocked it, and Richard sat down in the passenger seat, slamming the door shut. "The lab is only twenty minutes away," he said. "Think you can handle that without killing us?"

Luke started the Toyota and jerkily guided us out of the parking lot and onto the campus roads. "You need to tell me where I'm going," he said.

"Stay on this road until it hits the highway," Richard said. "I'll show you where." He kept his eyes on Luke for a long moment, the beginnings of a smug smile on his face, the smile of someone getting exactly what they wanted. I suddenly realized Richard knew Luke had no idea what he was doing; he was risking his own life just to see if, and how, Luke would crack. We drove down a long straight road lined with tall trees planted in military rows. It was very dark, and I had a momentary feeling of utter weightlessness as Luke pressed his foot down on the gas and we hurtled through black space. Richard cleared his throat. "You might want to turn your headlights on." Apparently his nihilism only went so far.

We merged onto the highway, thankfully empty of much traffic at this late hour. New Jersey scrolled by: gas stations, conference hotels, corporate parks. The opposite sides of the road were indistinguishable as Luke held the car steady and slow in the middle lane. Richard pointed to an exit only a short distance from campus, and Luke gingerly guided the car off the highway. Soon we were on a quiet road with few buildings and no cars at all. Richard had Luke park in the dark corner of a huge lot. Across the lot crouched a low, expensive-looking building.

"That's the lab."

"The lab for what?" Luke said.

Richard didn't answer. He just opened the door and started walking across the lot, leaving Luke trembling in the driver's seat. "That wasn't so terrible," I told him. "Pretty impressive, actually."

He exhaled loudly and slumped back into his seat. "Yeah," he said, "but we still have to get back."

We got out of the car and hurried to catch up with Richard, who bypassed the bright front entrance of the building and took us around to a side door, looking over his shoulder before he brought out a bristling set of keys.

"Be quiet," he said. "There shouldn't be anybody here now, but you never know." He selected a key and opened the door.

"Where did you get those?" Luke whispered.

Richard smiled slyly and tapped his nose. "Graduate students have bad habits too. And sometimes not enough money to pay for them."

Inside was a dark corridor and another door with a ribbon of light at its base. The first door shut, and that ribbon became our only guide. Richard selected a second key by touch alone and opened the inner door. Fluorescent light slapped my eyes; everything was gleaming white and spotless. "What do they do here?" Luke asked, shifting the strap of the Pentax from one shoulder to the other. Richard didn't answer. "Richard?"

"What kind of film is in that camera?" he asked. "Because black-and-white would be better. More reportorial."

Darkened classrooms and offices flanked the hallway. We turned a corner, and floor-to-ceiling windows ran along the left-hand wall. Another corner and another corridor before Richard's raised hand brought us to a halt. We heard distant voices from somewhere else in the building. "It would not be very pleasant to get caught," Richard said. The sound faded, and he waved us on. Finally, we came to a set of black double doors, which Richard used a third key to open. We entered the room and the door closed behind us.

The temperature was cool; blue bulbs cast an aqueous glow. I heard rustlings, low breathing, the sound of fingernails on metal. My eyes adjusted, and I saw rows of large cages running down either side of the long room. Dark shapes stirred inside the cages. I walked closer. "What are they?" Luke said. Suddenly, a pink face flashed forward and split open. Its scream was infantile and insane. The animal grabbed the bars of its cage, shook them once, and then retreated back into the shadows. A message traveled around the room from cage to cage, murmuring and activity, little shrieks of curiosity or outrage. The monkeys circled and sat and watched, stiff pink ears quivering.

"Researchers study their faces, their expressions," Richard said. "They play them music and show them footage of other monkeys still out in the wild. There is the looming event test. The measuring of the fear response." The monkeys smelled rich and familiar, probably not unlike people under similar conditions.

"There is something called the multisensory integration test."
The nearest animal scratched itself and snickered at me. Its pink
child-face floated in the dark. Wet eyes crinkled. "But the specif-
ics don't really matter," Richard continued. "The central question
studied here is what their faces can tell us about how they feel.
And what they can tell from each other's faces."

"What's the answer?" Luke asked.

"There isn't one yet. But I wish I could do these same kinds
of experiments on people to help figure it out."

The cages were stacked two high and ten long on either side
of the room, forty monkeys smiling and frowning. Some pressed
their faces against the bars to see us better; others stayed in the
corners with their backs turned as though ashamed by our presence. I stuck my fingers through the bars of the nearest cage and
wiggled them at a monkey's twitchy eyes until the creature
snapped at me, teeth flashing.

Richard pointed at the camera hanging off Luke's shoulder.
"We don't have all night."

Luke began to snap pictures. The flash illuminated wrinkled
fleshy cheeks, tufted chests, a rolling eye. Some cowered away
from the light while others reached out to touch it with leather-
skinned baby-hands.

"We need more action," Richard said. He picked up a broom
from the corner and walked the length of the room banging it
against the bars of the cages. The monkeys chattered and com-
plained. He banged it harder. They screeched and protested.
Luke took pictures. Richard swung the handle like a baseball

bat and rattled the cages. The screeching grew louder. Richard ran up and down the rows, his blazer flapping, his face red. I joined him, spreading my arms and letting my fingers run across the bars. The monkeys achieved a frenzy, throwing themselves against the walls of their cages, bawling, shrieking, the sound of many minds unhinged in exactly the same way. Then Richard pulled up abruptly and raised his hand. "Listen." Behind the monkey chorus was the sound of human voices calling to each other. We heard them approaching the door of the lab. "Quickly," Richard said. He grabbed Luke's wrist and dragged him to another door at the back of the room, and I followed close behind.

Again, the keys came out, and we slipped into another hallway. They all looked the same, these corridors: gleaming white walls, scrubbed linoleum floors. Richard sprinted away, and Luke and I struggled to keep up. Shouts echoed off hard surfaces. Richard turned left, then right, then left, and then we lost him. We spun around the corner of another hallway, but he was gone. Luke stopped next to me. "Where did he go?" I shook my head. I wondered if he had intentionally lost us, if this were some kind of joke. Suddenly his head popped out of a stairwell door we had somehow missed. "What the fuck," he said. We crashed though the door and into the stairwell, taking the stairs three at a time, the heavy camera bouncing on its strap around Luke's neck. On the ground floor, we burst through an exit and triggered a shrill alarm. We had come out behind the building, at the edge of a lawn. Richard waved us forward, and we jogged around to the front, where the parking lot waited, empty except for the Toyota in the far corner.

Luke paused in front of the car. "What?" Richard said. Even in the midst of our escape he allowed himself a cruel smile. "Is there a problem?" "Fuck," Luke muttered before he flung the driver's door open. He sped out of the lot and back down the dark local road, nearly taking out a row of miniature pines, his face twisted into a tense grimace. Out on the highway, the anxiety leaked out of him, and he slowed down, hugging the shoulder, shying away from other cars. As we approached campus, he refused to go faster than thirty miles per hour, and he stopped at the first sign of a yellow light.

"I'm done," he said. "I'm not going any further."

Richard grinned, triumphant. "Get us home, and I'll never ask you to drive again." He paused. "As long as you admit you're just a common liar like the rest of us."

Luke turned to look at him. "What?"

The light changed, and Richard waved at the road. "Go on. You've come this far."

The drive back took half an hour; I'm still not sure how we survived it. After Luke returned the car to its place in the student lot, Richard sauntered off to his dormitory, whistling and twirling his massive set of keys. In our own room, Nate snored on the top bunk and a letter waited on Luke's desk. It was a note from the dean of student life requesting a meeting to discuss a "lewd and possibly threatening incident." The Noh mask, of course.

Nate was apparently a squealer. Luke tore the letter in half and threw it in the garbage.

———◈———

Fall shuffled onward. Luke again grew distracted from his studies, skipping classes and assignments. The bad grades began to pile up, and I became concerned. Could he fail out? He ignored two voice mails from the dean's office, and I feared a campus security guard would show up at our door any day. Could the school ask him to leave? I would not allow this to happen; I needed this separation from Claire. We had to stay, and so I began to complete his assignments and improve his papers myself. He didn't argue with me; he just handed me the pen and paper, or set me in front of his computer, and he didn't seem to care either way. He didn't seem to care about much of anything. His mind was mushy, preoccupied. Only two things held his attention: his photography and his slavish devotion to the cult of Richard.

On Halloween day, we sat in our afternoon Shakespeare seminar. Luke stared at the ceiling while I crouched behind him doing my best to remember everything that was said. The students encircled a scarred wooden table and bent their heads toward the gray-haired professor. The wattles on the old man's neck shuddered as he spoke, and his eyes sagged behind thick-lensed glasses. Some girl compared Othello to Clarence Thomas, and then time was up and we were free to go. Richard waited for us outside, leaning against the building, rubbing his nose. "What are you doing tonight?" he demanded.

"I don't know." Luke shrugged. "I don't have a costume."

"Fuck costumes. I have something better."

"Oh yeah? What?"

"Think the lab, but creepier. Be in your room at nine. Don't wear anything too nice."

"Richard. What is this about?"

He looked at his watch. "I'm late for a meeting. See you at nine." He winked at us, and then rushed off through an archway and around a corner.

Back in the dorm, there was another message from Claire on our voice mail, the most recent of a dozen Luke had not bothered to return. She said the leaves were starting to fall again, and could Luke please come home to help her sweep them away. He erased the message. Nate sprawled out on the beanbag, holding an economics textbook over his face. He gave Luke a wary "What's up?" and then returned to his book. I could see he wanted to ask about the letter from the dean—it had been two weeks already—but he had not yet figured out how to bring it up. Luke refused to make things easy for him, and said nothing. Instead, he had adopted an attitude of spaced-out serenity around Nate, which just further unnerved his roommate. Luke sat at his desk now and looked through contact sheets from the photography lab until Nate left for an early dinner. The images were in grainy black-and-white, and only fragments of the monkeys' bodies—tails, eyes, teeth—had been illuminated by the flash. I stared at an open mouth howling in silent protest and then looked away.

Luke and I followed Nate to the dining hall, and sat alone at a back table. The setting sun streaked across a glass wall. Luke ignored the day's specials and instead prepared one of his staples, white rice mixed with Worcestershire sauce and mayonnaise, one of the few things he ate anymore. I pointed out that the globules of rice and mayo looked like fat squeezed from a clotted artery, but he shoveled it into his mouth anyway, saying it reminded him of home. I couldn't tell if he was joking. Back in our room, Nate had disappeared for the evening, and we passed the time until Richard showed up by playing chess. The knock came at precisely nine o'clock. Luke stood up to answer it, but Richard walked through the unlocked door first, followed by two girls.

"*Buenos noches,*" he said. He noticed the chessboard on the floor, looked around the room, and asked, "Who's winning?" then turned to the girls without waiting for an answer. "Ladies, I'd like to introduce you to Luke Nightingale, reclusive genius and photographic prodigy. His mother's family has been in America longer than Jesus." He turned back to us and winked. "Play nice."

The girls stood in the doorway until Luke recovered his composure. He swept a pile of paperback mysteries off the futon and welcomed them in. I inspected the pair. One was a girl from our pop art class whose name I remembered as Beth. She sat on the futon and crossed her bare legs demurely, as though her seat were lined with Italian leather rather than tatty flannel. She wore a sleeveless white blouse and a corduroy skirt, and a tattoo of a rat chasing its own tail decorated her upper arm. The other girl remained standing at the edge of the futon, looking anywhere except at us. She was small and thin, and seemed to be trying to make herself even smaller. She was dressed plainly, in jeans, a black sweater, and sneakers, and she had pulled her dark hair back into a utilitarian ponytail.

"Hannah?" Richard said.

The girl looked up. Her sharp features scrunched together in the middle of her face, and suddenly she was not shy or uncomfortable, but feral, vicious. She relaxed, and her face spread out again. She extended a tiny hand. "Nice to meet you," she said quietly. Luke took her hand, squeezed it once, then dropped it. My eyes stayed with her a moment longer. It was as though I could see inside her chest, where a tarry ball of need stuck to her rib cage. She swallowed things from the world around her but they only stuck to the ball, adding to its size.

"Now that we're all acquainted," Richard said. He slung a backpack off his shoulder and unzipped its outside pocket. He wore a black track suit over a white T-shirt instead of his usual blazer and jeans. Out of the backpack came his cocaine kit: the mirror, the razor, the glass tube. The powder itself was in a tiny orange-tinted vial. He locked the door and busied himself with chopping out lines. "I'm assuming you've scared away your horrific roommate for the evening?" Tap, tap, tap went the razor against the mirror. I stood by Richard's shoulder and fixated on the blade's notched edge. "How about a bit of music?" he said.

"It's dead quiet in here." Luke fiddled with his computer, and icy electronic rhythms marched out of the desktop speakers. I liked this music. It banished the human voice and its sloppy warmth, replacing it with precision, repetition, unsentimental intelligence. Such lovely rigor.

"I hate techno," Beth said.

Richard glanced at her. "Grow up," he said. He stepped away from Luke's desk. "Dinner is served." Four fat lines rested on the mirror. "Four?" I said. Richard held the glass tube out to Beth, who stood up from the futon and glided across the room. She bent over the mirror, took her line, and raised her head in one smooth, practiced motion, as though she had learned how to do drugs in finishing school, alongside curtsying and the waltz. Hannah stood behind Richard, her hands picking at the weave of her sweater. Beth handed her the tube and sashayed back across the room. I could tell the two girls were not really friends; they connected to each other only through Richard, but exactly how and why I could not figure out. Hannah gripped the tube like a knife and scraped its end across the glass as she snorted. After her line disappeared, she threw back her head and gasped. She licked a chapped fingertip, smeared it across the mirror, rubbed it into her gums. Her behavior was that of a starving child unsure of the source of her next meal. Beth sat on the futon and lit her cigarette like a queen, then Richard picked the tube up off the mirror, holding it out to Luke with a sly smile.

Luke frowned. "You know I don't do that."

"No, but perhaps there's a part of you that wants to." Richard spoke softly enough that the girls could not hear. I stared at the two remaining lines.

"Richard—"

"Listen," Richard interrupted, "we're all a team tonight. Do you understand? Don't screw it up."

I licked my lips. I wanted some.

Richard said, "You don't always have to be in such control."

Luke looked at me and then back at Richard. "You don't understand the alternative."

Richard grinned like a skull and opened his mouth to answer when Hannah said, "Whatever you're scared of, this will make you forget. You won't be scared anymore." She turned away from the window and looked Luke in the eye. Her angry face smiled, still angry.

"Fuck it," Luke said. He took the tube and snorted messily, pushing some loose tendrils of powder to the edges of the mirror. He drew back his head and coughed. "Jesus." Richard took his own line in two economical bursts, one for each nostril, and then he laughed. Hannah was still staring at Luke, but I felt like she was trying to find me and just didn't know where to look. The music hissed and clicked. Luke ran his tongue over his teeth and gums; his face focused to a sharp point that he directed first at Hannah, then at Richard, then back at Hannah. Nobody spoke for exactly seventy-five seconds, and then Beth stubbed her cigarette out on the floor and said, "Nothing could be more tedious. Let's go."

Outside, a murdered starlet and a priest walked by arm in arm. We headed down campus toward the parking lots again, where we found Beth's boxy old Volvo among the rows. Richard looked at the car, then nodded at Luke. "Don't get any ideas." I sat between Luke and Hannah on the cracked leather backseat. Beth—her window open, one hand on the wheel, the other holding a cigarette—took turns on the narrow campus roads at fifty miles per hour. Richard grinned through the windshield at the rushing tarmac. I felt my bones turn to iron, ramrod straight. I was strong, and then I was weak, and then I was strong again. I nudged Luke. He shook his head at me, swallowing heavily. His eyes were nervous but he was smiling.

Richard talked about physics, control groups, parapsychology. A mix tape of gloomy New Wave played at low volume. Once we were on the highway, Richard brought out the vial and tapped bumps onto the gold collar stay. Luke and Hannah snorted theirs aggressively, like animals. Richard held the stay steady underneath Beth's nostrils as she drove faster and faster. "Next exit," he said. Luke and Hannah did not speak once the entire drive. There was so much need and anger and anxiety boiling in Hannah's small body that I thought if Luke touched her his hand might melt. Beth drove us onto a dark local road. I saw a house with toilet paper tangled in the trees of its front yard. Cardboard skeletons advertised beer specials in the window of a darkened liquor store. Beth talked about Lichtenstein, Brooklyn, lecherous professors. Through the tinny car speakers, a singer defined grace and betrayal. Richard consulted a hand-drawn map. "Pull over here." He turned to the backseat. "You have to leave campus to learn anything at this school."

Beth parked the car off the shoulder of the road, partially hidden among some reeds. We got out, and she lit another cigarette. At first its glowing tip was the only thing I could see as I traced its languid course from her hip to her mouth and back again. Then my sight adjusted, and I saw the high half-moon and the thin clouds whipping across its face. The reeds swayed in time with the wind. We walked down the empty road, and our shapes took on sharp, dangerous edges. A prickly aura of tension flickered from person to person before settling on Luke, the hood of his sweatshirt pulled monklike over his head. His face retreated deeper into the hood's cavity, but his hands remained uncovered, bone-white and slim-fingered, worrying at the edges of his jean pockets.

The reeds broke, and in front of us was an empty guard booth and the start of a narrow road that wound its way along the left side of a flat field, past a squat redbrick building and a small lake, then beyond into a dark cluster of pines. The lit windows of a small house flickered distantly behind the branches, and I wondered about who lived there.

"Stay low," Richard said. "We're probably not the only people here on Halloween."

The wind rose up, and a raft of ducks lifted away from the lake, the sound of their wings echoing over our heads and then dispersing into the night. Richard pointed toward the building and told us to run from tree to tree as though dodging sniper fire. We covered each open space quickly and stopped at the foot of the building, Luke and the two girls breathing heavily, Richard unaffected. The structure was only two stories high, with a squat central block and two rambling wings. It was completely decrepit. All the ground-floor windows were boarded up and covered with graffiti; a few boards had been pried loose and hung askew like rotted teeth. Ivy and filth clung to the building's redbrick walls, and weeds pushed up through the concrete at its base. It had never before occurred to me that tearing something down shows more care than letting it slowly fall apart on its own. Neglect is sadder and more brutal than destruction.

Richard took two flashlights out of his backpack, handing one to Luke and keeping the other for himself. A pair of headlights appeared in the pines beyond us, and Richard sucked his teeth. "Security," he said. "Inside. Hurry." He held back a loose board and ushered us through. Beth went first, her skirt flying up as she vaulted into empty space. Hannah followed, and then Luke. The headlights swung around a bend and searched in our direction. I slipped through the small opening and fell to the floor. Richard came last, pulling the board tight behind him. The two flashlights played over a room covered with a thick layer of dirt and littered with beer cans and broken glass. I heard the muffled sound of the pickup truck passing by outside, and then continuing along the road.

"What's the story behind this place?" Luke said.

Richard shook his head. "Besides the obvious? I prefer not to know too many actual details. The stories I make up are better than whatever the truth may be."

"But what's the obvious?"

Richard gestured at the rows of filing cabinets resting against the back wall, and Hannah opened a drawer at random. Inside the drawer were reams of rotting paper sorted into dozens of folders. She picked one out, and dust billowed off it in a choking cloud. "Christina Liebing," she read. "Admitted August fifth, 1942. Residence: Trenton. Date of birth: April ninth, 1923." Hannah looked up. "She was only nineteen." The typed words were crammed onto the page in tightly spaced clumps. Hannah scanned down the form. "Diagnosis: Depression. Patient exhibited minor improvement following repeated ECT." Hannah placed the file back into the drawer and removed a second one. "Sean Blau," she read. "Multiple personality disorder. Patient vacillates between three distinct identities of which the authentic, or original, is at the time of current treatment impossible to determine." Hannah flipped through the fat file. "Patient is permitted to use spoons at mealtimes, but knives and forks are forbidden." Chicken-scratch handwritten reports followed the neatly typed cover pages. Richard took Blau's file from Hannah and stuffed it into his bag.

Somebody had scrawled a huge pentagram in red paint on the wall of the hallway outside the room and more crushed beer cans lined the floor. It was difficult to get a clear picture of what the place actually looked like, of its true dimensions. Our flashlights gave only partial accounts, illuminating a dirty corner, an empty light socket, a snippet of graffiti. The relationship between the inside and the outside of the building remained obscure.

"Look at this," Richard said. The rooms in the second wing were smaller behind thick and rusted metal doors. He directed his flashlight into one of the windowless chambers and let it play over an elevated slab of cracked leather, straps and restraints dangling off its sides. He stole sideways glances at Luke as he pointed out each new outrage, as though noting his responses.

We found the staircase in a large, high-ceilinged atrium. Upstairs housed the sleeping quarters. Most rooms lay completely bare, but some retained their raw metal cots; a few even had moth-eaten linens and towels folded on top of the cots as though awaiting new guests. I wondered what you had to have done to end up in here, and whether places like this even existed anymore. Richard led us to a dead-end hallway and reached up to grab a cord that hung from the ceiling. A trapdoor opened and a ladder slid down. We climbed up one by one.

The roof was flat with a peaked section in the middle and waist-high walls running along the edges. Even though the asylum was only two stories high, there was nothing nearby to block our view. Richard looked at Luke eagerly and with a touch of impatience, as though waiting for someone who was late to arrive.

"Here." He unrolled two blankets from his bag, spread one out, and tucked the other under his arm. "Sit." We sat. "Hannah?" He lifted an eyebrow, and she sat down next to us. Richard and Beth remained standing.

"Where are you going?" Luke asked.

Richard just said, "Have fun, kids," and then he and Beth walked across the roof, climbing over the peaked middle and disappearing on its far side.

Hannah slipped a flask out of her back pocket. "Just because King Richard won't drink doesn't mean none of us can." She took a swig and offered the flask to Luke. He grabbed it without hesitation and guzzled at the whisky, and Hannah laughed without joy. "Easy," she said, "we have all night."

The moon hung heavily behind her. Her face was a black oval in which white teeth flashed and then vanished as quickly as they had appeared. Luke took another slug before he handed the flask back to Hannah, his jaw clenched and his pulse beating furiously everywhere all at once. Hannah reached over me to put her hand on his thigh. "You're shaking," she said. "It's okay." She leaned back, a tiny body against the night sky.

Luke gestured toward the other side of the roof. "What are they doing?"

"What do you think?"

He shrugged, playing the bashful child. He looked around the roof and out onto the grounds. "I don't like this place. What are we doing here?"

"Does it scare you?"

He hesitated. "No. It's just a strange place to be."

"Compared to what?"

"Anywhere else I've been, I guess."

She paused, and then said, "You really want strange, check out the steam tunnels."

"The what?"

"There's a whole network underneath campus. Like an underground labyrinth."

"You've been down there?"

"Of course. You'll go sometime too."

"How do you know?"

Hannah shrugged. "Why miss out?" She glanced toward the other end of the roof. "So. What do you really think of Richard?"

"He's . . . charismatic," Luke said cautiously.

"That's true. But would you call him your friend?"

"Of course," Luke said quickly, then paused. "Why are you asking?"

"Because I think you need friends. You deserve them. But I'm not sure if he's the right kind."

"Are you?"

She ignored the question. "Don't you want to know what he thinks about you?"

"I suppose you're going to tell me either way."

"He finds you fascinating. Intriguing. But that's not a coincidence. I told him about you before you even got here. I grew up in the city too. I had plenty of friends at your high school."

Her voice was flat and I couldn't see her expression. I had no idea if she was lying, and if she was, I didn't understand why.

"Who?"

"It doesn't matter. Lots of people."

"What did they say about me?"

What could they have said? Luke had always been careful to conceal as much as he was able.

"That you were strange. That you had a fucked-up mother. That it seemed like you had a secret you'd been hiding a long time. All of it interested me. I wanted to meet you. They didn't know what your secret was, but I think I do."

Hannah smiled, that flash of white in the black. She pulled from the flask and then put it to Luke's lips. She cradled his head with her other hand and slowly tilted it back as though she were a mother administering medicine to her sick child. "There," she said. She took another pull herself, and then capped the flask and placed it to the side. I raised myself onto my knees at the edge of the blanket. Luke leaned toward her, and she grabbed his shoulders and pulled him in. Her mouth found his, and she bit at his lips. I stood up to look down on the two of them. She shoved him onto his back and straddled his hips. His hands reached up and tentatively felt at her chest, but she swatted them down, and then pulled off her sweater, and the T-shirt and bra underneath. Luke tried to sit up and she shoved him down again. "Try harder," she said. He pushed against her hands on his chest, and finally her elbows broke and he rushed up into her. She took off his sweatshirt and pressed her skin against his. I paced around the blanket and looked at them from every angle, unspeakably jealous. She pushed him back and undid his belt buckle. "I deserve this," I said to Luke, "not you." She yanked his jeans down so they bunched around his sneakers. She straddled him again, and bit at his neck and chest. He lay back and ran his hands gently along her back.

Suddenly she stopped and looked down at him. "Come on," she said. "Fucking do something."

"What?" Luke said.

"Fucking do something. This isn't crazy, this is normal and gentle and boring." She reached down and felt at his boxers. "What are you scared of?"

Luke opened his mouth but didn't say anything. His eyes rolled around until they found mine and that was it. "Enough," I said. I grabbed her shoulders and rolled her off Luke and onto her back. I pinned her arms down, bit at her nipples. She laughed, a harsh sound. "This is funny?" I said. I ripped off her jeans, and still she laughed. I heard the truck drive by. I heard Richard's schoolboy voice float across the roof. Hannah grabbed the back of my head and pulled at my hair. I pressed my fingers into her crotch, twisting the fabric of her underwear to the side. "Stop," Luke said from somewhere behind me, "this is all wrong." "Shut up," I said. Hannah clawed at my boxers and I tore her under-wear off. "There you are," she said. I hooked her knees around my waist and guided myself into her. I felt everything. My skin raged with feeling. And she felt me too. She hissed and dug her nails into the back of my neck. I started pushing against her, and once I started I could not stop.

2

THE NEXT MORNING, I woke up to a cold dorm room. Someone had left the window half open, and damp, chilly air swept across the floor. I rolled over on the bottom bunk; I didn't know why I was in Luke's bed. The end of the night was blurry, flecked with gaps. I had stumbled home at dawn from Hannah's room with coal in my throat and sand in my eyes, Luke trailing drunkenly behind me. I remembered doing a line of cocaine off Hannah's stomach. I remembered biting her cheek. I remembered fucking her on the bare wooden floor of her dorm room while Luke cowered in the corner hiding his eyes. After we were done, I remembered watching her fall asleep wrapped in a ball of blankets underneath her bed. She asked me to stay with her, but I knew she didn't mean it.

I stood up, and the room warped and bubbled like a melting photograph. I shuddered and walked over to the window, and then I saw Luke huddled in the corner, shivering with no blanket and a sweatshirt for his pillow. His eyes were squeezed tightly shut, but he wasn't asleep. On our desk, the telephone message light blinked insistently; outside the window, the sky was low and gray. A volleyball net sagged in its dirt pit in the middle of the quadrangle, and two students in ski jackets and wool hats hurried along the stone paths. I stared out the window for a long time, my head a bucket of cement.

I heard a rustling noise behind me and turned to see Luke rise unsteadily to his feet. His bottom lip was fat and cracked near the left corner, and a chain of purple welts stood out against the white skin of his neck. He raised a finger to his lips and picked at the split. "Daniel," he said. "What the fuck happened last night?"

I didn't know what to say, not only because I couldn't entirely remember, but also because I thought if I told him what I knew, he would never let any of it happen again.

"I don't remember coming home."

"Yeah," I said casually. "Things may have gotten slightly out of hand."

He shook his head, then suddenly rushed out of the room

and down the hallway to the communal bathroom, banging open the door of the nearest stall. I followed, just in time to see the vomit, thin, clear, and alcoholic. He hunched over the toilet until his stomach was empty and the dry heaves passed, then he walked over to the sink, ran the cold water, splashed it across his face. He straightened up and squinted at himself in the mirror. He reached out to touch the glass, his finger leaving smears over his nose and his wide, unmatched eyes. He felt at the welts on his neck, and the Luke in the mirror did the same. He turned away from his reflection then, and looked at me, fearfully, I thought, rubbing the welts and fingering his cracked lip as though he'd come to some new understanding of things. I didn't like what I saw in his expression, and I didn't like the silence that settled down between us, the only sound the humming of the fluorescent lights.

"What?" I said.

He opened his mouth as if to answer, then seemed to think better of it. Instead, he just shook his head again and walked back to the dorm room to sleep it off.

We spotted Hannah in line with a friend at the dining hall the next day. She looked tired and small in her hooded sweatshirt, but I thought of what was contained within that tiny body, its rage and its appetites, and I smiled to know what others didn't. She waved at Luke, and he flushed bright red, hurrying off with his head buried in his tray. He didn't notice it, but I saw the little twist in the corner of her mouth, and I knew she was thinking of me. I was suddenly filled with a new contempt for my own false shape, this image I had always so carefully groomed and maintained. It was irrelevant, no more permanent than Luke's childhood fantasies of dinosaurs and witches. I now understood Luke's body, brittle and flawed as it was, to be my intended and final home, and occupying it my only strategy for survival.

The call from Cassie came that evening. She was back in Providence, painting more canvases of distressed nymphs and mutilated teddy bears. We hadn't talked to her since the first week of school, and she wanted to know how Luke found college life. I leaned in close to hear her voice, and all thoughts of Hannah disappeared. "Ask her to visit," I said, and to my surprise Luke did.

"When?" she said.

"How about this weekend?"

"I guess I'm not doing anything special."

"No date with your boyfriend?"

She laughed. "No boyfriend. The cutest guys here would rather dress me than kiss me."

I don't think Luke knew what she meant, but he laughed anyway. It was decided: she would arrive Saturday afternoon. The ease with which she had spun back into our lives was startling, and it made me wonder if all my restraint had been misguided.

Luke went to Richard for help.

"Your stepsister?" He looked up from a battered copy of the *Physicians' Desk Reference*. "That's an occasion for a party, isn't it?"

"I hope so," Luke said.

Richard tossed him a flyer. "Good thing there already is one." An anime graphic of a cyborg clutching a laser pistol stared up at us with huge purple eyes. Amnesia VI, the flyer said. The Future Was Yesterday. "The design is shoddy, but you get the point." 10 P.M.–6 A.M. One tent, four DJs.

Out in the hallway, I said, "Cassie will think this is stupid."

"Yeah, well," Luke said. "Do you have a better idea?"

She arrived five days later in a billow of cigarette smoke and air kisses. She looked taller than the last time we had seen her—in August, at the Boathouse in Central Park—but she was probably just skinnier. She had dyed her hair blond and cut it into an asymmetrical bob, and replaced her tattered corduroys and Converses with tight black Levi's and snakeskin cowboy boots, but the apple cheeks were intact. I saw her, and she was perfect.

"Well," she said, taking in the sun-spattered quadrangles, "I guess all colleges really are the same." In our dorm room, she showed us a photograph of James Jr. He was almost four years old, holding a water gun in front of a pool somewhere and squinting into the camera like a thug. He looked affronted, as though the photographer were asking far too much of him. "He's a huge brat," Cassie said. "James spoils him to death." She inspected the photographs pinned on the wall above Luke's desk. She tapped a print of Hannah's naked torso arched backward over a couch, her head chopped off by the framing. I wanted to tell her I had taken that picture, and then talked Luke into developing it just the day before.

"Very 1920s. Man Ray. Brassaï. Who's the model?"

"I don't know her name," Luke said.

"You're lying, but I'll respect her privacy."

Embarrassed, Luke handed Cassie the rave flyer. "I thought we might go to this tonight."

"Wow. It's a shame I left the glow sticks in my high school locker."

Luke blinked at her dumbly.

"Sorry," she said, "bad joke. Sure, I don't care." She pinched his cheek. "I want to do what you want to do." She glanced around our dismal little dorm room. "By the way, where am I sleeping?"

⋅⋙⟨⟩⋘⋅

The tent stretched behind the social club that night, crawling across the lawn like a giant black caterpillar. Richard carried a leather satchel, inside of which was a plastic bag containing fifteen one-gram vials of cocaine and one hundred Ecstasy pills, the pills pale yellow and stamped with the Mercedes logo. He had opened the bag in our dorm room, and Luke had hesitated for only a moment before he held out his hand for two pills. Cassie had clapped and laughed. "Fantastic," she said. "So this is what the kids are up to these days. I'll take three, please." She swallowed the first one right there in the room and winked at Luke. "Claire doesn't have to know about this, right?" Already on the walk to the party, she seemed to have struck up some sort of friendship with Richard.

He touched her hair and rubbed the thin fabric of her sweater between two fingers, his accent flawlessly aristocratic, his words tumbling out of his mouth like laughing porcelain children.

We entered the tent and breathed in a mouthful of gamy air. It was pitch black inside except for a thread of UV lights strung above our heads and a handful of strobes placed randomly around the space, all madly blinking out of sequence. A gigantic disco ball studded with what looked like broken glass hung from the highest point of the tent, down at the far end of the long, twisting tunnel. Underneath it, a DJ hunched over two turntables and a collection of computers and beat-up electronic equipment. A wall of stacked speakers roared at an absurd volume. Everybody inside the place had been reduced to silhouettes, loose shadows spinning and merging and coming apart again.

Cassie leaned over to shout into Luke's ear. "Wild," she said. On her other side, Richard's fingertip traced the collarbone jutting out above the stretched neck of her sweater. He whispered something in her ear, making her laugh. I wanted to punch him in the face; how dare he trespass like this. The music staggered out of the speakers and Luke stared up into the UV lights. Spots of phosphorescent lint speckled his black sweatshirt, and the strobe glinted wetly across his eyes. "Well?" I said. He looked at me. "What?" "The pills." He took one out of his pocket and rolled it around between his fingers before swallowing it without water. "Why not?" he said. Next to us, Cassie and Richard were smiling, talking fast, touching each other gently like shy animals. She tried to roll a cigarette, but her fingers fumbled with the damp paper, and the tobacco flakes kept falling out of place. She gave up and took hold of Luke's arm. "This feels wrong, doing this with you here," she said. "But you're okay. You turned out okay." He nodded, and I would have given anything to speak to her, to tell her how I felt about her.

"Don't tell your mother I told you," she said, "but she called me up and asked me to come down to check on you."

"What are you talking about?"

Her pupils were huge, and she stroked Luke's sweatshirt as though it were made of silk. "She says you don't return her calls. She sounded frantic."

So this was why Cassie's visit had been so miraculously simple to arrange; I should have known better.

"She should mind her own business," Luke said.

Cassie smiled absently. "But Luke, you are her business, more than anything else. You always will be. Don't you know that?"

She touched Luke's forehead and turned away from us then, back to Richard and his offer of a cigarette. A mob of kids wearing parachute pants and sucking on pacifiers danced around us like robots. A second DJ elbowed the first out of the way. He wore a gas mask and no shirt, his chest sickly sunken and smooth, and he directed a searchlight around the tent as though hunting for survivors. Something buzzing and nasty whipped out of the speakers, followed sixteen bars later by a ferocious kick drum. Then everything dropped out except a simple piano chord, which grew and grew until it became something enormous, and people lifted lighters over their heads, and then the sound surged and exploded in another direction, the kick drum like artillery, a Klaxon wailing three hundred sixty degrees around my brain, absolute chaos inside and out.

After that, the passage of time became slippery and absurd, like a pig slathered in Vaseline. I kept losing track of Luke, and then he would suddenly show up at my elbow, saucer-eyed and lock-jawed. It was too loud to speak, and the strobes wobbled and shook. I saw Luke take the second pill, again swallowing it dry. I saw Richard trawling the space, drawing people aside, dipping into his satchel. His work seemed altruistic, selfless, and I wanted to tell him he was doing a good job. But I couldn't find Cassie anywhere. Luke appeared at my side, then disappeared just as quickly. The air grew stifling, heavy with smoke and sweat. I smelled pot and the burnt-rubber tang of amyl nitrate. I stood in front of an industrial fan with my arms spread out wide and my eyes closed. My sense of touch was outrageous, impossible. I could feel the sweat drying on my skin with agonizing precision, the moisture wicking away to leave a flaky crust, a snake's scales. I needed to get outside.

I went out the back way past the wall of speakers, pushing through a slit in the tent to suck at the cold, fresh air. I saw a kid sitting at a computer in one of the house's attic windows, typing. I had entirely forgotten that I was on somebody's back lawn, that for the rest of the world time had not slipped off its tracks. I turned around and looked at the tent. It seemed so much smaller from the outside that I felt myself to be a victim of some geometrical sleight of hand. Yet the world did not settle down as I thought it might. Objects retained auras; the streetlamps wore royal halos. Cassie, I thought. Where is she?

I wandered behind the house, off the grass into a small cement lot. Cars glittered as though glazed with sugar. My breath steamed, so I suppose it was cold, even though the air seemed to be the exact same temperature as my skin. I felt the space around me to be an extension of myself, my body turned inside out and opened to the world. My mind reached out and placed objects into my surroundings—I thought of a scarlet Jeep before I saw it; I imagined a cat before it darted by—so I was not surprised when I rounded the far corner of the building and found Cassie leaning back against a cement wall, Richard pressing into her, his hands hooked into the waist of her jeans, their faces joined sloppily together. I stopped twenty feet away and watched. Richard ran his hand underneath Cassie's baggy sweater and pushed the fabric up, exposing a flash of white skin, her stomach sucking in as she inhaled, the bottom row of ribs curving out. He said something in her ear, and she laughed, a high, clear sound, unexpectedly loud in the quiet parking lot. The leather satchel lay off to the side, slouched against the wheel of a station wagon. Cassie's dyed-blond bob left trails against the cement as she moved her head from side to side. I wanted to say something to stop them, but my jaw was fastened shut. My teeth ground against each other, and my tongue sat fat and inert in the middle of my mouth. I turned around and walked back the way I had come.

At the side of the house, a porch stepped down onto the lawn. I sat on the steps and looked at the tent. I heard the throb of techno, but I couldn't figure out if it was coming from inside the tent or somewhere in my own skull. I shook my head, and sounds spun out through the air to land here and there on the lawn. The eastern edge of the sky lifted. Kids walked past me on the porch, moving to and from the tent, the lawn, the inside of the house. At some point, the buzzing in my brain slowed and then ground to a halt. The music went quiet. I began to get cold, and I decided to go home.

I walked down the sheltered avenue, past stone-faced Georgian and Tudor mansions. A light occasionally shone in one of the second-floor bedrooms, but mostly they were dark, the houses withdrawing into themselves, giving away nothing. I turned toward campus, past the engineering quad, low and sad-looking, the computer science building, the technocratic black glass of the economics center. I came to the hushed street that marked the boundary between the school and the town. The quaint shops were shuttered, the immaculate sidewalks deserted. Two county police cars passed each other on the otherwise empty road. I kept my head down and walked on the university's side of the street, entering campus through iron gates.

I slipped into our dorm room just as the sun cracked above the buildings to the east. Nate was gone, probably at his new girlfriend's dorm doing his best to avoid us, and the room was empty. A sort of visual humming gave all the objects an unfocused restlessness, as though everything were just at a momentary pause. I sat down in Luke's desk chair and was suddenly, painfully exhausted. But I couldn't let myself fall asleep. Cassie had to come back here sometime, and I wanted to be awake to greet her. Meanwhile, I had no idea where Luke was. I had not thought it possible for us to be separated for so long, but at the time this idea seemed too complicated to consider clearly. Without thinking, I picked up a quarter off Luke's desk and rolled it across my knuckles, back and forth, the metal glinting in the bright morning light. I flipped the coin into my palm. It sat there, tarnished and solid, unremarkable. But something was strange: how was it that I held this thing? I looked at the hand underneath the coin; its skin was pale, nearly pellucid, its fingers long and delicate. I placed the quarter back on the desk and picked up a pencil. I held it between two fingers in front of my face for a moment, then took hold of it with both hands and snapped it easily in half, letting the two pieces clatter to the floor. I did that, I thought. Without permission or supervision, that was me. To know this was an odd and wonderful feeling. But before I had a chance to explore this new situation, the doorknob rattled, and the door itself shuddered and then abruptly opened to reveal Cassie, giggling and red-cheeked and gorgeous, struggling to extract her borrowed key from the lock. She yanked it free, then saw me and stopped, smiling, just inside the doorway. "Where have you been?" she said. She swayed slightly, and the door swung shut behind her. "I've been looking for you."

I stood, rising carefully out of the desk chair, the unfamiliar sensations of stiffness and sore pain throbbing through my jaw, my feet, the base of my skull. The light pouring through the window was stupidly bright, and it slapped across Cassie's face like an insult.

"At a certain point, enough is enough," I said. "Where's Richard?"

She shrugged and tugged at her sweater. "Crashed out in his room. We've all had enough, I guess." She pointed at the empty bunk bed. "That available? I'm completely shattered."

"Okay," I said. "Take the bottom."

She sighed heavily and removed her sweater and jeans. In her underwear and bra, her body was smooth and marble-white, much as I had imagined it to be. A tiny, fresh-looking tattoo of a compass floated on top of her left shoulder blade and a ring of softer flesh encircled her body just above the waistline of her underwear. I stood five feet from her and didn't dare move; I felt as though at the slightest twitch my body would go flying in ten directions and then crumble to the floor. She rummaged through her bag for a T-shirt and shorts, and then took out a pill bottle from an inside pocket. "Xanax," she said, popping one in her mouth. "For the comedown. Want one?"

"I'm fine."

"You have to sleep sometime."

"Yeah."

She looked at me for a moment, then lay down in the bottom bunk, propping her head up on the pillow and tucking the sheets under her chin like a little girl. I just stood there in the middle of the room looking at her; it was as though I had forgotten what, if anything, was expected of me. She licked her lips and pointed at the desk behind me. "Roll me a cigarette and I'll love you forever." I turned around like an idiot to stare at the pouch of tobacco flakes and pack of papers. I didn't know what came next, and she must have realized it because she said, "Don't worry. I'll tell you what to do." I listened to her instructions. I cradled the paper in my palm and sprinkled in the tobacco. I took it all between my fingers, and I rolled the tube back and forth, smoothing it out until it was even. Finally, I licked the edge and sealed it shut. It is hard to explain how this all felt. Everything seemed alive: the tobacco flakes and the paper in my hands, the glue strip vibrating against my tongue like the wing of an insect. I held the finished cigarette out in front of me, absurdly proud.

"Gold star," Cassie said. She reached out her hand, and I dropped the thing into her palm along with a book of matches I also found on the desk. I sat down cross-legged beside the bed and watched her strike the flame and cup it to her face, the blue smoke gathering around our heads like a thundercloud. I wanted to tell her who I was now, but I didn't know how to begin. She would look at me and she would see Luke; not only that, but she would see a Luke who had lost his grasp on himself, a Luke deluded and desperate. I needed time to reveal myself slowly, in pieces, so that when we reached the point at which I could tell her everything, already part of her would know. But I didn't have that sort of time. I felt sure my occupation of Luke's body was temporary; it had been too easy to be true for more than a few hazy and accidental hours. So instead I just sat there and said nothing. We were both silent through the smoking of her entire cigarette, the only sound the crackle of paper crisping to ash. When she was finished, she dropped the filter into a half-empty water bottle and rolled over to face the wall.

"Pull the shades, would you," she said, her voice drowsy, submerged.

I got up from the floor and did as she asked, the sunlight painting hot white edges around the dark green vinyl.

"You're a sweetheart, Luke," she said, and with that she fell silent. Her breathing grew long and regular in the dim room. I stood by the window for a long time, watching the shape of her body rise and fall underneath the sheet. Her dyed hair pulsed softly on the pillow as though it were a separate and remarkable creature. I took a step toward her, and suddenly I felt as though Luke were watching me, but from somewhere within, somewhere inside of me. I reached above his desk and took one of the Noh masks down off its hook. I placed the mask over my face and stretched the wire across the back of my head. The inside of the mask smelled of wood and rot, the musty odor of old books, and my breath echoed in my ears.

I walked across to the bed and stood over Cassie. Her body was slack as I turned her away from the wall, her skin giving off heat through the thin cotton of her T-shirt. A small drool stain on the pillow marked the place where her mouth had been, and there was not the faintest flickering behind her eyelids. The tranquilizers were doing their job, but still I was careful as I peeled the sheet off her body. Her shorts had twisted and bunched up around her hips, and the black edge of her underwear curved out from underneath. Her T-shirt, too, had ridden up above her belly, and I began the delicate process of lifting it away from her skin and drawing it toward her head and shoulders. She had removed her bra somehow without my noticing, and I paused when I reached her breasts. I held the T-shirt up with one hand and reached out with the other to lightly stroke first the left and then the right nipple, the skin there velvety and the color of wet clay, ringed by tiny, almost invisible white hairs.

I stroked her again, and she stirred, shifting her weight slightly but unmistakably from one hip to the other, and then there suddenly blossomed in the center of my forehead the sharpest, most excruciating pain I had ever felt, as though a burning-hot spear were forcing itself through the inside wall of my skull and out into the room. I lurched away from the bed, the pain spreading across my face. A violent wrenching feeling gripped my head and body, and I felt myself pulled sideways, angrily, with great force. I staggered into the desk, and when I regained my balance, Luke stood between me and the bed, the red mouth of the Noh mask grinning like a fresh wound.

<hr />

Eight hours later, Luke put Cassie on a north-bound train and then climbed the old sycamore in the courtyard behind our dormitory. Neither of us had slept. Luke had kept a vigil by the bunk bed through the morning and deep into the afternoon until Cassie woke up, disheveled and unremembering. I just leaned against a wall the whole time, watching him watch me; there had been no point in denying anything or making any excuses. We had not yet spoken a word to each other. Cassie kissed Luke's cheek, a kaffiyeh wrapped around her throat and giant sunglasses hiding half her face, then she boarded the train and was gone.

Now we were twenty-five feet off the ground, squinting down into the courtyard through a lattice of dead branches. The sun set, and we watched the streetlamps one by one fill with light. A bicycle—a Schwinn, originally painted some shade of dark green underneath the rust—perched above us, wedged into the crook of two branches as if marooned by a flood, its tires bald and a blanched tennis ball jammed into the front spokes. During our first two months here, Luke liked to climb up to sit near the bicycle and invent elaborate stories about how it got there: catapults, telekinesis, strange magnetisms. But this evening he said nothing and just stared down onto the heads of the students hustling across the courtyard below. Finally, I broke the silence: "So what happens next?" Luke leaned back against the trunk, his legs straddling a knotty branch and purple smudges shadowing his half-closed eyes. I suddenly feared he might nod off and topple out of the tree. "Well?" But he wouldn't answer me, and we stayed speechless high in the branches until the sky was completely black and the climb down was like sinking to the bottom of a well.

We were back at the campus train station by ten o'clock the next morning. After twelve hours of sleep, Luke no longer appeared ill, but he continued to keep his mind to himself. The ride into the city was the same as any other: the trash-littered embankments by the side of the tracks; the sad houses with their peeling paint and pathetic lawn toys; the brief, blurred glimpses of the clogged Turnpike; the massive shipping containers at the docks outside Elizabeth; the jets screaming overhead near Newark Liberty. Penn Station was just as predictable: dirty, foul-smelling, crowded. Infested by disgusting specimens of the human animal. I liked to imagine how these spaces would look wiped clean of people: an empty train, a deserted Eighth Avenue, a lonely Times Square. I couldn't think of a single place that would not be better off. Even Penn Station, grimy and maligned, would be ennobled by such a purging.

We took the subway to Ninety-sixth Street. Most of the people in our car looked like they would rather be hunkered down in their apartments, strapped into their beds, hidden away from the city and everyone in it. Their bodies assumed defensive postures; they clenched against the screeching movement of the train, the unwelcome attention of other passengers. Some slept, but with their mouths open, circulating bad air. At Columbus Circle, a horde of teenagers trundled shopping bags onto our car, and I shrank back against the far side doors. "What are we doing here?" I said. "I didn't want to come back." Luke said, "I don't care what you want," and then he clapped a hand over his mouth, as though he had broken some new rule he had set for himself.

We were the only ones to get off at our stop. The park crouched low and wet under leaden clouds, everything colored in shades of brown and gray. A doorman whose name I had never learned let us into the lobby and nodded at Luke. We walked to the elevator, and I felt his eyes follow us all the way across the marble lobby. Once the elevator doors shut, I said, "So are you going to tell me how long we're staying?"

Luke half-smiled. "Why, do you have other plans?" As soon as the words were out of his mouth, he banged a fist into the wall and said, "Fuck. Can you just shut up for a while, please? It will make things easier."

"Easier for what?" I said.

Luke didn't answer, and the elevator deposited us on the third floor. He unlocked the front door, and there was the familiar foyer: the charcoal Nightingale Press emblem, the obscure black-and-white prints. The lights were off and the apartment was empty. We weren't there long. Luke dropped his bag in his room and used the telephone to arrange some sort of appointment of which I couldn't catch the details. Then he walked into Claire's bedroom and opened the door of the second closet, where she kept Venetia's things. The closet was a walk-in, almost a small room of its own, with a mirrored back wall and racks of dresses and skirts and coats hanging two deep on either side. Luke reached up to pull the light cord, and the clothes gave up their colors, scarlet and turquoise and plum, in patterns of gingham and houndstooth and polka-dot. Tissue paper filled out their shapes, and their plastic wrapping rustled as Luke bent to brush his hands over the rows of pumps and boots and sandals lining the floor. He straightened and noticed the cocktail dress hanging off a hook on the inside of the closet door. He took a handful of the black silk, rubbing it between his fingers, and then he let it go. The dress slouched back on its hook, an empty sheath of cloth. He turned the lights off and we left the apartment.

We walked down Central Park West and turned right on Eighty-third Street, and I suddenly knew where we were going. "Is this really necessary?" I said, but Luke was done talking to me. In Dr. Claymore's waiting room, the receptionist gave us a starched smile: "I don't think he'll have an opening until later this afternoon, Luke." "You mentioned that on the phone," Luke said, "and I don't mind waiting." We sat down across the room from a woman holding a young girl in her lap. The girl, about six years old, squirmed and grabbed at her mother's hair, scrabbling her feet against the woman's thighs as though trying to propel herself into the air. The mother whispered something fierce in her daughter's ear, and the child quieted and turned around to face us. Her eyes roamed wildly until they found me, and then she grew still, folding her hands into her lap like an old lady. Her mother bounced her softly on her knees, but the girl barely seemed to notice; her solemn eyes did not break from mine until the office intercom buzzed and the receptionist called the pair into the back for their session.

We waited three hours and four patients until Claymore found a suitable gap for us in his schedule; the combination of boredom and expectant tension during these hours was, I felt, punishment enough for whatever transgressions of mine had so disturbed Luke, and I told him so. When we were finally called to the back, Claymore waved Luke to the patient's chair and steepled his baby-hands underneath his chin. "Well, this is a nice surprise," he said. "What's on your mind?"

Luke sat quietly for a moment, as though unsure how to begin, then said, "I want to talk about when my mother first brought me in to see you."

"Let's talk about it."

"I mean literally. When was our first session?"

"About thirteen years ago, I believe."

"But more precisely. You have it all written down in a file, don't you?"

Claymore frowned. "Yes, I'm sure I do. But why does it matter?"

"You're here to help me, right? That would help."

Claymore buzzed the receptionist, who a minute later dropped off a few fat manila folders. Claymore flipped to the back of one of the files. "You first saw me on April ninth, approximately thirteen and a half years ago." He looked up through his bifocals. "We started our weekly sessions immediately following that."

"What was our focus those first months?"

"I could list a range of topics, but that wouldn't really get at the substance of our sessions. The simplest answer is we talked about whatever was on your mind." He paused. "What do you remember us talking about?"

Luke rubbed his eyes with the heels of his hands. "Look. If I remembered well enough, I wouldn't be here asking you."

"Maybe it would be better to talk about what's bothering you now."

"What's bothering me now is that I can't remember how any of this started."

Claymore shifted forward in his seat. "Any of what?"

After a moment, Luke said, "We've talked about the dog. Midnight. Which was why, I think, my mother brought me to you in the first place. I don't blame her. It's a horrible thing, and I'm sorry, and I've said I'm sorry, even though I don't think I had any idea what I was doing. Look at your notes. That's why she called you, right?"

"That was the catalyst, yes. Although, as we've also talked about before, what worried her wasn't so much what happened to Midnight as your refusal to accept responsibility for your actions. Even if they were a mistake."

"She claimed this was a pattern?"

Claymore fiddled with the papers on his desk. "Is that how you remember it?"

"We don't need to talk about how I remember it when the facts are written down in front of you."

"Okay, I'll play along. What she told me, and what you yourself told me at first, was that you blamed Midnight's accident on an imaginary friend. Which was troubling to her, although, in my opinion, a not entirely unnatural response for somebody your age and in your position at the time."

"She talked about this friend with you."

"I feel like you know the answers to these questions already, Luke."

Luke clasped his hands together, suppressing some gesture of impatience. "I'm asking you when she first heard me mention him. I can honestly say I don't know the answer to that."

243

Was this the purpose of our tedious visit? Why didn't he just ask me? I remembered our first meeting clearly: the playground, the sandpit, the dinosaur fantasy, in which I participated and, naïve as I was, believed to be something other than childhood hysteria. Luke introduced me to Claire right there on the Fifth Avenue sidewalk, and I thought at the time that by acknowledging me she was doing more than humoring her son.

Claymore looked down at his notes. "Let's see," he said, thumbing through the sheets. "She said it was during the fall, soon after your father had moved out."

"Okay," Luke said. "Anything else?"

"Actually, yes." Claymore adjusted his glasses. "She said you first mentioned your friend on the same day your father made what she called his 'victory lap.'" He looked up. "I believe she meant the last visit he paid to your apartment in his effort to finalize the divorce."

"Do you have the date?"

"Nothing more specific than November, although I'm sure that's something your mother would know. Now, Luke, I would never discourage a reexamination of this time in your life. It's important. But perhaps we can move away for a moment from the dates and the particulars and talk a little about why you rushed back from college and sat in my waiting room for three hours just to ask me these questions."

"Isn't it good enough that I wanted to know?" Luke pulled a check from his back pocket and dropped it on the desk. "I have to go. Thanks for seeing me on such short notice."

"Wait a minute—" Claymore stood up, but by the time he was around the desk, Luke had already slipped out of the office and down the corridor to the waiting room, and we were out on the street before anybody could try to stop us.

"I could help you," I said to Luke. "What do you want to know?" He did his best to ignore me as we quickly walked west, keeping his eyes fixed straight in front of him. I looked down at my current shape: formless black pants and a droopy sweater-like thing covering up an indifferent body. I didn't even want to imagine what my face looked like. I had been neglecting my appearance ever since the night with Hannah had made it clear my fastidiousness was a waste of time. But perhaps this indifference made it too easy for Luke to dismiss me. I quickly cleaned myself up, straightening my shoulders and spine, sloughing off the loose, characterless clothing and replacing it with a slim pinstripe suit.

"Luke," I said. "Come on, we can figure this out together, whatever it is."

He looked at me, but if he appreciated my efforts to tidy up, he gave no sign of it. "This is the last thing I'm going to say to you today: keep your fucking mouth shut. I need to think." And with that he turned his back on me and headed into the park.

We walked the dull and muddy paths for the entire afternoon, not even stopping for Luke to eat. I hated every minute of it. I didn't understand his new obsession with things that had happened over a decade before. Worse, I didn't know how much, and for how long, I was going to pay for my mistake with Cassie. I had not been thinking clearly that morning, but my punishment so far—Luke's silence and his inexplicable behavior—seemed unreasonable, and held within itself the promise of more of the same. I had made such progress during our first months at college that it was especially painful to cede any ground now.

Finally it grew dark, and Luke became too cold to continue in his wanderings. We made our last push north and emerged across the street from Claire's building. Upstairs, the apartment was dark and quiet as before, but when we stepped farther into the room I saw a man's black leather jacket hanging off a doorknob. Its shoulders had a distinctive ribbed design I recognized but could not place. I was about to point it out when we both heard low voices coming from the back of the apartment. Luke walked across the foyer and down the hallway, the talk growing louder until we stopped in front of Claire's half-open door.

"Hello?" Her voice wavered in the stillness of the apartment.

Luke said nothing.

Then a man spoke: "Luke, is that you?"

"Herzen," I said.

Luke pushed open the door. Claire and Gregory Herzen lay together on the low bed. The shades were drawn, and Claire had pulled the sheets up to her chin. Her eyes were wide and glittering; her dark hair swirled around her pale face. Herzen sat up at her side. His chest was covered with a thick mat of black hair and his shaved head gleamed in the light of a bedside candle, and I was suddenly sure this had been happening for years.

"Sweetie," Claire said. She sounded as though she were choking. "You didn't tell me you were coming home."

Luke didn't say anything; he just stood in place with his arms slack at his sides. He looked stupid, soft-brained. The moment hung, suspended like a drop of water from a leaking faucet, until Herzen wrapped a sheet around his waist, stood, and circled the bed. He was thick, compact, a well-intentioned ball of purpose. He held up a palm in placation, like a politician or a priest. "Luke, buddy, I'm sorry you had to see this." He looked ridiculous, vaguely Roman, one hand in midair, the other clutching at the sheet. I watched his bare feet with their angry little clusters of hair on each toe. The sheet bunched as it met the floor, and I kept hoping it would catch his step, that he would fall face-first onto the mahogany just to complete the absurdity of the scene. But Herzen didn't trip. Instead he reached out his free hand to touch Luke's shoulder.

Luke slapped it away. "Don't touch me."

"Luke," Claire pleaded. She sounded like his cheating wife, not his mother. She moved as if to get up, but she couldn't really do anything. She was trapped in the bed, held in place by her nakedness. I laughed at these two people, supposedly adult, supposedly serious, but so ashamed of their bodies that they covered themselves up in embarrassment and were left looking like humiliated children.

"Can you please go wait in your room?" Claire said. "Just give me a minute, please."

Luke seemed ready to argue, but after a moment he turned and stalked into his bedroom, where he sat on the edge of his bed and dared me to say something.

"Don't be angry with your mother." Herzen appeared in the doorway, back in his uniform of black jeans and a black T-shirt.

Luke glared at him. "She's fragile, Gregory. What are you doing?"

"She's not a child. She can do what she wants."

"She doesn't know what she wants."

Herzen sighed. "That's not fair, or even true."

"You're a scavenger."

"You can think what you want about me, but your mother deserves better."

"Better than what?" Luke said. "Better than me?"

"That's not what I meant." Herzen frowned, deep furrows stacking up across his forehead. The skin on his shaved head looked soft and plastic, like flesh-colored Play-Doh. "There's nothing I can do about this now," he said, and then he retreated into Claire's bedroom, closing the door behind him.

Fifteen minutes later, Claire sat at the kitchen table drinking tea and wearing a black silk robe pulled tight beneath her throat. Herzen had been dismissed, and we were back to our familiar triangle, Claire and Luke facing each other across the table while I stood off to the side like some peculiar kind of judge.

Claire said, "Why didn't you tell me you were coming?"

"I wasn't sure if I was going to spend the night," Luke said. "I didn't want to make a big deal out of it."

"So instead we have this." Claire spread her hands in a gesture that could have included any number of things.

Luke shrugged. "If you're talking about Gregory, I'll get over it."

"You're angry. I can tell."

"Not at you."

"At Gregory, then."

Luke shrugged again. "This is not something we need to talk about now. Or ever, really."

Claire pulled her dark hair back into a severe bun, the transformation from sexual subject to mother complete. "Don't blame Gregory," she said. "I'm still alive. I make choices, good and bad. But either way they're mine to make." She was speaking as though she hadn't left scores of agitated messages on Luke's dorm-room voice mail; as though she hadn't called Cassie down from her cloud of pot smoke and acrylic fumes to pay Luke an investigative visit; as though she hadn't done what she had done and Luke didn't know what he knew. This was the fiction of Claire the competent, independent individual, and it was impossible to tell if she performed this sleight of hand on herself or if it was only for our benefit. Either way Luke let it pass, relieved she hadn't thought to ask what he was doing home in the first place.

As if to show he wasn't angry at anybody, Luke accompanied his mother to the press offices the next morning. On the taxi ride down, Claire halfheartedly asked whether he was missing any classes. He gave his head an emphatic shake—"Canceled. Would I be here otherwise?"—and as we pulled up in front of the familiar sooty building, she looked grateful to accept this nonsense. Upstairs, the office never changed: antiquated, cramped, busy with the crackle of phones, faxes, computers. I spotted Herzen near the back of the room, hunched over his keyboard, his shoulders drawn up to his ears as though by invisible hooks.

Claire made a fuss of presenting her son the college scholar, as though he had just returned from war or some perilous adventure. Her employees smiled and patted Luke on the back, apparently committed to ignoring the absurdity of the situation. Claire ushered Luke to the meeting table, presented him with a mug of coffee, asked if he wanted to look at some manuscripts for her. He shook his head: "I'm fine. Just do what you need to, Mom. Don't worry about me." Herzen turned away from his desk at the sound of Luke's voice and gave him a strange half-nod, half-shrug, somehow apologetic and defiant all at once.

I glanced at Claire, who had walked over to her own desk and was ignoring both Herzen and Luke. It seemed their affair was a secret—or at least had the pretense of being a secret—to the rest of the office. Herzen turned back to his work, and I searched Luke's face for a reaction. I saw only the slightest tightening in the set of his jaw, but it was enough. He hadn't forgiven a thing.

After a few minutes, when the office had absorbed the disturbance of our arrival, Luke stood from the meeting table and moved over to the bookshelf that hid the wall between the room's two largest windows. I inspected the dusty spines of the press's entire three-decade catalogue of detectives, double-crossings, and inexplicable, implacable evil, the simple nightingale drawing repeated hundreds of times in black, white, or red, like some discursive process of evolution. I saw the book Luke was looking for just as he did, but still he hid the copy of *Shadow Life* among a few other randomly selected titles, as though I somehow wouldn't notice it.

I stood at his shoulder as he read, but he angled the book so I couldn't see the words. It didn't matter; I remembered well enough, although this time the pages were unmarred by Venetia and Claire's scrawl. Luke found whatever passage he was looking for, and he copied out some lines onto a piece of computer paper. He read over the paper, then folded it into a tiny square and slipped into his back pocket.

While Luke continued to read, I watched Herzen work. He had a pile of manuscript pages at his elbow and he made marks on the pages with a red pencil, stopping every ten minutes or so to input his changes onto an open file on his computer. He had a habit of pinching and tugging at the skin between his eyebrows, twisting it as though it were a screw fastening his face onto the bone underneath. He took a phone call and propped his big black boots up onto his desk like some kind of cowboy. I watched Claire just a few desks away, ignoring her computer to scribble notes that she passed off to her staff, who circled and flowed around her desk with orchestrated deference. Despite its placement in a back corner, Claire's desk was unmistakably the center of the office, and I imagined the black hole of her absence on those days she stayed home.

At lunchtime, Herzen rapped the meeting table with his knuckles as he walked past. "Need anything from the outside world, buddy?"

Luke started from his book. "What?"

"Like food, I mean." Herzen flashed a grim smile.

"I'm not hungry. But . . ." Luke looked toward Herzen's desk. "Maybe I could use your computer while you're gone? I need to send an e-mail."

"Go ahead."

"And . . ."

"Yeah?"

Luke waved the copy of *Shadow Life*. "This author. Did she write anything else?"

Herzen took the book and looked at the back-cover flap. "Oh, yeah, her. It was before my time, obviously, but it's a bit of an in-famous thing."

"What is?"

"This girl, Alexandra Tithe, was twenty-five or something when she wrote the book. She sent the manuscript in, and then killed herself about a week before it was published."

"You're kidding."

"No. There were rumors that she seemed to consider the book in some ways autobiographical, which, if you read the thing, is rather frightening. She drowned herself, just like the girl in her story." He seemed about to say *And just like your grandmother,* but caught himself in time. "Here." He handed the book back to Luke. "Just another cheerful Nightingale Press anecdote. I'll be back in a few."

Luke watched Herzen leave, then returned the novel to its place on the shelves and walked over to the empty desk. Luke hated using computers and his e-mail turned out to be utterly uninteresting—a note to his photography professor about missing class—but it was while zoning out on the screen that I saw my opportunity.

"You don't have to answer me," I said, "but please hear me out." Luke said nothing, and I took it as my cue to continue. "You can tell Claire whatever you want, but I know you're still angry at Gregory, and I don't blame you. Your mother's a fragile woman. We've disagreed over our feelings toward her in the past, but there's no point in denying this fact. And Gregory is taking advantage of her. Think back to when she was home ill last fall. I didn't get the sense that his visit to the apartment was unprecedented, did you? And now—"

"Stop," he said, and then looked around to see if anybody had heard him. "I get it," he murmured. "I agree. So what?"

"So now's your chance to get him back." I pointed at the open file I had seen Herzen working on. "That's the first to go. Then all the rest."

Luke blinked at me, then glanced back at the computer screen.

"Hurry," I urged, "he'll be back soon."

We took a look together around the room: nobody was paying any attention to us. People were eating lunch at their desks or chatting on the telephone; a distracted mood was in the air. We saw Claire bent over a colleague's desk near the door, going over some kind of spreadsheet. "Fuck him," Luke said, and then he deleted the open file and dozens more, whole folders of edits and contracts in progress, the entire trove of Herzen's working materials dumped into the trash and then dispersed into meaningless bytes.

"Done," Luke said.

"No." I pointed to Herzen's open e-mail account. "This is the best part."

And so we quickly composed the e-mail to Claire—terse, vulgar, unforgivable—and I showed Luke how to postdate it until later that evening, something I'd learned from watching Nate screw with his friends, and for a moment it didn't matter that our trick would never hold up for very long, that it wouldn't be difficult for Herzen to prove his innocence. But at the time this seemed impossibly abstract and removed: we would be back at college and we would get a phone call. Claire would be furious, and so on, and so what?

We hit Send and then found Claire back at her own desk.

"Mom." Luke touched her shoulder. "I thought we could go out to lunch before I catch my train."

"Oh," Claire said. "I thought you were staying for dinner."

"Sorry. I have to get back."

"It's okay. Plans change." She stuffed some papers into her bag, then looked up at her son's face and smiled. "What did you have in mind?"

3

WE FOUND RICHARD in his dorm room
as soon as we were back on campus. He opened the door with a
bleary-eyed frown, but quickly flexed his smile at the sight of Luke
in the flesh. "Where the fuck have you been?" he said, ushering
us inside. Luke was sorry he had disappeared on Saturday night.
He was sorry he'd been MIA for a few days. He hoped there
were no hard feelings. Richard graciously inclined his head, told
us he'd been worried. "Rough night. I've been laying low myself."

Luke snorted a line with him to celebrate his return to the fold, and they laughed like jackals, the two of them, high as balloons in a cloudless desert sky, fucked up and flying at 6:00 P.M. on a November Tuesday.

"I owe you." Richard winked at Luke. "After you disappeared, that was the best night I've had in quite a while." You piece of shit, I thought. Just keep smiling. He lit a cigarette and leaned back in his desk chair. "Hannah's been looking for you too." He waggled his eyebrows at Luke. "She wants more of whatever you gave her."

"Yeah," Luke said. "But I don't know if that's going to happen again."

Richard narrowed his eyes, and I wondered how much Hannah had told him. "But the two of you are just getting started." He exhaled through his nose like a cartoon bull. "I imagine it only gets better from here."

"We'll see," Luke said. "I'll call her when I call her, right?"

"Whatever you say." Richard shrugged. "I'm just trying to help."

They spoke for a while longer, and I occupied myself by poking around Richard's painfully neat room, a room so spartan it seemed temporary, like a movie set. Eventually Luke took a bump for the road and made his excuses. As he turned to leave, Richard grabbed his arm. "One more thing." Richard looked off to the side, almost shy. "I neglected to get Cassie's number in all the rush. I thought maybe you could help me out."

Luke smiled. "I'll see what I can do," he said, and then we headed out into the damp evening.

"You're not actually going to give it to him."

"Maybe. I don't think it would bother me."

"But it's the same as it is with Herzen. It's arrogance. These are people who shouldn't be allowed to keep getting whatever they want."

"Maybe," he said again, but this time he sounded less sure of himself.

Drizzle slicked the stone paths as we made our way toward the heart of campus. Snatches of laughter and jagged music burst out from behind the drawn shades of the dorms; underneath the wet night pulsed a kind of subterranean energy, a covert charge. Luke lowered his head against the weather. He moved with purpose, and we arrived quickly at the doors of the glass-walled library. He flashed his ID, and we were through into the echoing lobby. We paused for a moment as Luke inspected the directory before heading down the stairs to the basement.

I wanted to ask what we were doing here, but I thought given the tenuousness of my current situation it was best to wait and see. The lower levels turned out to be where the university stored its vast periodical archives in filing cabinets full of miles of microfilm. Luke had never been down here before, and he wandered the endless rows of cabinets, squinting at the typed labels affixed to each drawer in a state of agitation. I couldn't help him because I didn't know what we were looking for. The floor was quiet and, as far as I could tell, empty, but Luke didn't seem to be in the mood to ask anyone else for help anyway. Finally, he stopped and opened a long, shallow drawer packed with small cardboard boxes, each labeled with a string of letters and numbers. The label on the drawer read "New York Times, 1990–1994," but he tucked his chosen box under his arm before I could read its individual label.

Luke took the box to one of the dozen microfilm readers at the back of the floor. He opened the box and then frowned at the spool of film, and I realized he didn't remember how it worked. There was a secrecy about Luke's project that I didn't like, and I felt, perhaps irrationally, that it wasn't in my best interests to help. But if the e-mail to Claire was the first step in regaining the trust I had lost with Cassie's visit, it was small gestures like this that would be the second. So I spoke up and reminded Luke how to unspool the film, how to slide it into the machine and snap it in place, how to scroll through the strip, how to rotate and focus and enlarge the image.

Luke scrolled through the entire edition of the first day he chose without giving any headline more than a cursory look. When he was finished, he scrolled back until he located the Metro section. He seemed to memorize where it was in relation to the rest of the day's paper, and as he moved forward to each consecutive day, he went straight to that section, his eyes bright and feverish in the light of the screen. But for the first two weeks of the month he had chosen, November, he came away from the Metro pages disappointed. I saw reports of rapes, muggings, and a budget crisis, of crack, Lotto, and all manner of domestic atrocities, but none of these were what Luke was after.

As the days scrolled by, I slowly realized what we were doing sequestered in this basement on a rainy Tuesday night. But this foreknowledge didn't help me when, a minute later, the familiar headshot slid onto the screen. I recognized it even before Luke zoomed in on the surly, blurred face. I took in his sullen expression, and a bilious feeling started somewhere in the center of me and spread outward in all directions, like oil poured into a frying pan. Luke stared at the headshot and then scrolled down to the larger photograph of police officers and well-dressed citizens staring down and out of the frame. I felt infected, corroded. It was as though looking at these photographs again had released a poison that was now eating its way through whatever sense I had of myself, as though my entire self-conception was softening and then disintegrating like paper in water.

Above the two images, the headline read: "Fifth Avenue Fall Ruled Suicide."

***

The secret smile appeared on Luke's face before he went to sleep that night and barely left it again the entire week that followed. If before he had moved through his days at college in a kind of anxious fog, he now glided above them, weirdly serene and untroubled. But this was not the way it was with me. I preferred to ignore things I didn't understand; yet this was not something

I could do when those things were thrown back in my face with such violence that they became all I saw.

I couldn't explain the anxiety the newspaper article awakened inside me. That sullen young man was just one of the dozens, maybe hundreds, of people who died in New York City every day. The article gave some personal details that added up to exactly nothing; there was only the coincidence of our proximity to his death. But I couldn't shake the feeling of recognition that grew stronger the more I tried to dismiss it as baseless. What bothered me even more than this was Luke's reaction to reading the piece; he seemed relieved of some heavy burden. Maybe on its own this should not have been worrisome, but by this point in our time together, I had to assume that any inexplicable change in his behavior was a reason for concern. But when I asked him what the article meant to him, he narrowed his eyes and said, "What does it mean to *you*?" and I had no answer. I needed to understand what bearing all of this had on the only thing that really mattered: the adoption of Luke's body as my own. I decided I had to force the issue, or else I risked things slipping entirely out of my control.

The day after we returned to campus the calls from Claire began and they didn't stop. Or I had to assume they were from Claire; Luke never answered the phone anymore, and he told Nate not to bother giving him any messages. Whomever they were from, they kept coming, the ringing insistent and unrelenting until Luke unplugged the phone cord. But even the thought of a furious and possibly unstable Claire couldn't shatter Luke's calm. He went to his classes as usual—and, as usual, let me handle most of the workload—yet his mind was entirely elsewhere. He stopped by Richard's room every evening for some cocaine and one-sided conversation, evading his requests for Cassie's phone number with increasingly implausible excuses. The eerily placid days passed until a week after our evening in the library I finally couldn't stand it any longer.

"Luke," I said. "Please. You have to tell me what's going on. Is it Cassie? Is that what's bothering you?"

We were walking through the woods behind the graduate college just before dusk. There had been a dusting of snow the night before, and Luke paused to carve an X with the toe of his sneaker into one of the shaded patches that had evaded the day's wan sun. He smiled down at his marking. "You think about Cassie more than I ever have."

"I mean what happened when she visited. Because I apologized already. What more do you want me to do?"

He looked up at me. "Nothing's bothering me, Daniel. You're the one who seems upset." He started walking again, and I hurried to follow. Over his shoulder he said, "Do you remember when we first met?"

"Sure. Of course. It was in the playground by the Met. We played a game with your water pistols. You were there with your mother."

"And you were alone."

"Before I met you, yes."

"Right."

"So what?" I said. "What's your point?"

He stopped again and turned around to look at me. "What were you doing that afternoon before you met me?"

I blinked at him. My mind raced back through my memories of that day. I could picture the playground in crystalline detail: the sickly gray shade of the sand, the chipped red paint on the slide, even the tread of the tire swings. I remembered the vivid fantasy of the tyrannosaurus, the cool feel of the sand on my stomach, the sound of Claire's voice calling out for her son. But I kept reaching further back, and Luke's face close in front of mine was the first thing I could grasp. Before that there was nothing. He knew it too, and nodded, satisfied.

We walked in silence for a few minutes until we reached the sharp cut of a stream. The stream didn't flow; it just rested, black and scum-flecked, in the basin of its raw trench. Luke leaned over to spit into the cut. He watched his saliva float on top of the water until a breeze scuffed the surface. Our reflections were blurred together as the wind rubbed the water, and then a cloud covered the sun and blotted us out like a bottle of spilled ink. Luke turned to me. "You said you wanted to help."

I nodded cautiously.

"I've been thinking about what you said about Richard. About his arrogance. I've been thinking about some of the things he's done, some of the things he's said to me. You might be right."

"Okay," I said.

"I just want to scare him," he said. "Like with Omar. Nothing more. Just to show him how it feels. And I want you to help me. Can you do that?"

I wondered why he would bring this up now, whether it was some kind of trap. But it didn't matter if it was; I had nothing to lose. "Of course," I said. "That's why I'm here."

⊷⊶⊷

The next night we led Richard onto the lawn behind the campus's newest dormitories—modernist white boxes, like overgrown building blocks—and crouched over a manhole sunk deep into the grass. It was three in the morning; there was no one around. Richard pulled on a pair of batting gloves and flexed his hands. "I've wanted to do this for a while, but no better time than the present, right?" He took a vial out of his back pocket and tapped a finger of powder onto his university ID. "Colombian courage?" He held out the card, and Luke took his bump with a gasp. Richard did his own quickly, without fuss, and then pulled the hood of his sweatshirt up over his head and curled his gloved fingers around one of the manhole's handles. Luke grabbed the other handle, and they lifted the iron disc out of its slot. It made a rough sound, like sunken ships scraping across the bottom of the ocean, and I peered down into a perfectly black circle. According to the rudimentary maps we had found online, the steam tunnels ran underneath almost the entire campus, a warren of maintenance rooms, water pipes, and ventilation shafts. Ever since Hannah mentioned them to us, I had wanted to see them for myself, and I convinced Luke they were perfect for our current purposes. This time I would go first. I swung my legs into the center of the circle and climbed down the ladder, moving swiftly into the darkness. I descended until I pushed my lower foot out for the next rung and found only air. I paused, but Luke kept coming, and Richard above him. I had no choice but to let go. I pushed off and found myself on all fours on a dirt-dusted cement floor. Luke joined me, switched on his flashlight, and told Richard to pull the manhole shut behind him. The disc fell into place with a hollow sound, cutting off what was left of the sky.

Richard took out his own flashlight and sprayed its beam around the space. We couldn't see much, but there wasn't much to see anyway. Darkness fell back to reveal patches of concrete and pipes running along a section of the low ceiling. The heat was savage, dry and suffocating. Everything was silent except for our breath and the sound of the steam rushing through the pipes, a soft hissing sigh, the labored inhalations of an asthmatic giant. There was something sad in the noise. Richard flicked the beam of his flashlight at Luke's face. "So we're down here. Now what?"

Luke looked at me to lead the way. The low ceiling forced the two of them to stoop like apes. Their flashlights played over the usual detritus of abandoned places, the same garbage we had found in the asylum: faded beer cans, broken glass, plastic wrappers. Earlier visitors had scratched slogans into the walls: *Ted Loves Samantha. Fuck Economics. We Were Here First.* Every few minutes the flashlights found a vertical shaft that led up to a manhole, and each time Luke lied: "Sealed shut. The one we used is the only way out." A film of dust had settled over Luke's clothes and face, sticking to the wetness of his eyes and mouth. I imagined him standing perfectly still until the dust covered every inch of his body, and then slipping out from underneath to leave a hollow shell in his shape. The tunnel took an abrupt turn and I held up my hand.

Richard pushed past us to shine his light around the corner. The passage dropped off, but it was difficult to see how far. The flashlight showed a snarl of copper pipes clotting the narrow space, and there seemed to be only a small gap through which we would have to lower ourselves. I grabbed one of the pipes and carelessly descended into the tangle below. I knew the pipes were hot enough to blister skin, but I felt no pain. The close, thick air, too, was a fact I noticed but did not truly suffer. I had grown used to the ease with which I could move through the physical land-scape and its blunt obstacles, but I now realized it was an illusory kind of freedom.

I stood below the pipes and looked up at Luke and Richard, two shadows behind the bright circles of their flashlights. I watched Luke's silhouette as he took a towel out of his backpack and wrapped it around the thickest pipe. He tested the strength of a pipe below him, balancing lightly on one foot before releas-ing his full weight. Every inch of his skin except his face was cov-ered, but he could burn himself even through his clothes. I watched the care with which he contorted himself around the hissing metal, the caution with which he used his body. Finally, Luke was through, and Richard followed his lead, stepping where he had stepped and grasping where he had grasped, all these acrobatics performed in murky gloom, like something seen at the bottom of a turbid pond.

We stepped forward, and the flashlights gave us a patchwork view of a large room out of which sprouted three tubelike passages. I saw corrugated metal and braces of pipes. Light bulbs in plastic mesh baskets had been placed at even intervals in each tube, none of them functional. In the room in which we stood, we found a few discarded generators, some stacked air-conditioning units, a junked pile of desktop computers. Richard said, "It's where appliances go to die."

The next tunnel forced Luke and Richard to crouch even lower, and they moved at half height. If before they were apes, now they had regressed even further, to something unnamed and forgotten. I led the way with Luke holding onto the tail of my suit and Richard following close behind. Other passages branched off from ours. They all looked the same in the partial vision of our flashlights, but it didn't matter: the layout of the tunnels had been branded onto my brain. The only map we had brought with us was in my mind.

"Wait." Richard bent down with his face between his knees. He looked up, and I saw in the beam of Luke's light his red face, his glittering eyes. He was not well. "What is it?" Luke said. Richard shook his head, catching his breath. In the sudden quiet of our pause I noticed a rustling sound, like crumpling paper. Luke illuminated the segment of the tunnel between Richard and us. A ring of something dark moved across the metal. I stepped closer, and saw that it was a flowing loop of cockroaches climbing up one side of the tunnel, clinging to its ridges as it curved above our heads, then scuttling down the other side and across in front of our feet. The beam of the flashlight shone through their translucent wings and gave them a strange orange glow, as though they were lit by little lamps from within. There must have been a gap in the metal tubing somewhere within their loop, because otherwise their path made no sense—it was just a circle repeated over and over and over.

Richard followed the beam of Luke's light, and he let out a slow hiss: "Motherfuckers." He braced himself to jump through, and then just as he went, the ring dissolved, and the cockroaches freed themselves of the walls, collapsing inward in a flurry of rasping wings. They rained down on Richard, and, howling, he beat them off, waving his arms and snapping his head around. He banged against the sides of the tube twice, once with his head as he straightened up too quickly, and then again with his flashlight, accidentally slamming it bulb-first into the ribbed metal. There was a crash, and then his light went out and we were left with only one weak beam. Richard stumbled by us, bouncing off the sides of the tunnel, cursing and flailing as we captured his spastic movements in badly lit fragments.

"Richard," Luke called out, "are you all right?"

"Motherfuckers, motherfuckers." Richard kept repeating the word, shaking out his hair, stomping his feet.

I whispered in Luke's ear: "Just a bit farther."

Richard shook the useless flashlight, saw its shattered bulb in the light of our own, and then hurled it back the way we had come. It clattered off the metal with a hollow clang that echoed down the length of the tunnel. "Can we get out of here now?" he said.

"But we've barely begun."

"I don't care. I've had enough."

"Why?" Luke said. "What are you scared of?"

Richard crouched in front of us, his arms folded and his shoulders pinched. The oddly angled light smeared purple hollows under his eyes and mouth, leaving him looking like a mourner in an El Greco painting. "I'm not scared of anything. I'm annoyed, and I'm really fucking hot. Now, what else is there to see?"

"There should be something up ahead," Luke said. "A maintenance room or something."

"Fascinating."

We moved quickly, and as we neared the tunnel's dead end, I put my hand over Luke's: "Now." He switched off the flashlight, and it was as though I had closed my eyes. There was nothing, not even the faintest shred of light. I heard Richard pull up behind us: "What the fuck?"

"Uh, hold on," Luke said, improvising his role perfectly. "Something's wrong with this thing."

"Luke, don't fuck around with me now," Richard said, panic in his voice.

Luke shook the flashlight so Richard could hear the batteries rattle around inside their cheap plastic casing. "I think the batteries are dead."

I heard Richard shuffle towards us. "What? What are you talking about? You didn't check them?"

"I guess I forgot."

"Tell him about the other exit now," I whispered in Luke's ear.

"You forgot?" Richard's voice turned nasty. "Oh, this is too fucking perfect. What else did you forget? Did you forget how to get out of here? Do you remember that, you fucking lunatic?"

"Stop it, Richard. There's an exit just ahead of us."

"I thought the way we came in was the only way out."

"Just follow my footsteps."

Luke started walking with an exaggerated, clomping gait. According to the maps, at the end of this corridor was another drop similar to the one we had navigated before, only a few feet deeper and without the tangle of scalding pipes. At the bottom of the drop was supposed to be a small room, empty except for a locked metal door. The original plan was to convince Richard to lower himself into the room before we did. Once he was stuck down there—no rope, no key—we would disappear back down the tunnel, only to return fifteen minutes later to his gibbered gratitude. The broken flashlight was a bit of luck that could only help us: the total darkness, the flood of relief when Luke returned not only with a rope but with light as well.

I guessed we were a few feet from the end of the tunnel. I reached out to stop Luke's progress. "My back hurts," Richard said from somewhere behind us. "All this fucking simian crouching."

The tunnel seemed tighter in the complete dark, squeezing in on us like a constricting vein. The darkness grabbed hold of my mind, shaking memories loose inside of me. I was a broken toy, curled up on the kitchen floor. I was a frightened shadow adrift in Central Park. I was a body falling through bright afternoon sunshine. I was nothing, an idea, a notion, a collection of feelings and inchoate wants. I could not feel the tunnel floor beneath my feet. "Luke," I gasped. "What is it?" he said, and then the world returned to me, and I returned to myself.

"Did you say something?" Richard said.

"Yeah. Get up here and help me with this grate."

Richard shuffled forward and brushed by me in the dark, cursing the dust, the heat, the dark, the cockroaches, the entire stupid fucking idea. "So there's a way out down there? Where are we, exactly?"

"Underneath the gym," Luke said. "That's a maintenance room. We lower ourselves down, and then there's a door that leads into the lockers by the pool."

"This is fucked," Richard muttered. He tapped the grate. The two of them tugged, and I heard the grate creak, that terrible sound metal makes when it complains. "Harder," Luke said, and then the grate came free all at once, sending them staggering backward. I stuck my hand out into the open space. I found Luke beside me by touch, and I whispered, "Now's the part where you play scared."

The two of them crawled forward and let their heads hang out over the edge.

"I can't do it," Luke said.

"What does that mean?" Richard said.

"I'm afraid."

"What's wrong with you?"

"I can't see anything."

"Neither can I, but you got us here."

"I can't go first, Richard. We can sit here all night. I won't do it."

Richard sucked in a mouthful of stale air and let it out slowly. "All right. I don't know why I should have expected anything better out of someone like you."

There was a scraping sound, and then he said, "I'm halfway out." I heard him moving slowly backward, his torso and arms dragging across the corrugated metal. I heard rumbling machinery somewhere below, a generator or refiner or some other huge contraption hidden away out of our sight, doing what we ask of it. Richard said, "Something feels wrong here."

"It's nothing," Luke said, "your feet are halfway to the ground."

"It feels . . . deeper."

"Just drop."

"Luke," Richard said, "maybe you'll stop being such a coward someday, but until then, you can go fuck yourself." And then he let go.

We waited half a second for the sound of Richard's feet hitting the floor, and when it didn't come I felt Luke tense up beside me. The full second elapsed, and still nothing, and then Richard's voice starting a sentence, "What the fu—," that he never finished because he hit the bottom of the ventilation shaft forty feet below, down beneath the level of the gym's swimming pool, where they kept the water purifiers and the tanks of chlorine and bromide. The loudest sound was of a sack of sand smacking against concrete, but around the edges of this sound were others, something brittle and something wet. This was not meant to happen. This shaft was meant to be at the end of an adjacent tunnel. I had misread the maps. I had made a mistake.

"Richard!" Luke yelled down. There was no response. "You're deranged," he said to me, "you're sick, you're a sick fuck." He fumbled for the flashlight in the front pocket of his sweatshirt.

"I didn't mean for this to happen," I said. "I got confused."

"I don't believe you."

Luke shone the flashlight down the shaft. It was a cheap light, and its beam was a weak milky yellow. The walls of the shaft were made of corroded iron, and the light picked out patchy stains of green spreading alive and growing across the darker brown. By the time the beam made it all the way down to the bottom, it could barely illuminate anything at all. What we saw of Richard was indistinct: the suggestion of a human body, no more than that. We had to fill in most of the details with our imaginations. There was no movement, no sound. Whatever it was, it was broken and it would not be put back together.

"We have to get help," Luke said. His voice was raw, stripped bare.

"We will do no such thing."

"I don't understand. How could you do this?"

"I said it was a mistake." How could I have gotten something so important so wrong? But then part of me thought maybe it wasn't all that important anyway. "We need to leave now. We need to get as far away from this as possible."

"I'm not leaving him down there like that."

"Don't be stupid," I said. "The longer until he's found, the better. We need to go."

Luke picked up the grate and struggled to put it back where it belonged. We shuffled back down the tunnel. I went left at one turn, right at the next. "I'm lost," Luke said. "You could be taking me anywhere."

"Do you have a choice?"

We kept moving. We were somewhere underneath the chapel now, and I thought of those hundreds of tons of stone pressing down on us. We had been underground for almost an hour and Luke was short of breath. The hot air and the dust were robbing him of oxygen; his movements had grown sluggish. Finally, in a bunker-like chamber we had not passed through before, he sat down to cry.

He sat cross-legged on the dirty floor, the light cradled in his lap. The beam lit his face from below: the gasping mouth, the snot-caked nose. I crouched down and put my hand on his slick forehead. "What have you done, Daniel?" he said. He lay back under the pressure of my palm. "I'm tired. I want to sleep." I thought, These are the words of someone who has given up. One eye—the green one, the Nightingale eye—flickered open and shut. It was time. I moved my hand down to his face as though blessing him. I said, "You wanted me to help you. That's exactly what I'm doing right now."

I took my hands and pried open his mouth. I felt his teeth, and the tough, wet tissue of his gums and the inside of his cheeks. I stretched his jaws as wide as they would go. He made a noise, something strangled and glottal that might have been an attempt at words. I pressed his tongue down, and the sluglike appendage struggled against my fingers. His eyes snapped open, and they rolled around in their sockets trying to get a fix on my face. I bent my head forward, and I looked deeper inside his mouth, and beyond, into his throat. My face went in first and was enveloped by damp warmth. I felt the sandpaper texture of his tongue against my nose, eyes, and lips. As I moved into the back of his mouth and farther down into the narrower passage of his throat, my features were smoothed out, licked clean. My shoulders followed, falling into each other; my chest collapsed, and my spine compressed. I felt his body struggle to absorb me. His flesh and sinews trembled; his bones creaked, opening themselves up. I tunneled down deeper, feeling my way blindly through tubes and viscera. My hips crumpled to fit into his mouth, and then my thighs, shins, and finally my feet scraped past his teeth and joined the rest of me inside his body. My shape became liquid. I spread throughout his limbs like oil spilled onto a parched slab of desert soil, the fluid filling every crack. He stiffened and then relaxed, and then stiffened again as I worked my way into each crevice. I threaded myself through every vein and every bone, imprinting myself on every surface. I enfolded each cell of his body until it became my own.

After a while he did not resist, and soon after that, there was nothing left to do the resisting. I filled out his shape. Everything was so rigid and inflexible, but perhaps this tightness was only a trick of my mind as I considered the body's new permanence. I opened my eyes and blinked out the dust. The flashlight lay at my side where it had fallen, and I picked it up, standing on shaky feet. I took a few steps, then looked behind me. A small child curled up on the floor in the beam of light. Dark-haired, smooth-cheeked: Luke, six years old, as I'd first seen him in the playground. His skin shone phosphorescently, and his hair was plastered across his forehead. His eyes were closed, his hands tucked up near his chin. He looked to be dead, or maybe sleeping, and I turned to let him be. I didn't mind if he slept there forever.

4

I FOUND MY WAY out of the tunnels and back to the dorm room. I guessed it was somewhere between four and five in the morning, and the campus was quiet. I was going to steal Nate's car. The thought of sitting on a hurtling train among all the morning commuters filled me with unspeakable panic. I didn't think I could behave for the entire ride; I wasn't sure I would be accountable for my actions. We had left the door to the room unlocked, and I entered to the labored sound of Nate's breathing.

The shades were open, and I could see the shapes of things by the glow of a streetlamp. I found the car keys inside a cigar box in Nate's bottom desk drawer, lying on top of his passport and checkbook. I thought about ripping out all of his checks and scattering them around campus. I considered doing violence to the shape under the sheets, then using his passport to board a plane to some obscure, forsaken place. We would disappear together, his name, Luke's body.

There was still no light in the sky as I started the car and eased my way out of the student parking lot. The campus roads were empty. I passed a county police cruiser idling with its lights on at the turn to the highway, but I felt nothing, no anxiety. I didn't feel like a murderer. I felt like a free man, a released convict who has served time for a crime he did not commit. The cop car shrank in the rearview mirror, and then disappeared around the backside of a bend. I stayed in the middle lane and held steady at exactly the speed limit.

Somewhere on the turnpike near the airport I was joined by a flood of merging cars. I let them flow around me on all sides, and I became part of the restless organism, enfolded yet separate in my own private metal box. The feeling was not unpleasant. We all drove together past an enormous power plant like a city plucked out of some dystopian future, with its infrastructure of pipes and catwalks and blinking lights, pilot flames burning at the top of chemical exhaust shafts. Beyond the Bayonne docks and over New York Harbor, a thin strip of lighter gray indicated the dawn. I took the exit for the Lincoln Tunnel and emerged onto West Thirty-eighth Street fifteen minutes later.

I found myself idling at a red light on Ninth Avenue, which seemed as good a place to leave the car as any. The radio clock read five to seven, and the street was starting to fill up with traffic. I left the engine running and the lights on. A few honks and shouts followed me down the street, but I paid them no attention. I walked for an hour, barely looking up to notice the sky progress through its infinite shades of gray. The body did as it was told. I fixed my eyes on the sidewalk in front of me, and I kept walking. I passed through Times Square and Bryant Park, and then I walked up by Rockefeller Center, where I paused to look at the statue of Atlas I had always admired. It was about strength and punishment, things I understood. But I didn't stop for long, continuing north on Fifth Avenue through a chasm of faceless buildings and harried people. I walked, and as I walked I told myself what I remembered of the story of my life. I mouthed the words as they came to me, getting used to the shapes my lips and tongue made when they chewed on the images in my head. It was a rehearsal for later, when I would say everything again, this time out loud to Claire. I wanted to speak without error. The walking calmed the anxiety that thumped around inside my rib cage like a spastic second heart. The people moving around me became pale gray shadows of people, and then nothing like people at all, just shapes and static.

Near Fifty-seventh Street I caught sight of myself in the reflective brass door of some hotel. I looked disgusting. My hair was filthy and tangled. My face was covered in a layer of grit from the tunnels, which also coated Luke's black sweatshirt and jeans. This was not how I wanted to present myself to the world. I felt around in the pocket of the jeans and came up with a credit card, as well as Luke's driver's license and college ID. I walked a few more blocks, sat down on a bench on the south side of the park, and waited for the stores to open. Finally, at ten o'clock I walked up Madison Avenue and into a boutique full of mirrored surfaces that reflected each bright ceiling light a thousand times over. A salesman dressed in black immediately attached himself to my side, probably hoping to get rid of me. I pointed at a rack of silk suits and said in a strangled voice, "Get me one in my size, and a shirt too." He said, "I'm not sure if this is the right place for you." I slapped the credit card down on the mirrored counter. "I want to buy a suit and a shirt. The sooner you sell them to me, the sooner I'll leave." My hands were shaking, and I clamped them together behind my back, leaving the card sitting there naked on the counter. I hated all the lights and mirrors. I did not want to look at myself covered in dirt and wearing rags. There was a conference between the salesman and his manager, and then they produced a suit—black, slim, three-buttoned—and said it would cost two thousand dollars, as though this would send me running out of the store screaming. "That's fine," I said. It was difficult to bend my mouth around the words. "Run the card."

I walked into the park with the new clothes slung over my shoulder. The terraces and stairways around Bethesda Fountain were mostly deserted, so I stripped off Luke's sweatshirt and jeans and stepped naked into the fountain. I splashed the frigid water over my body, rubbing the skin clean. When I had done the best I could, I stepped out and waited for the cold air to dry me off. The shirt fit fine, but the suit pants were too big around the waist, and the jacket's shoulders hung off the edges of my body. I realized I had not bought shoes and would have to wear Luke's dirty sneakers the rest of the day; in my rush to leave I had forgotten the credit card on the store's counter.

I had an entire day to fill before I could go to the Central Park West apartment. I didn't have the keys, and anyway, I did not want to wait for Claire in the empty rooms like some kind of petty thief. I wanted her to invite me in. I wanted us to meet as equals. I kept moving through the park, following its paths wherever they took me. Everything I saw was slathered thick with the grease of memories. I would have to do everything all over again to make any place entirely my own. I came out of the park at Sixty-eighth Street, on the East Side. This was the New York I knew best: Fifth Avenue's limestone-faced fortresses; the black-painted park benches; green awnings, bronze door handles, brass-buttoned doormen. The attitude and style had been passed down for generations without much change; like the buildings themselves, these things just received periodic touch-ups to appear cleaner, newer, more in line with the current era. Even now, right across the street from where I stood, a cleaning crew worked on an apartment building's grimy façade. They wore face masks and harnesses, wielded pressurized nozzles. Scaffolding protected the pedestrians below. The fast water beat against the limestone and the city's dirt was eradicated, but it would return, and then these men would be called in to do the same job over again. Limousines sat outside consulates on the cross-streets, the flags of countries rich and poor hanging like colorful corpses. People still walked around here pretending it was where history was made, but the city I knew was ingrown, incestuous. It had become diseased.

At noon I went to the Central Park Zoo. I bought a ticket with the last of Luke's cash and saw the seals and snow monkeys. A polar bear dove off a rock, swam in a circle, got out, shook off, did it again. The zoo was mostly empty, but I came across a group of schoolchildren outside the penguin house. They were very young, tiny little things in their parkas and caps. They milled around in the aimless way of all children, and I didn't pay them any attention until I saw Luke. He stood off to the side in a navy pea coat and penny loafers. He was looking down at a tuft of grass pushing up through a bulging crack in the blacktop; then he raised his head and saw me. His small face was mild, unworried. He looked at me curiously, as though I was the one who should not have been there. I stepped closer, but I did not know what to say. He turned away to join the rest of the children, and then the teacher swept them all into the penguin house. I followed the class into the chilled, fishy interior. Behind the glass, the penguins slipped and stumbled on slimy rocks, their stubby bodies much shorter than I remembered, their flippers tagged with bright yellow bands of rubber. I bent down and looked into the face of each child; Luke's was not among them. The teacher moved toward me, her mouth twisted up into a worried scowl. "Stay away," she hissed at my departing back. "Creep."

Later, I sat in a coffee shop on Amsterdam for two hours. I ordered a hamburger and fries, but I couldn't eat any of it, no matter how hard I tried, and even though I knew I would have to learn. The grease pooled underneath the meat and soaked the bun pink. I smiled apologetically at the waitress, told her I was finished. I could drink the coffee, though. I liked the bitterness; I had my cup refilled five times. There was nothing to read, so I just stared out the window and practiced my story for Claire. Luke walked by in his pea coat and loafers, his hands stuffed into the pockets of the coat, his face tucked into the collar. I waited until the waitress ran an order into the kitchen—I had no money to pay the check—and then I bolted. I saw Luke turn onto Ninety-third Street, but when I came around the corner, no one was there. I walked up and down the length of the block, but I found nothing.

What did I do for the rest of the afternoon? What does anybody do when they don't have any money and they can't go home? I paced the streets. I stared into shop windows. I went down to the river and watched the slow movement of the water. Like the sky with its layered clouds, the Hudson was many rivers braided into one. Strands split off and curled into eddies; certain bands of water slid south faster than others. I sat like a homeless person on a bench and watched the river move. There was a sunset without a sun, and the cars on the highway below turned into abstract things, white lights one way, red the other, their movement reduced to a colorful blur smeared over black canvas.

⚬⟞⟨⟩⟞⚬

Four hours later, Victor helped Claire out of a taxi and through her building's bright glowing doorway, and now here I stand in front of the brass elevator, my hands pinned behind my back, as still and straight as a rod driven into the earth.

Time thickens. The elevator takes decades between each floor. I am an old man before it is halfway down; I have lived three lives by the time its doors open. I step inside and press the button for the third floor. There is a leather bench in the corner. There is a mirror on the wall. The floor is covered by a black- and white-checked rug. I've noticed each of these things before, but my relationship to them has changed; I am now just one physical object among many, and I have to be careful of everything. The doors open. I walk to the end of the hall and ring the bell for 3F.

Claire opens the door and her eyes go wide, and it is as though I have never seen them before, they are so big and strange. "I knew you'd come back soon to apologize," she says. She smiles and opens the door wider, but I can't move. The arms like kindling, the purple veins: she is fifty-two years old and she is tired. She looks into the apartment, then back at me. "We need to talk about Gregory. Aren't you going to come in?" I just stand there in the hallway. Her smile hangs in the air, anxious and expectant and full of hope. The silence stretches out until it can't be drawn any thinner; then its thread breaks, and I open my mouth to speak: "Your son is dead."

Her face flies apart and then falls back together, newly composed. She says, "You should come inside." I do, and she locks the door behind me. We stand together in the foyer. "Come," she says, leading me toward her bedroom.

She is wearing the black cocktail dress, ropes of pearls, the diamond brooch in the shape of a butterfly. These things are all her mother's. I don't know if she wore them to work or changed into them as soon as she got home; the difference somehow seems important. Inside the bedroom, I find absolute order. She has scattered her energy all over the room like a dog shedding its hair. She gestures to two black Barcelona chairs, new purchases, facing each other in front of the wide open window. We sit down. Cold air rushes across the room but she doesn't seem to notice.

I say it again: "Your son is dead."

She blinks at me. "You said that already. But I don't have a son."

"Not anymore. That's what I'm here to tell you."

"No. I only have a daughter." She frowns. "And she's a bit of a disappointment."

"A daughter? What are you talking about?"

"I'm talking about Claire, of course. I'm talking about your mother."

She leans forward to the edge of the chair, crossing one leg over the other, placing an elbow on the top knee, resting her chin on her hand. The movement is practiced, precise, graceful, but it is foreign to me. It is the gesture of someone I have never met.

I say carefully, "I don't think I have a mother."

She flinches. "Don't be cruel, Luke. Claire may not have always been a faultless parent, but she doesn't deserve that." The familiar scars creep like worms over her wrists onto her palms and the backs of her hands. She is Claire, and yet she is not Claire. She says, "I suppose some people blame me for the way she turned out, and you can join them if you like. But I think you are smarter than that."

"My name is Daniel. I told you, Luke is gone."

Her face sags, and I see Claire alone for a moment. But then Venetia rises up to speak again: "I wish you would stop saying that."

"But it's the truth. I killed him. I left him buried underneath the ground."

"You haven't killed anybody," she says. "He's no more dead than I am."

"Claire, stop this. I came here to tell you my story and to tell you how things are going to be. You're going to have to listen to me now."

"I don't need to listen to you. I know your story. What is it you want to tell me? I know it all already. Your story, my story, Claire's story: they're all the same. We Nightingales can't escape our story. We stay in the same place, spun like a screw deeper into its hole, while everybody else keeps moving, and we have no-where to look except at each other. Listen. Your mother tried to make herself into something different. She tried very, very hard. She would have a husband who would love her. She would have a child whom she would love. And for a short while, this is how things actually were. But then the husband left when he saw what he had actually married. And you were your mother's child, and no change at all. I told her from the beginning it would do more harm than good to act as though she could be something other than what she was. But she didn't listen. She persisted with her hope, causing all this unnecessary pain to herself and to the people who believed in her. I went away for a while, and when I came back things were as I always knew they would be. So." She spreads her hands and gives a little shrug. "Don't tell me how things are going to be, because I already know."

It is freezing in the room, but neither of us moves to close the window.

"You can call yourself whoever you want," I say. "You can think whatever you want. This has nothing to do with any of that. I'm telling you this is the first and last time you'll see me. I've come to say good-bye."

"No." She shakes her head. "We're going to start over, Luke. I'm going to correct all of your mother's mistakes, every single one."

"There is nothing to correct. I'm leaving, and I'm leaving alone."

"You don't understand. You are never alone. All of us"—she gestures around the bedroom as though it is filled with people— "we are always with you." She stands up and puts her palm against my cheek. "I'm not going to make you stay. I can't. But you'll see it's the only thing left for you to do." She smiles, a smile I have only seen in family photographs, Claire's bones and muscles and skin somehow twisting to form this adopted expression, and then she turns away and walks out of the room.

I rise from my chair to stand at the open window. The park spreads out beneath me, pitch black, furtive. Streetlamps illuminate small pockets that only emphasize the greater darkness. I place my palms on the sill and lean out into the cold air. The park refigures itself as a bottomless body of water, the wind directing its currents. I feel a tiny hand at the small of my back, and Luke says, "There is no place for you here."

I turn my head to see him, and somehow I am not surprised. He is six years old, and his small face is not happy or scared or angry, it is just there, looking up at me. His little hand is made of iron. He presses it into my spine, and I push back against it, but my spine will buckle before his hand will give. He holds me there, unable to move, half my body hanging out over the ledge. He says, "You need to go."

"Leave me alone," I say. "You gave up already."

He shakes his head. "I should have done this years ago. I'm getting rid of you for good."

He adds a second hand to my back. My weight lurches forward, my toes curling to keep their grip on the floor. "Luke, stop, you'll kill us both." My fingers scrabble at the sill, tearing free splinters of wood.

"Yes," he said. "But that's the only way."

I fight against him, but his little body has so much strength. I feel other hands join his, uncountable clusters of fingers pressing into my flesh. They are too much for me.

"Go," he whispers, and I go, pitching over the sill, clutching and pulling his wrist with both hands as I fall. The world rotates, park then street then sky, his body flung out into space against mine. He grabs my throat and we are joined together falling. The sky, the park, the street. We fall together.

Epilogue

———✦———

THE AMBULANCE ARRIVES, and now everything's noise—the siren, the shouting paramedics, the chattering bystanders, and, above it all, that woman's wretched moan, a lacerating, ragged-edged thing—but at first the street was silent. Almost peaceful. For a moment, it was just me and the boy. I looked down at him, this pale teenager in a black suit and dirty sneakers. He lay on his back, his head turned to the side, one leg bent at an impossible angle. I crouched to look at his face. He was breathing through the corner of his mouth around a clot of blood and what might have been teeth. His eyes found me, and I noticed they were strange, the left yellow-flecked green, the right brown. They held me in place for a moment, then some man came running across Ninety-fifth Street yelling about a falling body, and the eyes rolled away to look up at the sky.

A police car joins the ambulance now. Two officers get out and force everybody back. The building's doorman has been holding the moaning woman upright, and she is too far outside herself to notice when one of the cops pries her out of the doorman's grasp and leads her to the ambulance. The paramedics slide a backboard underneath the boy, and I can see his eyes are still open and he is breathing, the movement of his chest labored and irregular as they strap him in.

I slip to the back of the knot of people, feeling suddenly unsure of myself until I glance behind me. A small, sandy-haired boy and his father are walking up the block. The son holds the father's hand. The man cranes his neck, but he can't see through the cluster of people. He hesitates, unsure whether he should bring his son any closer, but the boy tugs at his hand, and they keep coming until they stop next to me at the edge of the crowd.

The man wears a gray suit and a loosened yellow tie. A small cut, as from a shaving razor, shows red just below his left ear. He drops his son's hand and taps the shoulder of a woman standing in front him, asks what's happened. The boy looks at me and I smile back at him. His eyes widen; he quickly looks away. "We live down the block," I hear the man say. "I figured I should know." The boy looks at me again, and this time his eyes stay on mine, wide and blue and serious. People mill around us, beginning to disperse, but the father is still talking.

"Hi," the boy whispers.

"Hello."

"What's going on?" he asks.

I look into the street, where the paramedics are rolling the stretcher and its load out to the ambulance. They collapse the legs, lift the stretcher, slide it into its berth. They slam the ambulance doors shut, and I look back at the boy.

"I don't know," I say. "But I don't think it's anything we need to worry about."

About the Author